Sentinel of the North

Book 9 in the Border Knight Series
By
Griff Hosker

Sentinel of the North

Published by Sword Books Ltd 2020

Contents

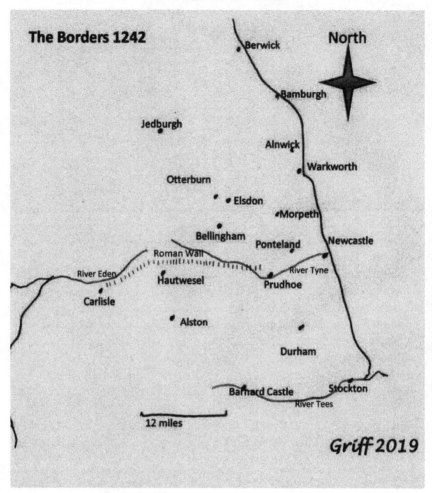

Part One

The Fragile North
Sir William

Chapter 1

My father and I had obeyed King Henry and taken part, on his behalf, in the crusade to the Holy Land led by Richard, earl of Cornwall, the King's brother. Our part had been something of a success but, as for the rest, it was proved, inevitably, to be a failure. We had regained Jerusalem but by the time we reached England, it had been lost again. To me, the land would never belong to Christians again and its loss did not worry me overmuch. I had suffered a personal loss, I had lost my squire, Matthew, and his death did not seem worth what we had achieved and then lost.

There were other, equally unpalatable changes too. My father had aged while we were away in the Holy Land. That was where he had made his name when he had fought at the Battle of Arsuf and I wondered if the memories had been too much. Certainly, he appeared to tire far more easily and he had allowed me to make more of the decisions towards the latter part of the crusade. I had learned then to lead larger numbers of men and I now understood a little more about being a border knight.

Since we had been away much had changed in the land we had left. Llewellyn the Great had died and, with his heir a prisoner in the Tower of London, then Wales became vulnerable. King Henry had ambitions but they were offset by the fact that his sister, Joan, had been married to King Alexander of Scotland, had died. There had been no children from the marriage and King Alexander had hurriedly married Maria de Courcy who was descended from Louis VI of France. Worse, she had borne him an heir, a child with French connections. That news filled me with dread for Queen Joan and King Alexander had both been sympathetic to an English alliance. There were many Scottish lords who sought to retake the huge swathes of England that my father and I had recaptured. Of course, the King also now had a son, Edward, and England had a hope for the future too.

I learned all of this as we rode north. We went, first to Stockton and then, after I was reunited with my wife and son, we headed to Elsdon, my castle on the border. My journey filled with information about the land I had briefly left. Our brief stay in Stockton showed me the changes that had been wrought in my family since we had been away.

My mother was loath to lose her son, grandson and daughter-in-law and sought to keep us in Stockton as long as she could. The fact that she had my dead brother's children living in the castle with her was not enough. As much as she adored Henry Samuel and Eleanor that would never be enough. She also had another five grandchildren living within riding distance too but I was now her eldest boy and Richard, my son, had spent longer with his grandmother than with his father! He was four years old and I had missed two years of his life. That, along with the loss of Matthew, made me angry. I had been taken by the King to perform him a service and, thus far, he had not even thanked us!

My mother managed to delay my departure to the north by a month for my father decided that Henry Samuel had done enough in the Holy Land to become a knight and I agreed. John, who had been a page would now become his squire and Alfred, my sister's son, would become my father's new squire with Thomas as his page. Mark, who had been my father's squire, would also be knighted even though he was still not quite ready. We had promised Matthew that his brother would become a knight and one did not break a promise to the dead! I knew that my mother was happy with all of this for it meant they would stay at Stockton and be safe. My manor, on the other hand, would not for it lay in the northern marches as close to the Scottish as any knight; I would be guarding the King's border. It explained why my mother kept me by her side for the whole of the ceremony. It was almost as though our roles had reversed and she was the one who needed protection.

She sat between my father and me at the feast held in the Great Hall of Stockton Castle. The castle had changed beyond all recognition since King John had died. My father had restored it to its former prominent position. We now had high walls and towers along with defences which were the equal of any in the north. The wall hangings and tapestries which adorned the walls were my mother's idea and reflected the glory of my father and his antecedents. The largest was of Alfraed, the Earl Marshal, defeating the usurper Stephen at the battle of Lincoln. Then there was one showing my father at Arsuf and another of him in the Baltic where he had helped Bishop Albert defeat the barbarians in Sweden.

My mother was joyous to have her whole family gathered under her roof and she chattered on while I listened. This was the first feast for a long time that neither Mark nor Henry Samuel had to serve and they were enjoying the situation. Mark was a tanner's son and his elevation to knight had been a remarkable one. Henry Samuel was witty and he was regaling the table with tales from our crusade. I was silent for I was still wrestling with the waste we had witnessed. The cost of the crusade, not only in men but also equipment had been unnecessary. If I was asked, I would not go on crusade again and I now knew why my father had been so reluctant to return to the scene of his greatest glory. Although I was silent, I was not unhappy for I was basking in the joy of my family all gathered together and the fact that I was home. In a perfect world, I would have a manor closer to Stockton so that I could see more of them but I knew that I was lucky to have what I did. My father had often spoken, somewhat bitterly, about how he lost all of his lands through no fault of his own and had to spend years regaining them. I had been handed my lands and I knew that I could lose them on the whim of a king!

My mother put her hand on my arm, "William, what bothers you?"

I smiled and patted her hand, "Nothing. I am quiet because this is not my night. This night belongs to the new knight in the family, Sir Henry, and I would let him enjoy it!"

"Your father told me of the attempt on your life." She shook her head and stared at the whitening scar along my face, "That there should be such wickedness in the world! And you almost died!"

"But I did not because God did not wish me to die." I did not say that the margins between life and death were fine. My brother had died because of such margins and yet I had lived because I saw some sweat!

Dick was giggling at something Sam had said and my mother smiled, "Your son is a delight. Make the most of him."

"I will do and I thank you for caring for both him and Mary."

"Mary is a sweet girl and you are lucky to have her." There was a sudden burst of laughter from Henry Samuel's sister and their cousin Elizabeth. My mother shook her head, "And young Eleanor needs a husband sooner rather than later for she is a little too wild for my liking!"

I sighed. My mother always preferred the boys in the family and Eleanor had lived longer with my mother than any other of the grandchildren. Inevitably, that led to conflict. "She is young and loves life. Henry Samuel is as frivolous at times."

"Nonsense! He is a knight and a sensible boy. He is nothing like his sister."

She was mistaken for they were almost identical but you could not argue with my mother. She was a strong woman but in this she was wrong.

"We will see. And you are in good health, mother?"

She smiled, "I am getting old, William. The young girl your father rescued in the Baltic now has grey hairs and does not sleep as well as she once did. It is better now that your father is home but I make the most of each day." I saw the sadness in her eyes as she said, "And I have grown very fond of your wife and your son. While I have missed you, their company has kept me young. With no bairns left in the castle, it will feel empty and lonely."

Just then Eleanor squealed with laughter at something Geoffrey, my squire, had said and a frown came over my mother's face. I loved my mother but I knew that once she took against someone then it was hard to change her mind. The only two of her grandchildren left in Stockton Castle would be Henry Samuel and Eleanor. I wondered how that would affect my father.

When I left the castle to head home, we were laden with wagons filled with clothes, food and war gear. I had left Elsdon under the command and care of Alan of Bellingham. He had been a hired sword who had come back to his home and was a good man. We had not taken any of my men on a crusade and I hoped that leaving almost thirty men in such a small castle would have been enough to deter the cattle raiders and border bandits who made life so hard for the English in that part of the world. I did not know how Alan Longsword and Tom of Rydal would fit in but the two men who had joined us in the Holy Land had more than earned their place at my side.

As we crossed the Ox Bridge, I waved at Padraig the Wanderer who had finally left my father's side to become a farmer. Both he and Richard Red Leg had suffered one wound too many and would now end their days peacefully as farmers. I hoped that my father would do the same. He had seen well over sixty summers and deserved, after a life of war, some peace.

For Geoffrey of Lyons, my new squire, Alan Longsword and Tom of Rydal the journey north was new to them. The country was far wilder than they had known heading up through England. Tom of Rydal, perhaps, had grown up in similar lands but as we left the farmlands of the Tees, then the Wear and finally the Tyne they saw fewer people farming. The farms also became smaller and meaner with less cereal and more sheep. As we neared the North Tyne, they witnessed the land almost closing in on them as narrow steep-sided valleys and huge forests which seemed to stretch to the horizon and beyond replaced the farms.

I saw Geoffrey's face as we rode just behind Tom and Alan, "And what do people grow here, lord? Trees and rocks?"

I laughed, "You come from a land of vines and rich fields of wheat. Here we grow barley and oats and we brew beer and eat black bread. Meat is rare for the ordinary folk and what animals we have we protect." His face showed his disappointment. "Do you regret accepting my offer of employment, Geoffrey? If so, I will happily release you for your service thus far has more than repaid me."

He shook his head, "No, lord, since my brother died our lives have been bound and I swore an oath. It is a poor warrior who breaks his oath because he cannot eat white bread. It is just that I cannot understand why such a great lord as yourself has not been rewarded with a greater castle. Your father's manor at Stockton is the one which should be yours."

"And when my father dies then I will inherit the castle if not the title but I do not wish his death. We will continue to serve here and you will find that the people who live here are as brave and loyal as any in the kingdom."

I wondered how Sir Richard, my nearest neighbour, had coped. He was the son of Sir William de la Lude and while his brother had inherited Hartburn Sir Richard had been given the thorn that was Otterburn. As a bachelor knight, it would have been a lonely existence for him. The only other castle which was close by was Rothbury. I knew that he was grateful to have been given the manor as I had been grateful for Elsdon but it did feel, sometimes, like living on the edge of the world.

Perhaps I was distracted by my worries for we were almost ambushed as I thought of what lay in the future and not what lay around. My father had sent some of his men to act as drivers but we had no archers. Archers were the scouts we normally used and the three warriors I had with me did not know this land. The four men who drove the wagons were all good men but they were driving wagons and their hands were occupied. Even though I was distracted some sense I knew not that I possessed came to my aid. We had just crossed the Wansbeck and passed through the small town of Kirkwhelpington when I sensed danger. We were climbing the road, which needed repair, through a wood which grew to a forest to the west.

The air on the back of my neck prickled; that was my only warning but I had not felt it since the assassin had tried to kill me in the Holy

Land. That brush with death was enough to make me draw my sword and shout, "To arms!"

I think the fact that Tom, Geoffrey and Alan had been so recently in battle and that the land through which we rode intimidated them made them react faster than my father's men who had been with the garrison in Stockton for two years. While my men drew swords and grabbed shields the five men at arms driving the wagons hesitated. John Golden Hair paid the price and he fell from the leading wagon. That was the one with my wife and son within.

Mary's father had been a lord but she was hardier than she looked. I heard her shout, "Dick, take shelter!" as she grabbed the reins.

I had turned when John had cried out and saw that the arrow had hit him in the right side of the head. I kicked my horse in the flanks and shouted, "Walter, you and the drivers protect my family! The rest of you men come with me!"

Walter was the next most senior man at arms and he shouted, "Aye, lord!" They had been lax once but they would not be so again. I could leave my wife and son under their protection.

This was not the Holy Land where it was rocks and gullies which hid ambushers. They were relatively easy to find. Here in the north, there were trees and undergrowth. Those who lived here beyond the law wore clothes which hid them in the foliage for they blended in. You looked for movement and I saw movement but it was the flight of an arrow. The hunting arrow slammed into my shoulder. It penetrated the surcoat and lodged in the mail. I left it there as I pulled my sword hand, behind me. The movement of the arrow had shown me the pale hand which held the bow. The man thought he had me and was nocking another arrow as I rode at him. He looked up in terror as my sword swept down to split his skull.

His cry alerted the others and they moved. Tom of Rydal was more familiar with this type of landscape. The Loughrigg fells close to his home were similar to this land and he had negotiated the undergrowth better than the other two. He was to my left and it was he who rammed his sword into the throat of the archer who drew back to send an arrow towards me. With two of their men dead and their ambush failed the others ran. As much as I wanted to get back to my family, I knew that we had to ensure that the threat from these bandits was ended. That they were bandits was obvious from the arrows they used. If they were warriors who served a lord then they would have used bodkins which had a chance of penetrating mail!

Geoffrey and Alan had followed Tom and I and, as the trees thinned a little further away from the light from the road, they were able to ride closer to us. The bandits were like a startled herd of deer and they spread out. They were, however, on foot and now that there was less undergrowth and fewer lower branches we were able to ride faster. I turned my sword so that when I struck the next man it was with the flat of my blade. He wore neither helmet nor leather cap and the smack from my sword into the back of his head propelled him towards a tree. He hit it and lay still. Geoffrey and Alan were keen to make up for their tardy start and both men swung their swords on either side of their horses' heads as they hunted the other ambushers. When I saw no more men before us and the forest was silent, I shouted, "Halt! Let us return to the road. When you find a body search it for evidence of their identity."

Geoffrey was confused, "My lord?"

"The coins they have will give us an indication of their nationality. If there are more Scottish ones than English then they came from north of the border. The reverse means that they are English and are local brigands. Look at their weapons. The Scots tend to have shorter swords and they like curved hilts and even curved blades. If they are English then I need to send to Sir Gilbert de Umfraville from Prudhoe Castle as this is his manor and he is duty-bound to keep it clear of bandits."

Our progress back was slow. When we reached the man I had laid unconscious I saw that the fates had conspired against me. I had wanted a prisoner and thought to render him unconscious. When he had fallen, he had impaled himself on a broken branch of a tree. He was still alive when I dismounted, but barely.

He was bleeding from the wound and I could see that he had but moments to live. Before I could question him, he spat a gob of bloody phlegm in my direction, "Bastard Englishman!"

He was Scottish. I stayed far enough away so that he could not pull some hidden blade and lunge at me, "You must have been desperate to attack armed men. You were asking for this death!"

He laughed and his body was wracked with pain as he did so, "We didn't see your mail! We thought the wagons were filled with goods we could steal. I…" His own laughter had killed him. The fact that we had so recently been used to riding abroad with mail beneath our surcoats had saved us.

By the time we reached the road, it was the middle of the afternoon. We would be hard pushed to reach Elsdon by dark. Walter had put the body of the dead man at arms in the back of one of the wagons. I looked up at Mary, "You and Dick are unhurt?"

9

She smiled and nodded at my son. He held in his hand the dagger which my father had brought back from the Holy Land and given to him, "He was ready to defend his mother to the death. Who were they?"

"Countrymen of yours. But I think there was nothing sinister in this. They saw the wagons and thought I was a merchant. Tom, you had better take charge of this wagon."

My wife nodded as Tom climbed up and Alan tied Tom's horse to the rear of the wagon. "We have come back to the frontier, husband. This is a timely warning of what we can expect." My wife looked frail and seemed as though a good wind would blow her over but she had an inner strength which made her stronger than many men. She kissed our son, "And thank you for being my protector!"

I took my shield from the wagon and rode with it on my arm and I pulled up my coif. I did not think we would have any more attacks for within a mile or so we would be within range of Alan of Bellingham's patrols but it paid to be vigilant. A lack of vigilance had cost one man his life already. As the sun began to set ahead of us, I wondered if we would have to travel the last few miles in the dark for we were travelling slowly in case there more ambushers. Then I heard hooves and was relieved when John the Archer and Idraf of Towyn appeared on the road ahead.

They looked both surprised and pleased to see me. "We did not know you were home yet, lord. Captain Alan will be pleased."

I nodded, "And while it is good to see you, John, we have been attacked within the last mile or so by Scottish bandits."

In answer, they both unslung their bows and loosely nocked an arrow. "The road is safe twixt here and Elsdon, my lord, and we will be your rearguard!"

Knowing that the road was clear meant we could ride hard and we did not spare the horses. They could rest for a good week before we sent them back to my father. The sun had just dropped below the western sky as we rode through the village and headed towards the gates of Elsdon Castle. Villagers came out when they heard our horses and men who served me and their wives greeted us as we rode towards the twisting path which led to the gates. As I looked up at the keep of my castle it made me realise that while Stockton was a castle which was comfortable, Elsdon was a castle in a war zone and the accommodation was functional at best.

Alan of Bellingham ran down from the fighting platform to greet me, "My lord, it is good to see you and my lady! Welcome home!"

"And good to be home but I need to tell you, Alan, that we were attacked by bandits. It was not on my land but that of the Umfraville family, however…"

"Aye, lord. And we have had trouble further north where Sir Richard has had some encounters with Scots. He was uncertain if they were bandits or if it was something more sinister."

"We leave that for the morrow. Tonight, we need food and our beds."

"I will have the cook prepare food and my wife and I will move back into our quarters."

Elsdon Castle did not boast a huge number of sleeping chambers. There were just three sleeping chambers in the keep and the men had their own warrior hall. Alan and his wife had a small house attached to the warrior hall. His wife also helped in the kitchens. Poor Dick was exhausted and almost asleep on his feet. He was past the time when he needed a nap but he was still young and the attack had wearied him. He barely finished the food before my wife took him to his bed. Since I had been away, he had moved into a room of his own. One of Mary's two women, Beth, slept in his room with him. We had few servants for Elsdon did not warrant them.

After we had eaten, I sent Geoffrey to his own small chamber while Alan and I caught up with events. He was a soldier and was keen to know the details of the crusade while I wished to know what had happened along the border. It soon emerged that it had been quiet until the autumn. Whilst that time of year was the time when bandits tried to steal animals for the winter October had seen more raids than normal and Alan thought that Sir Richard believed there was another reason. I knew that before I could see my own manor, I would need to ride to speak with Sir Richard.

"And the men who married the Yalesham widows and the other newly married warriors; what of them?"

He grinned, "Like my wife and I, lord, they are all content for, thanks to you we all have land we can till. They have all been busy making new warriors for the manor. Cedric's son, Cedric, has strengthened the farm where his father and brother died. He now has a small tower, a good wall and a ditch with a bridge he can remove if he is attacked. We learned from the treachery of the Scots and Sir Eustace."

"And Brother Paul?"

"Still as happy as ever, lord, he loves the village and that heartens us all. We went too long without a priest and life is too parlous here on the border to be without one. We need someone to intercede with God and we are happy that Brother Paul can do that for us."

11

With clean bedding on our bed, my wife and I lay in each other's arms and we snuggled, "I liked staying in Stockton Castle for it is comfortable and your family are all kind but for all its limitations this is the place I feel most comfortable for it is ours. In time I will make it as Stockton Castle. I have money of my own left by my father and I could use it to make this into a fine home as well as a strong castle."

I kissed her, "I think, my love, that this will always be a bastion. Whoever is master of this castle will be the sentinel of the north. Our task is to be vigilant and to warn the Bishop, the Sherriff of Northumberland and my father of danger from the north. We are the old-fashioned chamberlain who lays across the door of his master's bedchamber to warn of danger."

She pulled away from me a little, "Then you do not think this will always be our home?"

"No, my love, for I am heir to the manor of Stockton. My father was wounded on crusade. We did not tell my mother for fear of frightening her but he spent longer than I expected recuperating. He did no fighting towards the end of the crusade and that is right and proper for he has done more than enough in his life. I will need to help him when the time is right. My nephew will need a manor and my father will send him here but for now, we live as though this is ours until the end of time!"

She laughed for we were as one. I had not seen her for a long time but once we were together then it was as though we had never been apart and I was content.

Chapter 2

Young Dick had not known Elsdon and the next morning plagued both his mother and me to allow him to explore. I had too many tasks which needed my attention and so my wife took him around the castle. I first met with my men at arms and archers. I had made a profit in the Holy Land and I shared what I had gained with them for they had kept watch on my home. While I spoke with them, I discovered not only the details of their families but also their insights into the dangers they had found in the land. I was not criticising Alan of Bellingham but I knew that he would not have done so. By the time it was the middle of the morning I had spoken with them all and now had a much clearer picture of my manor and the dangers which surrounded us. The archers had told me of all that they had seen whilst hunting and scouting while my men at arms had observed the people who travelled my roads.

Geoffrey sat at my side the whole time for it was important that they knew who he was and that he knew them. I had watched him listening to men's tales. Geoffrey's English had improved but I still had to explain some of the northern words that were used: beck, bairn, fret and others. When the last man had left us and I had told Alan when to arrange the next assize I stood. "Come, we will ride to Otterburn and I will speak with Sir Richard. He and I need to be of one mind." Just then my wife and son appeared.

"I will have food readied for you, husband."

Shaking my head, I said, "I will eat later. Geoffrey and I must ride to Otterburn and if we are to be back before dark then we should leave now."

My son asked, "Can I come?"

As much as I wished to take him with me for I needed to be with him as much as I could to make up the time I had lost, I knew I needed to ascertain the dangers first. "Not today for you have no mount but I will have Alan find you a pony and we will teach you to ride. When you can ride then I will take you on short journeys."

It was not the answer he wanted but a better one than he might have expected, "Good! Then I will be ready tomorrow!"

I laughed, "Aye, ready to groom her perhaps!"

I took ten men with me; five men at arms and five archers. There was already a patrol of four men riding the road to the south and I had sent a message to Gilbert de Umfraville telling him of the problems we had encountered on the road. He was a baron and therefore my senior so I

13

couched my words carefully, it would not do to upset a powerful neighbour even though he failed in his duty to the King and his people. Being an English lord of the manor meant you had to be aware of politics at all times.

Geoffrey found the landscape through which we travelled, as we headed to Otterburn, even more intimidating than the road north of the Tyne. It was like the land in which he had been held a prisoner by the Turks but with cold grey skies and the memory of the ambush freshly ingrained upon his mind, he was silent as we rode. I also had Alan Longsword with me for I had a view to making him my captain of men. He rode with Stephen Bodkin Blade and me. Stephen pointed out the various places we had battled the Scots when we thwarted their attempt to take this land. He also gave me information about where my men had found intruders. Visitors and travellers were always welcomed but intruders came to my manor for one of two purposes: to steal or to cause trouble.

Otterburn manor was in an even more exposed position than Elsdon. With a small beck close by and the border just a couple of miles away Sir Richard would find trouble sooner than anyone. His tower keep was always manned and we were spied as we headed towards his castle. He was there, at his gate, to greet me when we reined in. When I had left, he had been a newly promoted keen young knight who was full of life and energy. Now he looked to have aged and he appeared to carry the weight of the world upon his shoulders. When I dismounted and he greeted me, however, I saw in his welcome the young squire I had known a lifetime ago. We had played together as children and he was that most rare of things here on the border, a friend.

"Sir William, you look well and it is good to have you back." I heard the message beneath the words. He had been isolated and had to do the work of two knights.

I nodded, "My men have told me all and I am sorry we could not return sooner but my days as a crusader are now behind me and I look to the border. This is my new squire, Geoffrey of Lyons. Mark and Henry Samuel are now knighted. I have much to tell you."

He had his servants fetch us food as I regaled him with the tales of the crusade. When I had finished, he nodded, "And yet you say you achieved nothing?" I nodded. He then told me of the problems which had recently surfaced, "The peace we had lasted only until Queen Joan died. The new Queen has French connections and while I have no doubt that the King does not wish a war, he is surrounded by treacherous men who do and, as far as the King of Scotland is concerned, worse, for some seek his crown."

14

The King and Queen of Scotland had been responsible for arranging my marriage to Mary and I still viewed King Alexander as a friend. I also knew both from my experience and from the Scots I had met on my way to and from the Holy Land that there were many men who sought to either undermine or usurp the young King. Now that he had an heir, Prince Alexander, then he appeared to be in a slightly safer situation.

"Now that I am back, I intend to protect the border aggressively. Until King Henry orders me to do other then I will assume that the Scots wish mischief."

"And that is a sensible course of action."

"Who are the main amongst his enemies?"

He laughed, "I believe that we could be here for some time but the one I would fear if I was King Alexander is Walter Comyn the Mormaer of Menteith. He is ambitious and married to get Menteith! He is cunning and has an able Lieutenant in Stephen of Blair Atholl. That man was a mercenary who fought in the Baltic crusades although it was after your father's time. It is rumoured that he has connections amongst the Knights Templar too. Comyn uses his lieutenant to distance himself from any underhand actions. I have heard that they have raided and murdered some folk who live on the borders of Comyn land."

"Scots?"

"Aye, for Comyn is ruthless."

I nodded, "How did you discover this?"

The Count of Atholl, Alan Durward, told me. He is the avowed enemy of Comyn and they have had many fallings out. He is an English sympathiser."

I had heard the name when we had stopped in York, "But he is Count of Atholl!"

"And Stephen of Blair Atholl claims the title." He shrugged, "Who knows the truth of such matters; it may be just another of Comyn's plots and plans."

There was much to digest. I turned to Geoffrey who had been serving us wine and fetching fresh food but he had just stood watching. His face showed me that he was rapt. "Well Geoffrey, what are your thoughts?"

"My lord, I fear that we have stepped into a nest of vipers." He smiled, "But, at least life will not be dull, eh, my lord?"

For the next month, I rose with the sun and went to bed long after it had set. I rode every inch of the border as far as Alnwick and Jedburgh. I had patrols riding through every hidden trail that we could find. In the first days, we found traces of Scots but they were cold camps. They had left but that merely encouraged us to be vigilant. I wrote to my father to keep him apprised of the situation and I visited with de Umfraville at

Prudhoe. He assured me that he now had patrols in place and he had managed to catch and hang four bandits. I wondered how many nameless travellers had died because of his lax attitude.

I still found time to be with my wife and son. We found a pony for Richard. It was about the time we found the pony that the folk in the castle began to call him Young Master Dick. I had called my son Dick since I had returned from Crusade but that was family. That was the fault of Alan of Bellingham's wife. Her father had been called Dick and she took to calling my son, Young Master Dick. As she saw him every day when Anne served food at the table and Alan also used it, it stuck and, to be fair, the boy liked it. Henry Samuel had been Sam for a long time and Dick would be Richard when he became a squire and that was some time off. I also had Geoffrey begin to train him to be a page and then a squire. He played the hoop games with him and also made him a wooden sword so that he could practise. My wife totally understood that he would have to become a warrior one day and she was happy.

By the start of May, he was ready for me to take him with me to ride my lands. We had him a stout leather jerkin made and a leather helmet. Geoffrey kept a halter on the pony and we did not ride more than six miles in any one day but for Dick that was enough. He was at that age when he asked why not once or twice but eight or nine times until he received the answer he wanted. Geoffrey found it infuriating but I knew it had purpose for it made me question things that were right in front of my eyes. He innocently questioned my defences around the castle and it was only when I had been through all the 'whys' that I saw we had left things in place just because they had always been that way and, actually, no longer served a purpose. He made me look at the buildings we had erected and question their design. I realised that if we had an internal wall and gate in the inner bailey then we could slow down an attacker and make it harder for an enemy to take the keep. Sometimes his questions led nowhere but I did not mind answering them for he had the fresh eyes of a child untainted by what he had been told and taught. We began to work on the internal wall and gate. As we toiled, I could not help but feel that we were not just building a wall, we were building us into a closer body of brothers.

Brother Paul had an assistant, Father John. An earnest young priest, he had come to us because he had displeased the Bishop of Durham. It was easily done but the punishment of Elsdon Manor was not the punishment the Bishop thought. Brother Paul was a good priest and enjoyed the pastoral care of the manor and we employed the priest to teach Dick. Father John blossomed and my wife enjoyed his company too. The women of the castle were good women and my wife adored

16

them but they had little refinement and sometimes my wife wished to talk as she had done in Stockton Castle where my mother, a well-travelled and incredibly clever woman, did not suffer fools gladly. It was one reason she and Eleanor butted heads so much. Mother wanted a more serious and sober young lady rather than the giddy thing Eleanor played. I knew that my niece had hidden depths and that she was far cleverer than she appeared to those who did not see beneath the surface.

It was in May that we discovered that my wife was with child once more. Margaret of Yeavering, one of the Yalesham widows, was the midwife to the village and she confirmed what my wife suspected. I knew then that our lives would change and my wife threw herself into nest building for the new child. I had men toiling in the bailey and others in the hall and the news of a new child made us work even harder.

We had friends amongst the Scots for we never raided their lands and, if those along the border found themselves under attack from bandits, then they knew that they could send to us. The days of fearing our neighbours had gone. King Alexander had replaced the aggressive lords of his border manors with more reasonable men. It gave us a buffer and any danger came from further afield.

Sir Richard heard a rumour, as high summer approached, of movements of Scots, not towards our borders but west, towards the lands close to Carlisle. The firstborn of Scotland was often called the Prince of Cumberland and now that the King had a son, he had attained that title. I did not think, for one moment, that the King had sanctioned the movement but there were those who would see it their patriotic duty to try to regain the land for the baby prince. When he told me, at my castle, we discussed what this might mean. They say that two minds are better than one and we had three for my wife was clever and, being Scottish, understood the politics of Scotland better than we.

"Without disrespecting you, Sir Richard and my husband, this is poor land which my countrymen do not really want. It is more of the same land they till. The land around Carlisle, Westmoreland and Cumberland is far richer and the title, Prince of Cumberland, is still significant. My father told me how when King Stephen ruled England, he gave Cumberland back to the Scottish king. That was just a couple of generations ago. This military presence to the south and west of us makes sense to me."

Her words persuaded us.

Sir Richard and I decided to take a small conroi and head west to ascertain the threat. At the very least we could let the Constable of Carlisle Castle know the danger and it would also let us test the Scottish defences. I took just ten men at arms and ten archers. The rest would watch my walls. Sir Richard took half that number. Before we left, I wrote letters to my father and the Bishop explaining my actions for I did not want them to think that we were breaking the terms of the treaty. We left in the middle of June, close to the longest day of the year. Dick had asked to come but I asked him to watch his mother and our unborn child. He was a bairn himself but he nodded when I asked him to be the sentry to my wife's chamber.

I took with me a courser, Lion. I had named him thus for his colouring. I had seen a caged lion in Jerusalem and the name seemed right for a warhorse. I wore just my short hauberk. The land through which we would be travelling was rough and hard enough on our horses without adding extra weight. The men we took were all experienced and thanks to Alan of Bellingham and Sir Richard they were used to working with each other. We crossed the debated border and the river and headed south and west. Once we passed Bellingham we were in a desolate land. There were no villages and few farms which was why we rode the road. Any signs of numbers of men would indicate that the rumours were true.

I had no intention of riding for seventy miles through empty land if there was no need. My castle needed work and my family needed me but we had to investigate every danger. To fail to do so might result in a catastrophe such as had resulted in the death of Cedric the farmer and his son. I say the land was desolate but that is not quite true. It was virgin land. The tiny road cut through a huge forest. I suspected that the forest teemed with game as there was no lord, that I knew of, who hunted there. Alan of Bellingham told me that there the wolves which had disappeared from other parts of the land prospered. As we rode along the road, we kept archers some fifty paces from us in the forest for this was ambush country.

Geoffrey was keen to learn about this land and he asked me why the forest had not been cleared and farmed. "I confess, Geoffrey, that I know not for certain but I suspect that there are so few people here and the rocks are so close to the surface that it would be hard for a farmer to make a living and then there are the bandits and raiders. Some men do not like to work for themselves. They prefer to have others do the work and then they take the fruits of their labours. If Otterburn and Elsdon were not protected by castles then I fear our valley would soon revert to this."

There was but one place of any size, the village of Hautwesel. It lay south of the Roman Wall and while there was no castle there, we would be able to pitch our tents. We found evidence of raiders once we left the last stone covered section of road and headed across the drover's trail. Cattle were bought in the south and brought north while some of the Scots used the trail to drive their cattle to market at Carlisle where they would fetch higher prices than in their own country. Had we seen signs of cattle then we would not have worried overmuch. What we found were fires and evidence of a large number of men camping rough.

We first found the fires close to one of the patches of water north of the wall. It also confirmed, in my view, that these were bandits who were intent upon mischief. The main road from Newcastle to Carlisle passed south of the wall. There were still Roman buildings on the old wall which afforded shelter but they could be spied by the men who travelled the road on the King's business. The signs we found told us that there were Scots abroad and they were loose close to England.

We also found evidence of their presence further south in Hautwesel. As we approached, we saw that the village had been made defensible; there were carts and wagons formed defensively around the centre of the village. My castle was just thirty miles north and both my livery and my name were well known. The headman, Robert of Hautwesel, looked relieved to see me, "This is a happy accident lord for one of the outlying farms, old Walter's, was attacked three days since. We only heard last eve for Walter used to come into the village once a week. We found him and his dog slain. His cow and sheep had been butchered." He shook his head, "It was the Scots!"

"Any trail that we could follow?"

He pointed south. "They were heading for the road. My guess would be they intend to raid the richer farms further south."

Sir Richard and I concurred. We camped in the centre of the village and the folk there shared their food with us. Our presence meant that they could now get back to their lives. A couple of days defending their village could cost the farmers dear.

Geoffrey was like my son and he had question after question. He only knew the Holy Land and warfare here in the borders was a different prospect, "But what do these Scots hope to do, lord?"

"The Eden valley is fertile and the defences of Carlisle protect the river. By crossing the wall here they are able to strike at the rich heart of the valley. It is high summer and animals will be on the higher pastures grazing in these long days. They can strike and take large numbers of animals. You have just travelled for more than a day from Elsdon. How many people have you seen?" His face told me that he now understood the problem. "We could wait along their route and capture them but then men like Old Walter might pay the price. We need to catch them."

Sir Richard nodded, "But they have three days start."

We had seen their camps and the hoof prints were outnumbered by the prints of clogs and buskins, "They are on foot, Richard, and tomorrow we push our horses. When they have crossed the road south of the wall then their trail should be easier to see."

I sounded confident but now that they were south of the wall there were many places a large warband could ravage and raid. Barnard Castle was to the east, Carlisle lay to the south and the only obstacle to the South was Sir Humphrey Vieuxpont's at Brougham. It was a strong one but the River Eamont could be passed both up and downstream by raiders. We left before dawn and had the luxury of the road for a good five miles during which we made good time. It was Garth Red Arrow who found their trail where they had left the road to Carlisle to head towards the Alston pass. There had once been bandits at Alston but my father and I had cleansed the land there of them. It had yet to be strongly settled and the route of the Scots made perfect sense to me.

Alston had been raided. We found the folk there still tending to the wounds and hurts of the men who had fought the raiders but at least we now had the numbers we might face. Tom Guisely had been a soldier and he had led the defence of the large village. "There were more than a hundred of them, lord. They were more than bandits for a lord led them. I saw his spurs. They had men with hide armour and they fought with purpose. Had we had more to take then they might have stayed longer but they butchered our animals and then left. That was yesterday."

I nodded, "And how did you survive the attack?"

He pointed to the only building with two floors. It had once belonged to a lord of the manor, "We holed up in there. It is made of stone and they could not burn it. They made mischief and then left. We will rebuild but, my lord, if you catch them then hang the bastards!"

I nodded, "That we will."

We carried on south, now on an old Roman Road where we could make better time. Tom's words disturbed me. I had thought this was just the usual band of bandits taking what they could but mailed men and a knight was something different. We reached Melmerby and found the Scots. They had been stopped by the tower there which was manned by a handful of men from the le Denum family. Our approach caught both them and us by surprise.

The road from the north descended and twisted through a wood. It was as we emerged that I saw my archer scouts unsling their bows. Although it was not good for them, we travelled with strung bows and it was good that we did. Abel Millerson shouted, "My lord, the house is under attack!"

20

Sir Richard was younger than I was and I had recently led large numbers in the Holy Land. I took charge, "Archers, dismount and support us. Baggage, stay here. The rest, draw weapons and follow me!"

I had no time to fit my shield and so I just donned my helmet and drew my sword. I dug spurs into Lion's flanks and led my men down the road. As soon as I passed Abel and my archers who were dismounted and loosing their arrows, I saw the Scots. The tower was not a large one, it was tiny compared with Otterburn, and there were barely a handful of men defending it. The Scots were busy placing faggots around the door. My archers had alerted them and they turned to face us.

I saw the knight for he was mounted with half a dozen of his men. He began shouting orders and the warriors who had been preparing to fire the door picked up their weapons to face us. A few desultory arrows flew in our direction. One clattered off my mail and I felt one strike my leg. I was ahead of Sir Richard and our squires and I drew their first flights. The nature of the road and the houses in the village meant that I hit the Scots first closely followed by Sir Richard, Alan Longsword and then our squires. A handful of Scots ran at us with spears and pikes. I had fought the Scots many times and one thing could not be denied they were the most fearless men to fight. Their recklessness, however, was their undoing for the three of us who hit them first were both well trained and controlled.

The Scots were so keen to get at us that they did not allow enough room to swing their pole weapons and when the rear of their shafts rattled against each other their aim was no longer true. One spear struck my right leg and broke some links on my chausse but my sword was already cleaving his skull in twain. Lion snapped at them, while Sir Richard on my left lowered his sword and as the Scot turned in fear, he was skewered by Sir Richard's sword. Alan Longsword's horse clattered her hooves on to the knees of the next Scot and with shattered bones, he crumbled to die beneath our horse's hooves. Alan's longsword swept forward and almost hacked another Scot in two.

We were through their first attackers and onto the green before the castle. It allowed us to spread out and race at the lines of Scots who were trying to form a shield wall. As arrows fell amongst them, thinning their ranks, their lord and his horsemen turned to race west along the Penrith road. As much as I wanted to catch him, we had almost eighty men to deal with. Geoffrey had joined me and he used his dead brother's sword with deadly efficiency. He leaned from his saddle to hack through bones and bucklers to maim and wound. I used Lion's hooves to smash through the Scottish warriors' defences and shatter bones and end lives. By the time my archers and men at arms had joined us it was all over. The fact that none surrendered showed just how brave the Scottish warriors were. Even as the last one was slain, I heard, from the west, the sound of a clash of arms.

"Garth Red Arrow, take command of the archers. The rest, with me!"

Galloping down the road I wondered what the clash of arms ahead meant. As we crested the rise and looked towards the village of Langwathby I saw a conroi of knights and men at arms. From the standard, I knew that it was Humphrey Vieuxpont and his men from Brougham. Even as we closed with them, I saw Sir Humphrey strike the Scottish knight with his war axe and the rest of the horsemen were slain.

The fighting had ended by the time we reached them and I reined in next to the knight and took off my helmet. "Well met, Sir Humphrey."

"And to you, Sir William. We heard that Melmerby was under attack but what brought you here?"

"Rumours of Scottish raiders. They were justified, it seems. They attacked Hautwesel and Alston before they attached the tower of Melmerby." I pointed at the man. "Who is he? I do not recognise the livery."

"I think he is a member of the Atholl clan. His livery looks like he is related to the Earl of Atholl. Padraig was the Earl but he was murdered eight years since. This could be one of his cousins."

I nodded, "And that makes sense of a rumour which has come that Walter Comyn is using Stephen of Atholl to cause trouble for the Scottish King. Will you tell his family of his death?"

"Aye, I will send them his body with armour and sword. It is what I would wish if I should die far from my family."

I nodded and gave him my arm to clasp, "Fare ye well and know that I will continue to watch the border by the Tweed for I am King Henry's sentry."

"And I will do the same here. Between us, we should be able to keep the peace."

And so I thought too, but I was wrong.

We had lost no men although we had suffered wounds. We helped to repair the tower at Melmerby before retracing our steps back to Elsdon. The loot the Scots had taken we returned, where we could, but they had not yet had time to capture many cattle and had eaten the ones that they had. The horses from the Scots were divided between Sir Humphrey and my men while the weapons were given, by me, to the villages which had been attacked. They would be able to defend themselves.

Chapter 3

It was July when we reached Elsdon and I was relieved to see that all was peaceful. My wife and son were pleased to see me although I saw that Mary had taken too much out of herself and looked tired. I sent her to her bed and I took over the work in the hall. I changed that which she had planned; her improvements would not give us more room and with a new child on the way that was what we needed. We could not build out but we could build up and so I added a pair of sturdy and spacious towers. In a time of war, they would give elevation to my archers but Dick could use one for his bedroom and when we had our next child there would be another room for them. We kept working on the dividing wall in the inner bailey for the Scottish attack had shown me that danger had not gone. I kept my mother and father informed of all that went on. I did so by sending a rider to Prudhoe who then sent my missives on to Durham and thence to Stockton. It was not a speedy form of communication but it was contact and I knew that my parents would appreciate the news.

We actually finished one of the new towers in less than a month. The internal walls needed plaster and the access to the fighting platform on the tower was just a ladder but we would be able to put a bed inside by the time September came. Dick was so excited at the prospect of sleeping in a tower that he asked to move in directly. My wife forbade him.

It was August when we had unexpected visitors. I was stripped to the waist helping to build the second tower when Geoffrey shouted, "Sir William, I see wagons approaching from the south and there is a knight with them." He peered out and shouted, joyfully, "It is Sir Henry! It is your nephew!"

I wondered what had brought him to the north.

Then Sir Geoffrey shouted, "And there is a lady in the wagon although her face is covered and I know not who she is!"

The thought crossed my mind that Sam had married but why would he bring his bride here?

I donned a tunic and headed down to the inner bailey to greet them. Passing through the hall I said to my wife, "We have guests. My nephew is here and there is a lady. I am guessing that they are here to stay for a while."

As I stepped into the bailey, I saw that the lady was Sam's sister, Eleanor. Before I even had time to try to work out the reason for the

23

visit my nephew had jumped from his horse and given me a hug, "Uncle! Vanquisher of the Scot! It is good to be here!"

I laughed, "And you are more than welcome, let us help your sister from the wagon and then you can tell me the reason for this most unexpected yet pleasurable of visits."

He gave an apologetic shrug, "There is much to tell and I also bring great news but it can wait until I have slaked my thirst with some of your beer! I hear that the waters of the River Rede make for good ale!"

"That they do and the Yalesham widows make the best of ale."

I held my arms up and Eleanor leapt into them. She buried her head into my shoulder, "Uncle, I am such a fool! My father would have been so disappointed in me."

I kissed the top of her head and put my arm protectively around her, "That I doubt. You never knew your father but I did and he was the most understanding of men. Whatever you think you have done we can sort it out." As I led her towards the hall, I wondered what could have caused my happy, cheerful and lively niece to become so unhappy.

My wife and I understood each other well and, as we entered, I used my eyes to warn her of Eleanor's condition. She gave a subtle nod and then beamed, "It is so good to see you, Eleanor. I do not know how long you can stay but it cannot be long enough for me. Come, we have a room with water where you can freshen up."

As she left, I asked Sam, "What is going on?"

He shook his head, "I only know half the story and my little sister refuses to give her side of it. I just know that she and grandmother had a huge row. There was much shouting and tears. I was already coming here and my mother said it would be best if Eleanor came so that she could help Mary with the birth of your next child." I handed him a beaker of ale, "That is all I know, I swear. I tried to find out the cause of the argument on the way here but I failed. My little sister was tight-lipped."

My wife and Eleanor returned. Mary had her arm around my niece and she said, "Henry Samuel, you can sleep in the new nursery chamber and Geoffrey will need to sleep in the warrior hall. Eleanor will have Geoffrey's room. Richard shall have his wish and sleep in the tower but Beth will sleep with the other servants. I will take Eleanor to her room." She gave me a pointed look and I nodded.

I waved over Alan of Bellingham and Geoffrey. "Help my son move into the tower and then shift your gear. You do not mind, do you?"

Geoffrey grinned, "It will help my English. The men know many words that you and Lady Mary do not use!" Of that I was certain.

Left alone I said, "And your visit?"

"There is good news for you. You are made a Baron for your service on the crusade and your work here." I nodded but without any enthusiasm. "I thought you would have been happier, Uncle."

"Elsdon is too small a place to support a baronetcy. It is a title only. All that it does do is allow me to have a voice in the county but I suppose I should be grateful. At least I will now be the equal of de Umfraville."

"I am just a bachelor knight and such things are new to me but I have news about me and the other knights of the valley. King Henry has summoned us to go to France to fight with his relatives against the French."

"He fights for the Lusignans?" He nodded and drank some more ale. "Then watch your back for they are a treacherous lot. Who else goes?"

"All of the knights from the valley. The King thinks we have the Scots under control. Only my grandfather will remain in the valley. Sir William de la Lude of Hartburn will lead our men."

I was less than happy with the news. The Lusignans wanted one thing, power. They were just as keen to get the English crown as the French one. "And how does my father feel about this?"

He laughed, "His reaction was just like yours and your words echo his."

"All that I am saying is for you to be wary. King Henry is no warrior and there are many who would like to see him brought down. If he is with the army in France then he is in danger. Watch out for yourself."

He looked at me seriously, "Uncle, I am the next generation of knights in our family. Thomas and Alfred will not be going on campaign although Alfred's father, Geoffrey, is summoned. There are four grandsons who will remain in England and that should be enough. I know that it is my time to shoulder responsibility and I will do so. Fear not, you and grandfather have trained me well and the hot sun of the Holy Land has not just darkened my skin, it has tempered me as a warrior. Mark feels exactly the same. We have a duty to Matthew to be the best knights that we can be and we shall be."

I smiled, "You are right and although I know that you will acquit yourself well, I still worry about you."

He stood, "Come, I have seen improvements since last we were here. I would have the new Baron show them to me!"

I heard the mocking tone in his words. It was typical Sam! "You are not too big that I cannot clip you!"

Laughing he scampered out of the hall, like the young squire he had so recently been. "To do so you must first catch me!"

Henry Samuel made me feel young. I could see why he was so popular in Stockton Castle. As I took him around it was as though I was seeing the improvements for the first time and I was pleased. He approved of all the improvements. When we reached the tower, we found Dick and Alan of Bellingham arranging my son's bed. I shook my head, "It will be cold here at night, even in summer. There is no fire within and the tower is not on the same side as the chimneys."

"I will be all right!"

Henry Samuel tousled my son's head, "And if you are cold then come down the stairs and sleep with me, cuz! If you can stand the snores!"

Dick giggled. Henry Samuel was good for us all!

Neither my wife nor Eleanor came down for some time. Alice brought word that cook should begin the food and the two would join us when time allowed. Henry Samuel and Geoffrey seemed oblivious to the obvious upset and I tried to speak normally to the three of them but I hated the not knowing and I also wondered, somewhat selfishly, if this was good for my wife and unborn child. When the two did descend they were both in obvious good spirits. I looked at my wife and asked a question with my eyes. She shook her head. I was to say nothing. I could beard any number of enemies but I would not cross words with the females in my family. If my wife wanted the tears ignored then ignored, they would be.

Geoffrey and Eleanor had got on well in Stockton and they resumed their playful banter. I think in Geoffrey's case it was a little flirtatious but Eleanor had not yet met anyone as exotic as Geoffrey whose English was accented and who had foreign looks about him. The table was filled with infectious laughter for Alfred's children both had a great sense of humour. I took Dick to bed while the drinking and the witty banter continued. Normally it would have been a hard job getting him to bed but he was excited about his new tower.

Alan of Bellingham's wife, Ann, had brought extra blankets. Beth came with me to ensure that her charge had all that he wanted. She looked around and gave the tower a critical glare. Shaking her head, she mumbled, "The bairn will catch his death of cold in here!"

"Beth, it is August and even though I have spent the last two years in hot climes I still find it warm!"

Dick happily grinned, "I like it! It is like my own cave! I will be fine!"

Ann wagged a finger, "And no walking around in the night. I do not want you falling down the stairs. Use the garderobe if you need to make water!"

I could see that he tired of her comments and wished just to snuggle down and pretend… I know not what but I had done the same when I was his age. I shooed the women away. "Dick, if you need aught or you are afeared then there is no shame in shouting for us. Your cousin meant what he said, you can sleep with him if you need to."

He nodded and pulled his blanket up around him. "Good night, father!"

As I descended the ladder, I realised that I had missed his vulnerable years when he had learned to walk, to make water, to eat with a spoon. I had gone away when he was little more than a babe and come back to a young child. I would make up for it with my next one.

When I entered my hall, they all stood and raised their beakers, "The Baron of Elsdon!"

I shook my head and my wife said, "Why did you not tell me?"

It was on the tip of my tongue to remind her that I had not seen her since I had been given the news but instead, I said, "It went from my head." I sat next to Eleanor. "I just hope that you will not find it dull here on the wild frontier!"

"Uncle, you do not know what a relief it is to be away from critical eyes and tongue."

I had inadvertently said the wrong thing and so I changed the subject, "And how long do you stay, Sam?"

"A couple of days at the most. I have to speak with Richard for I have messages from his father."

I understood. My father could deal with much of the work of Hartburn Manor but Sir William of Hartburn would like his son to visit, at least once while he was away.

I had to wait until my wife and I were alone in the bedchamber to discover the cause for the argument which had driven Eleanor hence. As I suspected it was a clash of wills between my mother and Eleanor. Both were strong-minded characters.

"As with all such family arguments, husband, it began small and the embers were quickly fanned by two women who are very similar in nature. Your mother made the mistake of comparing Eleanor to her brother and Eleanor threw back that Henry Samuel was your mother's favourite. Your mother compounded it by telling your niece that she could do worse than model herself on her brother. Eleanor called her grandmother an old witch!" She sighed in the dark, "Both are in the wrong but now that the carrot is out of the ground it cannot be replaced. Eleanor does not like the fact that she is compared to her brother for she thinks that he has been given more chances at life than she has. That she adores her brother is obvious but your mother risks driving a wedge between them."

"Aye, you are right. She barely spoke to him on the way up. Both my mother and my niece will miss him while he is in France. Perhaps this enforced distance will help them."

"Perhaps, but it has upset our domestic arrangements. I like not that Dick is in a cold tower alone!"

I laughed, "He is loving it but I will push on with our work and besides, Henry Samuel is only here a short time. It will be a two-night summer adventure for Dick!"

The next morning, we rode to Otterburn. It was close enough that I could take Dick but I ensured we had enough men at arms and archers with us for protection. I was still enjoying the conversation and atmosphere from the previous night. It had been good to hear Eleanor laughing again as Geoffrey amused her with his impression of one of the French knights we had met in Caesarea; he was a good mimic and anything that raised the spirits of my lively niece was welcome, in my view.

Henry Samuel had served with us and knew the land well. Even though we chatted as we rode, like me he was vigilant. "And, nephew, and how are the squires you and Sir mark now train?"

He nodded, "John, Sir William's sergeant at arms' son, is t mine and he is now at home being given instruction by Sir William of Hartburn and Sir Ralph, who was Sherriff of York's son. He is a good warrior for his father, Johann, has great experience. I believe that Edward, is working hard too."

"Then there will be many inexperienced men going to war for the King." He nodded and I could see that the thought had crossed his mind. I knew that my father would have brought all of this up with the King. "And the ones who have experience have not fought since they last followed my father here and that was some years since."

My nephew grinned, "You sound so much like grandfather that it frightens me! Aye, you are right and between you and me, grandfather worries that it is Sir William de la Lude who leads us for he has grey hairs and has not warred for even longer. But, despite that, I am hopeful for we fight in France and Sir William held a manor there for some time. There are others who will make the major decisions and our company has heart. I am looking forward to fighting alongside our grandfather's men for that is what we will be. Think on it, uncle, for the first time since Sir Samuel led the knights of Cleveland to follow King Richard, there will be a company of knights, men at arms and archers who will fight on foreign soil for England and its King! Great times lie ahead!"

You could not dampen the enthusiasm of youth but, like my father at home, I feared for them and knew that if either my father or I were there then they would have a greater chance of success. England had torn itself apart in civil disorder and there were few great knights left. The days of William Marshal and the Earl of Cleveland were long gone!

Sir Richard was, of course, delighted to see my nephew for they had grown close in the grim campaign which had seen us wrest the border from the Scots. Neither Sam nor I minded when he took his father's missive and devoured it. After he had finished and folded it up, he frowned and spoke to me, "I should be at my father's side when he goes to war."

"I know and I should be there too but if we left then the back door to England is left wide open. Our little foray to the wall has shown me that. One Scottish knight and a handful of followers cut a trail of destruction through the border."

He nodded, "Yet the destruction was not complete."

"And that was because of us. We have a duty here and my recent journey to Jerusalem has convinced me that watching our borders and fighting the Welsh and the Scots is of far more importance than a crusade or trying to get back lands thrown away by the wilful King John."

Henry Samuel was trying to be positive when he said, "Now that King Henry has a son he may grow into his role as a leader of knights."

I knew my father's view on that. "Perhaps, and I confess that King Henry does give some hope for unlike his father he has yet to alienate his lords. His preoccupation with King Edward the Confessor, however, worries me for that King was not a warrior king and that is what we need. We need another Henry such as the Warlord followed."

We then spoke of the border and Sir Richard confirmed that it was quiet. My own patrols had come to that conclusion. It would not make us complacent for it was like the weather here; more often than not it rained and when it did not rain there were clouds and that meant rain was on the way. Even a clear day made us suspicious.

"You must come tomorrow evening for we will enjoy a farewell meal with Sam here. You shall stay the night."

Sir Richard smiled, "Aye, it will be good to enjoy the company of Lady Mary. This is a bachelor castle in every way. Save for Anna, the wife of my steward, and the cook of the castle, there are no other women within these walls."

Riding back to Elsdon, Henry Samuel was in a reflective mood. "It is a monkish existence for Sir Richard and yet when he first came here, he was full of joy for the manor he had been given."

"And when you impress King Henry, as I know you shall, then he will give you a manor but it will not be an easy one in the south of England with a good income and a peaceful land. It will be somewhere he can use your sword to defend England. If not here then in the Welsh Marches."

"But Llewellyn the Great is dead!"

I laughed, "Do not use that appellation near to the King! You are right but his sons are not dead and only one is in the Tower. I have fought there and I can tell you that the land is hard to tame. It needs castles not like Elsdon but like Prudhoe, Warkworth and Stockton to defend it against the border raiders."

My men had been hunting and had managed to bring down deer fat with good grazing in a wet spring and hot summer. My father had sent wine with Henry Samuel and the feast promised to be a good one. We invited Brother Paul and his curate, Father John. Cedric, whose father had been slain protecting the manor and Alan of Bellingham were also invited. Geoffrey would not have to serve. We used the daughters of the Yalesham widows who were eager to earn an extra coin or two and to enjoy the company of the local great and good. For my wife this was a perfect opportunity to show to the leading local women, the improvements she had wrought. Now showing our new child she did less work on the hall but the last months had seen a transformation. We did not have the quality of tapestries and wall coverings my mother enjoyed but they were superior to any that the two guests had seen.

Eleanor, too, had improved spirits. I could not say anything to Sam about the cause of the row but I know that my wife had spoken at length to my niece about the situation and I think that Eleanor now knew that her brother had nothing to do with my mother's attitude and the distance between Stockton and Elsdon was a good thing. She and Geoffrey got on really well and he was also a changed squire. It had taken some time to get over the fact that his brother had been a traitor and that, now, Geoffrey was alone in an alien land. The two of them complimented each other and it was good.

Sir Richard was the last to join us and I could see why. I guessed that Anna, who was a motherly sort of woman, had helped to dress the young knight for he looked resplendent and had had his hair and beard trimmed and groomed. His surcoat looked to be new and he looked every inch the young errant knight. When Eleanor laid eyes on him it was as though she was seeing him for the first time. Hartburn and

Stockton are close and the two of them had occasionally played together
as children. Richard had been keen to enjoy the company of boys and
had largely ignored the young and awkward Eleanor. Now they were
grown and Eleanor was a woman when they saw each other I could feel
the excitement between them. My wife saw it too and smiled as she
nodded at me. I wondered how she had colluded with Anna. I also saw
the disappointment on Geoffrey's face. It was only then that I saw that
he and Eleanor were of an age and that he, too, might have had
romantic intentions.

The night made it clear that Richard and Eleanor were both smitten
by each other. My wife even sat them together as though to encourage
it. Brother Paul and Father John made up for Geoffrey's silence and the
table was lively despite his face. As Henry Samuel told a story of the
Holy Land and Jerusalem I said, quietly, to Mary, "I see your hand in
all of this!"

She smiled, "You men plot and plan wars but we have other plans.
Queen Joan saw that you and I were meant for each other and it was she
brought us together. Since I have come here, I have got to know
Richard and there is much to like about him. Of course, he is a man and
does not take enough care about his appearance. Mistress Anna was
more than happy to take him in hand. As for your niece, that is simple,
she is ready for a husband and children. She was sent here for a
purpose. Her mother, Matilda, could have done the same but the row
with your mother stopped that so that this is meant to be. The Yalesham
widows are philosophical about their state. They see the hand of fate in
all of this. They lost their first husband and you and your father brought
new men into their lives. They do not forget their dead menfolk but they
enjoy their new lives."

"Then you planned all of this from the moment that Eleanor
arrived?"

She shook her head, "No, I planned all of this in Stockton when I saw
then the discord between your niece and her grandmother." She smiled
and patted the back of my hand, "See, they are in love, are they not?"

I looked at them and saw that were bound in each other's eyes,
"Perhaps, but let us take this slowly, eh, matchmaker?"

She laughed, "Of course for there is no need for haste." She patted
her burgeoning belly, "We have a winter for them to grow close."

Henry Samuel left the next day and the parting between brother and
sister told me that any rift which might have existed was now healed.
That between my mother and niece would still remain but I would let
others worry about that. Sir Richard was also sad when Henry Samuel
left for I think he wanted the opportunity to fight in a war which was a

31

little more glorious than hunting down cattle raiders. The parting between Sir Richard and my niece was also a hard one for both of them. She was a maiden and he was a bachelor knight. They had to be formal and a kiss on the back of a hand was all that was permitted. That they wished to be together was obvious but Richard, especially, was aware of the niceties and protocols of the situation. As the eldest son of Sir William de la Lude, he had to be above board in all that he did.

My wife helped in her usual and practical way. As the two waved goodbye Mary said, "And now we can begin to prepare the crib and gowns for the new babe. We have much to do as we may have a girl and she may need clothes which are smaller than those which we had for Richard. It is best to be prepared. Any we do not need will not go to waste for we can give them to the mothers from the village!"

And so, we kept Eleanor busy. When she was not preparing for the baby, she was watching our son. It allowed me to finish the tower and the internal wall before winter set in.

Chapter 4

We knew, by the beginning of November, that it was going to be a hard winter because autumn had been wet and many farmers had crops which had failed. We were luckier than many other border farmers as ours had harvested earlier than was usual; that was as a result of Cedric and some of the other farmers having a feeling about the harvest. It was smaller than normal but not as poor as the ones who had it ruined by flooded fields. However, as most of our farmers raised animals it just meant we would have to be careful over the winter. When the first hard frost came in late October, I sent men to copse our trees for winter firewood. It was just a precaution but proved, in the end, to be justified. The second week of November brought the first snow. I was told, by Alan of Bellingham, that it often did this but when it was still snowing and had not relented by the end of the last week in November then we knew we were in for that hardest of winters, a wolf winter. There was a danger that we would be cut off from Sir Richard and so, while the road was still barely passable, I went with Geoffrey and four men to ride to Otterburn. It was one of the hardest rides I had ever undertaken.

We went wrapped for warmth and not for war. Upon our heads, we wore the hats made from rabbit skins and I had well-made sheepskin-lined gloves upon my hands. The buskins I wore on my feet were the oiled ones which would keep my feet dry. With woollen scarves wrapped tightly about our faces, we rode in silence for speech was almost impossible. For Geoffrey snow was something he had only seen on the tops of the mountains towards Swabia. He was finding it hard to stay warm. I think he was getting over his infatuation with Eleanor but seeing her each day could not have helped. I wondered if he regretted choosing to be my squire. If I had an alternative, I would, once more, have offered him the chance to leave my service for he was obviously unhappier than he had been.

Folk had used the road and so the snow did not lie as thickly as it did elsewhere but I knew that when the snow finally abated and it froze then the road would be impassable. I needed Sir Richard to keep his end of the road clear and I would keep mine. We either both did it or neither.

We had already brought every animal we could into the outer bailey. Cedric had learned from earlier raids and he had built stone enclosures which could be guarded against predators both human and animal. What we had we would keep. Some farmers still had the houses with a barn

33

below the first floor. They would have the advantage of heat from the animals and a greater likelihood of keeping what they had. As we had ridden north, I saw some of Sir Richard's animals still in the fields.

I was weary beyond words when we neared the castle and I was as cold as I could ever remember. Once we were in the hall, we took off our cloaks to dry them out a little. They were oiled but damp had a way of seeping through. The first thing I said to Sir Richard was, "You must have your farmers bring in their animals or you must have them inside your bailey or they will die."

I saw his face fall. Once I had said it then it was quite obvious but he had not initiated the thought himself. "You are right. I was fooled by the last two winters which were benign. Each day I think that the snow will melt and all will be well!"

Shaking my head, I said, "I fear not. I know my farmers for they have farmed a long time and they tell me that this will be a hard one. I cannot stay long for I need to return to my wife and the weather is not becoming any easier. I came here for you and I must make a decision. Do we keep the road open or abandon all communication until the thaw?"

I had deliberately couched it in stark terms and it had the desired effect. He shook his head, "I do not wish to lose touch with you and Elsdon. This is a lonely enough existence at the best of times. Had I wished to be a priest then I would have joined the monks at Fountain's Abbey!"

I smiled and knew that Eleanor had been much on his mind and the thought of being cut off from her would be hard to bear. "Then we will need to start tomorrow while the snow is still soft. Once it becomes frozen then we will shift nothing."

His Captain, Oswald of Otterburn, smiled, "It will be good for the lads, my lord. Stuck in the castle with no way to get rid of energy leads to fighting. This way they will be too tired to do anything else!" We headed back through the snow.

We began work the next day even though we were working in blizzard conditions. The men of the village cleared the village itself while my men and I, along with Geoffrey, took shovels and wheelbarrows to clear the road. The total distance was a mere three miles and so we just had one and a half miles to clear but, by the end of the first day we had only managed to clear just over half a mile and when we returned the next day snow had fallen on the part we had cleared. Of course, it did not take long to clear it for there was less of it and by the end of the day we had a mile done and we were able to shout to Sir Richard's men. Despite more overnight snow, we were able to join together the next day but we realised that until the snow stopped, we would need men clearing the road each day.

In the event, we had just three more days of the snow and then the land froze so hard that we spied some birds frozen to death. We would not need to clear the snow and we could reach Otterburn. We would be able to walk using wooden shoes with nails hammered through the soles to give us purchase on the ice but we would now need to use our reserves of timber and food for cold such as this needed heat for homes, animals and for life itself.

And then my daughter, Margaret, was born! She came on the second day of December. My wife was a hardy woman but it was not an easy birth. I think if we had not had so many experienced midwives living in the castle it might gone ill but Margaret was born healthy and the first to cradle her was Eleanor for my wife was weak. That instant changed Eleanor for Margaret was the first baby she had seen delivered and certainly when Mary of Yalesham put the swaddled, yet bloody bundle in her arms, Eleanor knew that she wished to be a mother and I saw her coo and whisper to the child. The two became as close as any and even when Eleanor had her own children then she and Margaret remained close.

My daughter changed all of our lives. Dick became very protective towards his little sister and we discovered, over the next months and then years, that Margaret had a forceful personality. What Margaret wanted she got! She was a demanding baby or, perhaps, the fact that my son had been born at Stockton Castle with my mother and all the other ladies to help I had not noticed how much our lives changed. In one way, however, her arrival was timely for it was just before Christmas and Brother Paul was able to christen her on Christmas Eve and that seemed appropriate and, somehow, symbolic. The church was packed and I think that was because Margaret was the first child to be born in the castle for a very long time. Despite the lively nature of my daughter the women of the village took her to one of their own and could not do enough for her and my wife. In spite of the sleepless nights, I could not help but thank God for delivering us of our daughter. Within a short time, she became a symbol of Elsdon and long after she had grown into a woman the people of Elsdon still thought of her as their own.

We still had Christmas to celebrate and I ordered the slaughter of one of our cattle. The animal should have been culled in October with the other weak ones but, somehow, she had sneaked through. She was an old cow and had not given milk for some time. The meat would need long and slow cooking. That did not matter for the cooks were happy to be in the warmth of the kitchen where the fire was warm and the ladling of juices over the animal was not a hardship. The women had made all the other Christmas treats well before the festive period and so we had puddings, pies, tarts and all manner of delights which would enliven our palates. The fact that my father and I had brought so many spices from the east was seen as a boon. I was generous with them and every house and farm on the manor benefitted. While in the rest of the country such spices were reserved for the richest of nobles, in Elsdon all shared in the bounty we had brought back. The crusade had done some good!

Of course, apart from Margaret, the castle was graced with love for Sir Richard spent the three days around Christmas with us. He was Margaret's godfather and Eleanor one of the godmothers. Thus, they were able to stand close together in the church, holding the babe and they could look longingly and lovingly into each other's eyes.

Sir Richard's last day with us was the feast of St. Stephen. The cooks had prepared the bread which encased some of the meat left over from the previous day's feast. As I broached another barrel of the wine Sir Richard came over to speak with me, "You know, Baron William that..."

I had drunk well and I smiled at him and held up my hand, "We have fought the wild Scots together. We raided apples from old Osbert's orchard at the Grange Field together, I am Will!"

He grinned, "Sorry, Will, I do not know if you are aware but Eleanor and I... your niece Eleanor that is..." I smiled. As if there was another. "Well, we have feelings for each other and I would ask you to intercede with your father on my behalf."

I clapped him about the shoulders, "Of course we are aware! The whole manor knows of it and we are all joyful." I lowered my voice, "She is a maiden and vulnerable. I would have propriety!"

"Of course."

"We shall have to wait until the snow thaws to send a message to Stockton. It may be Easter before you have your reply."

He grinned, "I care not but you may find me a regular visitor once the snow has departed." He looked happy, "May I tell her?"

"Of course."

Eleanor was seated with my wife. Beth had taken Margaret to her bed and Dick, despite all his best efforts to stay awake, lay asleep before the fire. I watched the two as he told her his news. They could not help themselves and threw their arms around each other. The room erupted in a cheer for all knew what it meant. All that is, except for Geoffrey, I suppose he had always known that she could never be his but until there was some sort of announcement, however informal, then there was hope. That hope was doomed to be dashed.

The wolves came in January. Cedric and Alan told me that the folk of the valley had not heard them for more than ten years. Alan went back twenty years to the last wolf howl he, personally, had heard in the forests. Perhaps they had decimated the herds of deer further south or it may have been such a harsh winter that they were driven close to the homes of men. Whatever the reason we had to do something about it. There were still isolated farms and a pack of wolves could do much damage. And, of course, they could attack the animals we had kept alive through the snow and ice. The ones in my village and Otterburn were safe but not so Cedric and the outlying farmers of Otterburn Manor. I took Alan of Bellingham, my archers and we headed into the remote areas of both manors.

I sent a rider to Sir Richard for this would need both of us and our men to remedy. The ten archers I took were my best and we reached Otterburn at noon. Sound travels a long way in winter and the frozen ground seemed to amplify the noise. As we headed for Otterburn, we heard the wolves, in the distance, and Idraf seemed to think that the wolves were to the south and west. Idraf had grown up in Towyn, in the shadow of Snowdon, the mountain he called Wyddfa where they still had many wolves. I trusted my men's instincts added to which it made sense. The wolves had proliferated in the land to the south and west of us. If their food supply had dried up then our land was the one which promised the most.

My rider had alerted Sir Richard and he was ready to ride. Our archers would be the most effective weapon we had and they all had good arrows with a barbed hunting arrowhead. We had spears. If the wolves decided to attack then they were the best defence. The sight of a wolf's gaping maw coming towards a man could empty his bowels rapidly. A spear was better protection!

We crossed the river and headed for the farm of Old Edgar. He, his wife and his widowed daughter lived alone. Ada had lost her husband in a Scottish raid. She had never married and the three of them lived a lonely existence. Although but a couple of miles from Otterburn, they were seen infrequently. I know that Sir Richard feared for Ada once her parents died. I dreaded finding a gaping door and three bodies for Old Edgar had seen more than fifty summers. To our great relief, when we found the door it was closed and we had to bang to attract attention.

When we told him our purpose Edgar laughed a laugh which had more lost teeth than ones he could use to chew, "Fear not, lord. We need not open our door. I can get to my animals through the back door of my home but it was good of you to think of us. We shall remember you in our prayers."

Relieved we continued south and west. The frozen snow made a good surface upon which to ride. None had walked upon it and it saved us having to twist and turn down a road. We rode towards the sound of the wolves. They howled but not regularly. We had to change direction a number of times but we kept drawing closer. We crossed the North Tyne which was a chillingly cold crossing. Once across we were in the land of the Scots and many would have asked why we did not turn around. The answer was simple; when there were wolves then there was no border for they were an enemy to all!

I was unfamiliar with this part of the border. I had fought north and west of here and we had travelled further south and east when we had followed the Scottish raiders. When I saw the farm, in the distance, then I knew that something was amiss. There was no smoke coming from the farm. No-one could go without a fire in weather like this. Our archers spread out in a large semi-circle and Sir Richard and I, along with our squires approached, with great trepidation, the farm. I dismounted and handed my reins to Geoffrey. I could not smell wolf but I drew my sword and dagger anyway. Sir Richard walked to my right.

The door was open and some frozen snow had blown into the farmhouse. That, alone, told me that the house was cold. It was still daylight but it would not last long and the light from the sun showed what had occurred. There was a great deal of blood on the floor. I shouted but received no reply. As there were no body parts then I guessed that the family had been attacked and their bodies taken by the pack. The family was dead and I made the sign of the cross and said a silent prayer for their souls. They were Scots but they did not deserve that as an end. When I emerged, I shouted, "Idraf, where did they go?"

He pointed west, "That way, lord."

Turning to Sir Richard I said, "We cannot catch them before dark. Let us return to your castle and tomorrow, we will leave before dawn. We fetch food and we can use this farm to rest and to sleep. The dead will not mind for we shall avenge them!"

He nodded, "Aye, we must scour the land for the safety of the people, all of the people."

The journey back was as hard as the journey out and I knew that we would have two more hard days. We were a little cramped in Otterburn but we did not mind for the cosy nature of the accommodation meant that we were all warm. It was also a comfort as we heard, in the distance, the howling of wolves. I found it hard to sleep for I had a vivid imagination and I could not put the thought of my daughter, Margaret, at the mercy of the wolves. A man, even a woman or a child could defend themselves but there were the old and the extremely young who would die. The picture kept me awake.

We reached the farm well before noon and the sun, although lower in the clear blue sky told us the time. We left our spare horse and the food we had brought in the farm. We were all warriors and could ignore the blood but if my men were like me, they would picture the deaths that had followed the attack.

The landscape was not the one we usually encountered in this part of the world. The snow evened out bumps and hollows. The frozen snow made the land one huge road which made travel a little easier. I relied on the locals, men like Alan of Bellingham and he pointed to a piece of high ground to the west. It lay more than two miles away but we could all see the trees and the rocks which were the perfect place for a small pack of wolves to hide. We knew it was a small pack from the tracks we had seen. Wolves follow in a single line but if you know wolves you can still determine the size of the pack. Alan of Bellingham knew wolves. We knew that they would, in all likelihood, be there for there had been a blood trail which had led in that direction. The further from the farm we came then we found less evidence of blood but an occasional smear showed us that we were on the right track. To the north and west, about four miles away lay another farm. The lack of smoke disturbed me for it meant that the people who had lived there were no longer at home. I hoped that they might have gone to stay with relatives but, in my heart, I knew that the wolves had claimed more victims.

As we headed towards the heavily forested high ground Geoffrey asked, "Lord, I do not understand this. Wolves have no hands nor do they have weapons. How could they get inside a farm and kill those within? I know they are fierce beasts but if I was in a farm, I would bar the doors until they had gone!"

Alan of Bellingham shook his head, "And that is what I would do, Master Geoffrey, until I needed some water or one of my animals cried out. When we get back to the farm you will see a pail which is frozen to the ground with ice. It told me the story as soon as I saw it. The wolves are cunning creatures and the pack would have waited for they are patient. Someone came out of the farm to fetch water. While the door was open then they struck. Even warriors do not keep weapons to hand in their own homes."

With that sobering thought, we rode closer to the trees. The archers unslung their bows and each readied an arrow. Idraf was our wolf expert and it did not take him long to find the wolves' trail. The covering of the trees and the passage of the animals made the trail through the woods slightly easier to see. As the ground rose it became harder for us to ride for the frozen trail was slippery. We dismounted and tethered our horses to trees. We left our two squires with the horses for what we were about to do was not for those who had never hunted before. I took off my cloak, despite the cold for I needed free movement with my arms. I had my sword but it was the long spear I carried which would, I hoped, keep me safe.

The archers were choosing their best arrows as I asked Idraf, "How many animals do you think, Idraf?"

"Not a large number, my lord. A large pack would have more signs and the farm looked to me to have had just three people within."

He was right. I had seen just two beds and the evidence was of a small family who lived in two rooms. I turned to Geoffrey, "You two stay here and keep watch. You are more likely to smell a wolf than to see one. If you smell anything which you do not recognise then stand back to back and watch for the creeping shadow of death that is a wolf."

As we headed up the trail Sir Richard said, "Creeping shadow of death? Were you trying to terrify them?"

I nodded, "Aye, I was!"

I followed Idraf and Alan of Bellingham. Alan and I both had spears and if we found the wolves then we would stand before the archers. The trail was clear now to see and wound up through the trees which were thicker here than they had been. Our breath appeared before us as we laboured and I found myself actually sweating despite the fact that I had discarded my cloak. When Idraf stopped I sniffed and I detected the distinctive smell of wolf. The wind was coming towards us and that meant that even if they had a sentinel, he would not smell us.

Idraf did not turn but waved us forward and the three of us with spears moved past him. As I was the leader and I took the fore, Sir Richard and Alan walked just behind me, their spears protectively poking before me. I looked ahead and saw the jumble of rocks and scrubby bushes which hinted at a den. I saw my archers and Sir Richard's begin to spread out behind the three spears which we carried. Hitherto we had followed Idraf and his footsteps but now I had to look down so that I neither slipped nor stepped on a piece of wood which might break and give warning.

The trees stopped just twenty paces from the rocks and, when we reached the clear area, my two companions stepped forward. As they did so I pulled up my coif for the rocks ahead were at head height. I knew that wolves liked to leap from above and I wanted the protection of my mail from the sharp claws of any wolf which chose me as its victim. We moved closer, gingerly, hardly daring to breathe but, of course, our breath appeared before us and, I think, that was what gave us away. I heard a growl and I stopped. The trail led to my right but the growl came from ahead of me and that told me that the entrance to the den was hidden.

Pointing my spear to the right I led Alan and Sir Richard. The growling had stopped and that was worrying for it meant we were being hunted. This was the wolf's domain and the animals knew it better than we. Wolves are not only fierce but they are clever and they hunt as a pack where each one knows what it must do. Were we the hunters or the hunted? It was as we saw the trail turn that we discovered that it was we who were being hunted. The four animals all leapt at us at the same time. We later learned it was the leader of the pack and three young adult male wolves. I heard the twang of arrows behind us but the wolves had taken my archers by surprise. I held my spear before me, however the leap of the wolf which attacked me was higher than I anticipated. I adjusted my spear and it found flesh but the teeth of the wolf were already snapping at my head and its claws were raking my hide jerkin. I was saved by two things: my spear found flesh between its hind legs and tore through something vital and my coif protected me from the animal's teeth. Had I not raised my coif then I would have had more marks on my face than the scar from the assassin's dagger! The weight of the animal knocked me to the ground and the breath was sent from my lungs. I could hear the sound of the others fighting and Garth Red Arrow's voice as he shouted, "Sir William is hurt!"

The animal was unceremoniously lifted from my body and I took Garth's outstretched arm and pulled myself up, "Not hurt but it was close." As I stood, I saw that the four animals all lay dead. The leader of the pack had been struck with five arrows and Alan's spear was embedded in its chest. It had died hard!

Retrieving my spear, I headed along the trail towards the den. Richard and Alan flanked me. The stink from the cave was one of wolf mixed with the smell of death. Behind me, Idraf said, "Lord, I think the females, the old wolves and the cubs fled."

"We take no chances." The cave was dark but we heard no threatening sounds. "Flint! We need light!"

My archers all carried the materials to light a fire and Garth Red Arrow knelt to light his kindling. As the flames flared, we saw a scene of horror. The wolves had gone but the bones of their victims remained. While Garth fanned the flames, Abel added dried twigs and wood to encourage the fire. We walked inside and saw the skeletons of the dead. Some still bore remnants of their hair and clothes. We would have to burn their bodies for there was no way we could bury them.

Turning to Alan I said, "Have the remains put together and we will burn them in this cave."

"Aye, lord, this is sad. I see only one man and two women. The other three are all young bairns."

I nodded for I, too, had seen the size of three of the skeletons. It made me think of Margaret and Dick. "Skin the wolves and put the carcasses with the bodies. We cannot leave them here for they will attract vermin and we cannot carry them back with us." We would use the skins to ward off other wolves.

It was early afternoon when we headed back down the trail. A pall of smoke rose from the cave and drifted above our heads. We could smell the burning wolves. As we had piled the carcasses upon the fire Idraf had said, "That may be the end of the pack, my lord. We killed the males. There might be a couple of females and an old wolf but they cannot hunt enough for the cubs. They will head for the forests and shun this land. We will not hear the howling again." In that he was correct but it was not the end of the tale.

Geoffrey and young Garth were pleased to see us for they had heard the sounds of the attack and did not know the outcome. As we headed for the deserted farm it was Geoffrey's sharp eyes which spotted something we had missed heading west. The sun was quite low and its rays lit up an unusual formation of what appeared to be rocks. We had not seen it heading west for our attention had been upon the trail of the wolves. What we noticed was that there was no snow upon the rocks.

It was an anomaly and as such, we had to seek an answer, "We will investigate. It will not slow us up for we can head directly for our shelter. Archers, nock an arrow."

As we neared the pile, we saw that it was not a pile of rocks but a pile of bodies. They were men. It became obvious what they were as we neared them. They were frozen stiff. Dismounting we saw that there were three of them: one older man and two younger ones.

Alan said, "I have seen this fellow before. He is, or was, a Scot and he farmed north of here. He brought some sheep to sell in Elsdon last year. As I recall he had three sons and two daughters."

I nodded, "And looking here I would say that two of his sons are with him. Search for the others although I fear I know the tale."

As our men began to search Sir Richard asked, "You know the answer?"

I shook my head, "I deduce only. There is no evidence here of his daughters and I am guessing that they were taken from their home and this farmer came hunting the wolves. They froze to death. That is all that I can see."

Idraf said, "Lord, it looked like there were four of them who came here and they came from the north."

I nodded and wondered what had happened to the fourth. Perhaps he had gone for help. Garth Red Arrow asked, "Do we burn them or take them back to the farm?"

"As much as I want to bury them night is falling. We had better burn them. Find wood."

Alan said, "Easier said than done, lord. This is open land and it was what killed them. They did not have wood to burn."

I sighed. Untangling frozen bodies would be an unpleasant task but we had little choice if we could not burn them. "Then try to separate the bodies and we will have to see if we can take them back on our horses." I knew it would slow us but the farm we would use was less than two miles away.

It was as the first body was lifted that I heard a cry from one of Sir Richard's men, John, "Lord! There is a fourth, a boy and he is alive but only just!"

Even as the men tore at the other two bodies to reach the child my hand went to my cross. Had I burned the bodies then I would have burned alive a boy. I thought back to Dick of Yalesham who had been the boy brought us news of the Yalesham widows. He had managed to survive in the cold and I should have been more careful!

"Garth Red Arrow, take two men and ride to the farm. Light a fire and put water on to boil! We have little time. Give the child to me! Alan, I leave you and the others to bring the dead."

I remembered how we had saved Dick of Yalesham and I would do the same for this child who needed the warmth of my body. I mounted my horse as John and Idraf carried the boy who looked to be little more than eight summers old. His body was cold, almost icy but as I reached for him a soft sigh slipped from his mouth. He was alive. I cradled him as I would my baby and wrapped my cloak around him several times. I could feel the cold against my body and I spurred my horse to follow Garth and the other archers who were already far ahead. As I rode, I knew that God had guided us to this boy. His mother and sisters were obviously dead. We had seen their corpses in the cave and I had now accounted for the folk who had fallen foul of the wolf pack. If Idraf was correct then we would have no further trouble from the animals. That their attacks had only hurt the Scots was cold comfort. These were farmers and not brigands.

When my stomach no longer felt icy then I knew that I had given the boy some of my heat. Dick of Yalesham had been given a hot bath by Brother Abelard and that had revived him. Of course, Dick of Yalesham had not been in as bad a condition as was this Scottish boy. As I neared the farm, I saw that the horses had been abandoned and the door was open. Abel heard my horse and rushed out. I handed him the child. "Hold him tightly while I dismount." The child's life would be measured in moments and not hours.

Garth had a fire going in the hearth but, as yet, there was little heat. I saw two of my men filling a pot with water. We could not give the child a bath but we had to find some way to keep him warm. I cursed myself for it suddenly came to me that we had four wolf skins which were with Alan and the others. The fur would have warmed the boy. As I looked around I realised that the wolves had not destroyed the furniture nor the bedding. "Abel, fetch me all the bedding you can find and place it next to the fire." I held the child tightly, "Fight, boy! Fight for life!"

Since the sigh, I had seen no signs of life but I had to believe that he was alive. If I had to hold a frozen corpse all night then I would so long as there was a chance that we could revive him. I could feel more heat from the fire and Abel brought in the straw-filled mattress and the blankets. These were not the soft, warm blankets we had in the castle. These were thin and threadbare but they would have to do. When they were laid on the ground, I had Abel take off my cloak and then I lay with the child on the mattress while my archers piled the blankets and the cloak on top of me covering us completely, even our heads. I blew my warm breath on to the face of the child.

I heard my other men arrive. "Where is Sir William and the child?" I recognised Sir Richard's voice.

"They are under the pile of blankets, lord."

I shouted, "Fetch the wolf skins and use those too." I began to feel hot but the child still felt like ice. He had not eaten or drunk for days and he needed heat from within. I shouted, again, "Is there some warm broth we can give him?"

"Not long my lord. It is not yet boiled."

I moved the blankets and cloak a little so that I could speak and see to whom I spoke. "It does not need to be boiling nor to be ready. We need a beaker of some warm liquid to warm from within."

Garth Red Arrow nodded, "Sorry lord!"

Idraf looked down at the top of the child's head, "It is like Dick of Yalesham, lord!"

I nodded; Idraf had been the one to find Dick and I knew that the two were still close. "Let us hope this also has a happy outcome."

Alf Broad Shoulders was the largest archer we had and was well named. He said, "Lord, if it is heat from a large body you need then let me have the child."

44

He was right, "First, let me give him some liquid and then you can take over."

When the child swallowed the warm ham and venison infused broth, we knew he was alive. That did not mean he would live but we could try to keep him alive. The broth was not just for the child and he was not the only one who was frozen. Once we had all eaten, we gave the child more broth and then took it in turns to lie and keep him warm during that longest of nights.

I was asleep and was woken by Alan of Bellingham. "Lord, the child is awake and he speaks. He is alive!"

Chapter 5

We headed back to Elsdon the next day for the boy appeared to be a better colour and had taken some food. Rather than risking the child alone, Alf Broad Shoulders rode with him and held his tiny body close to his. The child had spoken just one word. He kept repeating the word, *'wolf'* over and over. No matter what we said to him he would answer nothing else and he clung to Alf as though he was life itself. I discovered that when he had opened his eyes it had been Alf who cradled the child and spoke softly to him. Alf was a fierce warrior but that night I saw a gentle giant. We left Sir Richard at Otterburn and we headed for my home. There was but one woman at Otterburn for few of Sir Richard's men had married yet. They were, like him, young and bachelors. In addition, I knew that Brother Paul was a fine healer and the boy would be better in my castle and home.

I sent riders ahead to warn my wife and Brother Paul of our imminent arrival. The Yalesham widows knew what to expect for they had experienced this already. Alf Broad Shoulders had married one of them, Mariann, and she had been close to Dick of Yalesham. As we rode through the gates of the inner bailey it was Mariann and Margaret of Yeavering who greeted us. "Leave the child with us, my lord, we have a room prepared. Lady Mary spoke to us and we will watch over him."

As I dismounted, I said, "That is good, Mariann, for he appears to have attached himself to your husband."

She beamed at Alf who was truly a gentle giant, "Aye, he is the kindest man in the manor, lord." She suddenly realised what she had said, "Saving yourself, your lordship!"

I laughed, "No, Mariann, you had it right the first time. Alf, let me know when you learn anything for I would know this boy's story and that of his family. They may be dead but Brother Paul can say prayers for their souls."

We learned later from Alf, when the boy began to speak, that the men from the family had heard the wolves howling, obviously when they were attacking the other farm, and the men had gone to collect their animals. When they returned, they found the mother and the girls had been taken. Donal, for that was the boy's name, said that his brothers tried to dissuade their father for they knew that their mother and sisters were dead already, but their father, Ardhal, was a wild man and not one to be crossed. They followed the trail. The blizzard hit them and they had to stop. With neither flint nor kindling their father had made a mound around the youngest. Donal had survived but he had watched his father and his brothers die to keep him alive.

When Alf told me I said, "The boy will need a great deal of care. If you wish me to…"

He shook his head, "Lord, the boy was sent to us. My wife lost her bairns when the Scots raided and, thus far, I have failed to give her another. God sent this child to us. There may be problems but we cannot ignore the Good Lord's wishes. We will care for him."

I gave him a gold coin. "And here is a start in life."

"Thank you, lord, but there is no need."

"I know and that is why you will take it for I do this for a friend and it is not charity."

The two new children: my daughter and the waif and stray seemed to galvanise my manor. Through the long hard winter, we all pulled together and there were neither deaths nor disagreements. When the snow finally left us, it was almost March. I sent a rider to my father with a missive. It was a long one and it was detailed for I had much news to impart. And then I turned my eyes to the manor. Winter had been a time of watching and now it was the time for working. We had lost animals over the winter even though we had brought them to places where they were sheltered and fed, the winter had been so harsh that we had lost some. As soon as the snow cleared, we put them out on to pastures that were close to our castle and our village. At the same time, I had my men begin training for what I knew would be a hard summer. The King had taken many men with him for his foreign foray and the Scots would try to take advantage of that.

We realised that when, in May, I received a message from the Sherriff of Westmoreland. Sir Humphrey Vieuxpont had been murdered. He had been visiting one of his knights when the wooden hall they had been in had been burned to the ground. There was clear evidence that it was murder, pure and simple. While the Sherriff appeared confused about the killers, I knew that it was the Scots and it was a blood killing. He had killed a Scottish knight and they were having their vengeance. I had been with Sir Humphrey and I knew they would come for me. I rode to Sir Richard to warn him and we both initiated our patrols once more. We spoke of what we needed to do.

It seemed to me that the attack on Sir Humphrey had been both callous and cunning. They did not try to take him when he was abroad with his men and, instead, had waited until he was isolated and vulnerable. "One thing that we can do is to ensure that we only spend nights away from our own castles in either this castle or mine."

"Agreed but how do we protect our own people?"

"What do you mean?"

"They will try to get at us through them."

I could almost read his thoughts. He was thinking of Eleanor. It was common knowledge that the two were enamoured of each other and we would have to assign someone to watch her and that meant watching my daughter. My wife had grown used to having Eleanor watch over the child. There was much to think about. We initiated the patrols and I had Alan of Bellingham assign two men at arms to be inside the hall at all times to guard my family. I did not tell my wife for I knew that it would do little good as she would only worry. It was better that I do the worrying for her.

I had Dick's first armour made for him. It was made of hide but he was so proud of it that it made no difference to him. Along with his leather helmet and dagger, he strutted the inner bailey as though he was a warrior grown. On the border, children became warriors far sooner than in the pampered pastures of the south.

Eleanor knew that I had written to my father about her and Sir Richard and each time a messenger came from the south she watched for my reaction. The letter came in June, I knew that she was waiting for the reply and I sent for her as soon as it came and I read it while she was present for I could not keep her in the dark. "Your grandfather has agreed that you may marry." She squealed with delight but I held up my hand, "However, you must return to Stockton and Sir Richard must travel there too so that he may ask for your hand formally." She looked disappointed, "This is good news. Surely you did not expect that they would simply say marry in Elsdon for we are happy about this news?"

She laughed, "Not expected but hoped."

I rode to speak with Sir Richard, "So you and Eleanor can ride south to Stockton any time you choose and I will watch over your manor for you."

He looked delighted and grinned and then, even as he reached for the jug of wine to pour us both a celebratory beaker he said, "If we are in danger, Baron, then the journey south means we must take more men to protect Eleanor and me and that will leave less for you to watch a border where we know there are enemies seeking your life."

I had already worked that out but it showed the changes in Sir Richard that he had also thought them through. "I know and we will manage. The attack on Sir Humphrey was when he was far from his home and he was lured there. I will stay close to my home and be surrounded by men I can trust. I will not be caught so easily. When you go south you can stay at Prudhoe, then Durham. You will be safe there and as for here? Secondly, we will simply be more vigilant on any

48

strangers and we will watch closely those that we do not know." I looked him in the eye, "You trust your people do you not?"

He nodded, "I do!"

"Then all is well. You do, however, have one problem which I do not think you have thought of."

"And what is that?"

I smiled, "You are a bachelor knight with a castle which suits you. You are getting a bride and, inevitably, that will mean a family. I am not sure that you are well prepared for such an event."

He handed me the beaker of wine he had poured and lifted his to toast me, "And you are right, I have not thought of this but it is now high summer and the best time for me to travel to speak with Sir Thomas. We must set off by July at the latest."

"Agreed."

"I will set my people to making the improvements in my castle so that I may bring a bride back here."

"And I will escort you as far as Prudhoe. That will mean you need to take fewer men with you for the road from Prudhoe is a busy one and I think you will be safe on that part of the journey."

We realised then that Eleanor had grown so close to Margaret and to Dick that as much as she wished to set the date and return home, she was reluctant to leave the children. As we sat before the fire having ensured the two were asleep, she spoke to my wife and I listened.

"I know, Mary, that they are yours but they feel like mine too. Is that not strange?"

My wife had wisdom and an insight which I, as a man, did not. "You are ready for your own children, Eleanor, but you will always be close to Margaret and to Dick but it will be Margaret who will hold your heartstrings and that should give you comfort." She nodded to me, "When your father was killed, even though I was not there, I know that my husband took a special interest in your brother. Even now, although Henry Samuel is a man grown and a knight, Will here worries about him. You will be the same with Margaret, even though you will have children of your own."

That seemed to ease her mind. After she had retired, my wife and I sat together and watched the fire die. It was high summer but Elsdon was a cold castle and the fire was comforting. "I shall miss Eleanor, husband, for we have grown close. I wonder if this was all planned by some higher spirit than we know."

I laughed and patted her hand, "You have been speaking overmuch with the Yalesham widows! I swear that they all have something of the witch in them!"

"You mock me but they have lived here in the north longer than we have. Their folk were here when the Romans built the wall and the land is in their blood. We can learn much from them. You be careful when you ride to Prudhoe. I know you will do the journey there and back in one day but do not take chances."

"And I will not!"

Sir Richard must have left Otterburn while it was still dark for he reached our castle by dawn. We were ready to ride for we had a fifty-two-mile ride ahead of us. Had we not had the threat of an attack we would have taken two days for the journey although, as Alan Longsword pointed out, if we did not have the threat then we would not need to escort them in any case. I took six men at arms, Geoffrey and six archers. We had four spare horses and we rode for war. The journey south would take us longer than the journey back for we had a wagon for Eleanor and her bags. She said she would ride but my wife would have none of it, "She is about to be wed and that makes her a woman. She will be the wife of a knight and should be accorded dignity!" My wife was not a woman to be crossed.

Richard was distracted as we rode south for he and Eleanor chattered like magpies but my men and I, along with Sir Richard's men were vigilant. We knew the places an ambusher or a killer might lurk and we watched each one with the eyes of a hunting hawk. When we reached the fortress that was Prudhoe, I sighed with relief for we had delivered our charges. We still had a hard journey back but this was July and the days were still long. Gilbert de Umfraville listened to my news as we ate a hurried meal and promised to send an escort to Durham with Sir Richard. I think he still felt guilty about the ambush at Kirkwhelpington.

Eleanor was tearful as we parted, "Uncle, you are like a second father to me and I thank you and Lady Mary for all your kindnesses."

"They are no more than you deserve and I thank you for all that you have done for my children. Fear not, Richard, I will watch your land for you."

The sun was in the western sky as we changed to the spare horses and headed north and west. When we neared Kirkwhelpington we were especially wary for despite the new lord of the manor there it was still dangerous country. There were eight miles to go after Kirkwhelpington and so we changed horses once more and drank some of the lord of the manor's ale and ate some bread. He offered to put us up but, even though the sun would set shortly, we were anxious to reach my castle. I fretted at leaving them alone.

We had Dewey of Abergele and Ged Strongbow as scouts. I had chosen the two of them to come with me as they both had small holdings to the south of Elsdon and knew the road and woods well and they hunted there. The sun had set and we were negotiating the twisting road carefully when Ged stopped and said, "A stone in my horse's shoe, Lord William."

There was no stone for the use of the title Lord William was to tell me that there was danger ahead. All of my men heard it and knew that there was trouble ahead. The archers strung their bows. It was dark and they would be able to see little but any shadow they saw would be either an enemy or an animal. Like my men at arms and Geoffrey, I pulled up my coif and donned my helmet. It was pitch black and if the danger lay ahead, they would see nothing.

I had just pulled up my shield and drawn my sword when Ged said, loudly, "All done, my lord. Sorry for the delay."

Continuing to act as though there was no danger I said, cheerfully, "It will not harm us for we are almost home and soon will be within my walls." Those waiting for us would assume we were less than vigilant whereas we were the opposite. Without a word being said, Robin Greenleg would lead my other archers around my two scouts to approach the enemy silently. The road was stone but they could ride on the earth where the sound of their hooves would be dampened. I peered into the dark and could see little but, when I sniffed the air, I could smell the enemy. That was what had alerted my scouts and it confirmed that there was an ambush. All men stink of their homeland, the food and drink they eat and their bathing habits. We could smell that these were not friends and an innocent traveller would have called out when he heard the horses.

Dewey of Abergele managed to loose one arrow before one of the hidden warriors rose from his place of concealment and hacked through his leg with an axe. I spurred my horse; I had changed to Lion at Kirkwhelpington and he leapt forwards as though stung. I held my shield tightly and heard the cries as Dewey's arrow hit something and Ged avenged his friend with a flight sent at a range of two paces into the head of the axeman. Alan Longsword was on my right and Geoffrey, brave as ever, was on my left. Alan's longsword swept to the side and it was almost a blind strike for we could see nothing but he managed to tear through an eager bandit's flesh and the man screamed like a castrated pig. Alan whirled his horse to finish him. An arrow thudded into my shield and a stone clanged off my helmet making my ears ring. I had no protection to my right and so I headed Lion into the undergrowth and, as I did so, a shadow loomed up out of the darkness.

Lion snapped his jaws and I struck blindly down. My sword cracked into a helmet and then slid down to tear through mail and into a shoulder.

I knew that my archers had surprised the ambushers for a brigand had his bow pulled back to send a bodkin into me when an arrowhead suddenly sprouted from his chest. This was now a confused battle. All that I knew was that my men were mounted and the enemy were on foot and so I kept my eyes down. A warrior suddenly lunged up at me with a spear. He had been crouched behind a hawthorn bush and the spear came from nowhere. The angle of his strike meant that it came upwards and it caught in the links of my chausse. I could only make out the spear and so I had to guess where his head was. When my sweeping sword struck flesh and then bone, I knew that I had torn my sword across his face.

I was suddenly aware that I was alone and so I reined in Lion and began to back him away from the bush. There were sounds of fighting but they were deeper in the woods and further north. When I reached the road, I found Ged trying to fashion a tourniquet around the stump of Dewey's leg. Even in the dark and from the back of Lion I could see that the Welshman was dead. "He has gone, Ged."

He nodded as he stood, "I just hoped that he was not."

I cupped my hands around my mouth for I could hear that the sounds of fighting were fading, and I shouted, "Elsdon, ho! Return! Elsdon, ho! Return!"

I heard hooves and I readied my sword but it was Geoffrey. His face was bloody, "Are you hurt, Geoffrey?"

"It was a hawthorn. The man hid behind it but it availed him little for he is dead!"

I nodded, "The two of you, search the dead. Find out who they are. Collect any weapons. We have no time this night to move their bodies but I would not have the ones who escaped benefit."

My men returned in dribs and drabs. None had been lost and the wounds were minor. When we spoke of the fight their words confirmed that these were, indeed, Scots. Dewey's body and his severed leg were placed on his horse. We would bury him whole in the cemetery. We rode in silence for a mile or so in case there was another ambush. Alan Longsword said, as we headed along the road to the village which lay just ahead, "We slew twelve men, lord, and lost but one."

"That is not a trade I like, Alan Longsword. The one we lost was a warrior. The men who attacked us were brigands and should have been hanged." Even as we entered our gate, I knew that I would have to ride

52

to Scotland and speak with the King. I doubted that he could stop these attacks but I had to try something before more of my men died.

My wife heard us as we entered the gate and came, with Margaret in her arms. When she saw the body being carried from the horse she gasped and seeing Geoffrey's bloodied face said, "Is anyone else hurt?"

"No, but we were lucky. These men were south of the village." Alan of Bellingham was listening and he nodded for he understood my meaning. Our patrols were to the north and now we would have to stretch them to the south.

The next day I went with my men to clear the bodies. We would bury them but not in our churchyard. They would be buried outside of the wall in the area reserved for heathens, witches and suicides. Brother Paul was a kind man and he said a prayer as the bodies, there were fourteen, were interred. Two others had succumbed to their wounds. Their bodies told a familiar story. All had been warriors at one time or another and one bore the remnants of a livery which could have belonged to the Comyn clan. While it was fresh in my mind, I rode to the most remote farm in my manor, Cedric son of Cedric's. I told him what we had discovered as a warning.

He nodded, "We learned our lesson, Sir William, and we investigate any footprint which we do not recognise," he chuckled, "and even some that we do!" Then his face became serious, "It is you should watch out, lord, for it seems to me, simple farmer though I am, that it is you who is in the most danger."

"Perhaps but I intend to try to do something about it."

Once back in my castle I summoned Alan of Bellingham and Alan Longsword. My wife and Geoffrey were also in attendance. "I intend to ride to Scotland to speak with King Alexander. I wonder if he knows of the murder of Sir Humphrey and the attack on me. It may be that he does and that he has changed but I am more inclined to think that he is in the dark."

My wife knew the King better than I did and she shook her head, "I know the King and he is true to his word but Scotland is a country filled with men who seek the throne. It may be that this is all part of a plot. I think, however, that you do the right thing for it will be better to speak with the King directly so that there is no danger of misinterpretation. But you need to be careful, my love. Who will you take?"

I looked at Alan Longsword, "I would take the men who went with me to Prudhoe. Most are single and, I think, will be eager to avenge Dewey for he was a popular man."

My wife nodded, "And he was courting the eldest daughter of Margaret of Yeavering. She will be hurt by this."

I nodded, "Then it is settled, we leave on the morrow."

Chapter 6

We headed for Jedburgh. If it was a perfect world then we would find the King there for he enjoyed the peace and tranquillity of the place. The monastery there imbued the palace with calmness and an atmosphere of reflection. Sadly, it was not meant to be for he was not there but the Abbot remembered me and had known my wife and her family. The Kerk family had been well respected in Scotland, especially by the church for her father had endowed many churches and monasteries in the hope of intercession with God to give him a son.

"The King is in the castle of Edinburgh." I cocked an eye at the priest for Edinburgh was a place where a King went if he felt threatened. There were other palaces which were more like palaces. The Abbot shrugged, "There are many men who wish to usurp the King. He now has a son and he and the Queen feel safer there, my lord. You know the world of men and politics better than I."

We left the next morning for the ride north. We were travelling through lands in which I had fought but, with a peace treaty in place, we were ostensibly at peace. My banner marked me for who I was and it would be a foolish lord who risked the ire of King Henry and, more importantly, my father. The Scots feared my family. My ancestor, the Warlord of the North, had defeated them, along with Bishop Thurston and chased the handful of men who survived the slaughter north to the borders. It was said you could mark their trail home by the bodies that were left.

While we were not attacked, we were hardly made welcome. It was my wife's name and her father's reputation which gave us accommodation in monasteries and priories which marked the road north. I had no doubt that other riders headed north to warn the King of my approach and that suited me. When I reached the city walls I was expected and escorted, by twice our number, to the great castle which was perched on the rock which was known as Arthur's Seat. I knew that I would never have dreamed of trying to take the castle. His steward, Richard de Brus apologised to me, "I am sorry, Sir William, but we have no accommodation for your men in the castle, however, we have arranged chambers for them in an inn which is close to the wall. It will be at the King's expense."

I smiled as I nodded; they had been forewarned.

Alan Longsword looked less than happy about the situation. "My lord, you just have your squire with you." He glared at the Steward, "If aught happened to you!"

The Steward flushed and I said, "I am safe here, Alan Longsword, for the King is a friend, is he not, Steward?"

The knight had recovered his poise, "Of course, Sir William, and any hint of treachery is an insult."

"Sir Richard, we were attacked during the last week by Scottish bandits and we lost a man. You can understand Alan Longsword's fears."

The Steward sniffed, "Here you are safe!"

We were taken to our chamber. As I expected it was not close to the King's but that did not worry me. Water and towels were made available and I changed from my mail and the dirty surcoat which had endured the roads to a better one. Geoffrey helped to groom me for we were meeting a king. I counselled him, "Keep your wits about you and listen. The Queen is from France and there may well be French courtiers. Do not let them know that you speak French. In fact, say as little as possible."

He smiled, "I should pretend to be stupid."

"If you can manage it then, aye. You may not have to serve but if you do then listen in the kitchens for there you may hear gossip which is always useful."

As our last stay on the journey north had been but ten miles from Edinburgh, we had arrived in our rooms shortly after noon. The King and his Queen would be eating and so I took Geoffrey to walk around the castle. I did not think that we would have to take it but I had been taught by my father that there was no such thing as useless information. It was just information you did not need, yet!

Geoffrey was clever and he noticed the strengths of the castle immediately. "It is built on rock, lord, and you cannot mine. There is no chance of using towers for there is only one entrance and the gatehouse and barbican look as strong as many a castle."

"Aye, Geoffrey, and yet the chambers are small. This is not a palace, it is a fortress, so why is the King here?" I answered myself, "It is because he fears someone in his Kingdom. Perhaps it is Comyn; we shall discover all, I hope."

We made our way down to the antechamber near to the Great Hall. The steward preceded us into the Great Hall and I joined the nobles who waited for an audience with the King. When I had been on the Baron's Crusade my father's position meant that I had frequently been privy to meetings with high and powerful men. No matter who was with the

56

King I would not be intimidated. We were made to wait but that did not surprise me. I had seen King Henry do it frequently. While we waited, I listened to the conversations of the other courtiers who were waiting to be admitted. It would be interesting to see if any of them was admitted before me as that would tell me much about their standing with the King. Looking around the colourful surcoats I saw no liveries that I recognised. Which meant the Mormaer of Atholl was not in residence nor were any of the Comyn family. The talk appeared to be about the Viking kingdoms of the Isles. The Vikings had long disappeared from England and the only vestige of Viking power lay on the island known as Man. Perhaps this was good news. If the Scottish were casting their eyes to the north then the borders might become safer. Even as the thought flickered across my mind, I realised that this contradicted the raids and attacks we had recently endured.

The doors opened and the Queen left the room. I guessed it was the Queen as everyone bowed. The young Prince Alexander was carried by a servant. She glanced at me as she passed. I assumed that the King and Queen had discussed my arrival. All the other courtiers stepped forward, eagerly. I just stood and waited. I would remain impassive no matter how long I was made to wait. I understood the games kings, princes and courtiers played.

De Brus nodded to me, "Baron William, the King will see you now."

Word of my elevation had reached King Alexander. I was not surprised for many Scottish nobles held land in England and would have heard.

The King was seated at the table where they had just eaten. Servants had already cleared it and a scribe was placing documents while a second was seating himself at the end with a wax tablet and a stylus. There were two others in the room I did not recognise except to notice that they were both lords and from the trim of one of the nobles' beards he was a Frenchman. The other was a younger man and looked Scottish. King Alexander looked like a man well past his fortieth summer. He had aged and that was no surprise. Until his new wife had given birth to a son he was in a parlous position. His eyes, however, still sparkled, reminding me of the man who had helped to arrange my marriage, and he stood to hold out his forearm. I saw the noble I took to be a Frenchman frown at the gesture.

"Sir William, it is good to see you. And Lady Mary, how is she?"

"She is well, King Alexander, and we now have two children."

He beamed, "I know. My Joan," he made the sign of the cross, "would have been delighted. She said that you two were a match made in heaven and was one of the things she did of which she was the proudest. She saw it, like us, as a union of England and Scotland! Ours did not flourish but hopefully, yours will."

"And you are due congratulations, King Alexander, I saw your son and he looks healthy!"

"Aye, he is." The smile I saw was one of real pride. There was still hope for King Alexander. "I pray you sit. This is Sir Alan Durward."

The Scot held out his hand, "Mormaer of Atholl."

The King shook his head, "Alan, I have told you, that matter is in dispute. Sir Walter Comyn also claims that title and he has the support of the Earl of Fife."

He did not seem put out at all and he smiled at me, "I have the castle and the loyalty of the men of Atholl so I do not see a problem."

This was confirmation of the dispute between Durward and Comyn. As my father had once said to me, the enemy of my enemy is my friend and I warmed to Alan immediately.

"And this is the Count of Lisieux, Raymond de Courcy who has been sent here by King Louis for he is a cousin of my wife."

The Count made no attempt to move and so I merely nodded. The Count spoke in French and, more importantly, took great delight in delivering what proved to be disastrous news, "What you may not know, Sir William, is that your King Henry has just lost the Battle of Taillebourg. I myself brought the news. There was a great loss of life, amongst the English and their Lusignan allies."

He had a supercilious smile and I just wanted to hit him but instead, I said, "In war, many men die. I know for I have recently returned from the Crusades where I witnessed death many times." I would not give him the satisfaction of showing that I was upset although inside me I feared for the worst. Sir William de la Lude of Hartburn, who had led our men, was not the same master of the battlefield that was my father and King Henry had yet to show that he had any skill at all.

I saw that my lack of reaction had discomfited the Frenchman and I took that as a victory. The King nodded and waved to a servant who poured us wine. "So, Sir William, or perhaps I should use your new title, Baron."

I nodded and spread my hands apologetically, "I agree with Sir Alan here, a title is just that a title." I looked pointedly at the Frenchman, "It is how men view you that counts and, along the border, I am well respected and feared by my enemies."

Sir Alan nodded vigorously, "Aye, Sir William, I have heard of your exploits. When time allows, I would speak with you for I met the Lord of Otterburn, Sir Richard, and he told great tales of you and your father."

The Count said, "We have much business to discuss, King Alexander, and this distraction is unnecessary."

I began to see a sinister purpose to the visit of this Frenchman. I did not doubt that there had been a battle and the French must have won. Did this mean that the French were going to try to turn King Alexander from paying homage to King Henry to actively fighting us?

King Alexander frowned, "Sir William is an old friend and an hour of diversion hurts none. However, I do not think that this is a social call, is it, Sir William?"

"No, Your Highness." I recounted the story of the raid Sir Humphrey and I had defeated and then the murder of that knight and I concluded with the story of the attempt upon my life.

The Count waved a hand and said, rather too quickly for my liking, "They sound like brigands to me and you cannot hold King Alexander responsible for the action of all of his subjects."

I turned to the Count and, keeping my voice as steady as I could I said, "Count, I will take your opinion on anything to do with France for you are a Frenchman but this is not France and I believe that I was talking to the King of Scotland about his subjects and his land. I beg you to keep quiet!"

That I had stunned him was obvious and I am not sure what would have happened next had not Alan Durward burst out laughing and then said, "Well said, Sir William! You have put the popinjay firmly in his place."

The Frenchman coloured and stood. He bowed to the King and said, "I have been insulted and I cannot stay here and retain my honour."

I said, "And if you would like redress, Count, then know that I am one Englishman who has never been defeated by France and I will happily give you satisfaction!"

The King stood, "Peace! I will have no fighting in my home. Count, you are excused. Sir William!"

I nodded, "I apologise to you, King Alexander, for you are a gentleman!"

That did nothing to improve the Frenchman's mood and he glowered at me as he left.

King Alexander said, "I see that you and your father still have much in common." I nodded. "I was sorry to hear that your King lost his battle. I like Henry but I fear he is out of his depth as a general."

I said nothing for that would have been disrespectful to my king.

The King sighed and spread his arms, "I think that the Count is correct. I cannot control all of my men and I can only apologise."

I heard, in his voice, a plea. He did not wish conflict with England so who was he afraid of? I put that thought to one side and gave him the message I had intended to deliver. "The main reason I came here was to tell you that I will hunt down and kill any enemy who tries to hurt my people, my family or me. If that means hunting them down in Scotland then know that I will do it. We have some evidence that Walter Comyn's family is behind these attacks on Sir Humphrey and myself." I saw the King about to excuse himself, "Your majesty, I know that this may well be done to undermine you but you must realise that if King Henry has lost a battle and his ambitions of regaining his French lands are doomed to failure then he will not look kindly on a French alliance and his subjects being attacked."

"You are blunt but I can say, for I trust you both, that Walter Comyn has many allies and the French are my only support."

Sir Alan shook his head, "Your Majesty....!"

"You mean well, Durward, but I cannot have a civil war. I know what it did to England." He looked at me and I saw that his eyes pleaded with me, "Tell your King that I do not wish war and I will do all that I can to prevent it but you, Sir William, must help me."

I nodded, "And out of respect for Queen Joan and the debt I owe you for the wife I have I will do as you ask but let Comyn know, Your Majesty, of the strength of my views."

He smiled and looked heartily relieved, "Of course. I shall do so firmly for I will not have my lords undermining a peace so dearly bought. I also have good news for you. We have the revenues for the last two years from Creca, your wife's estates. The Earl of Fife still seeks them but the people there are loyal to Lady Mary's father. I will have them ready for you to take when you leave."

I wondered if this was a bribe and then remembered that both the King and Queen had promised me the income before I had even married Mary.

I rose, "And now that I have taken enough of your time, I will let you get back to affairs of state."

"You will dine with us this evening?"

"Of course, King Alexander, it will be an honour."

Alan Durward also stood, "And I will beg your leave, Your Majesty. I need to return to Atholl. This has been a most instructive visit."

It was obvious that he wished to speak with me and we left together. He looked at Geoffrey as we left the hall and passed through the waiting nobles, "Have your squire ensure that none draw close to us. I would speak with you in private."

Geoffrey had heard the Scot's words and nodding, he moved so that no one could get close behind us and overhear our words. The Scot smiled and led me up towards the battlements. That he was well known was obvious as the sentries all snapped to attention as we passed but, more importantly, none hindered our progress. He said nothing until we were clear of the press of men and standing on the eastern side looking towards the river.

He turned to face me when he spoke. "You are right in your suspicions, Sir William. The French seek to put a dagger in England's back. Having defeated your King Henry, they think they can force King Alexander to fight the English. Comyn and de Courcy are close collaborators. You put the Frenchman's nose out of joint but now that the Queen has given the King one son he hopes for more and he is her thrall. The French have him and as much as he does not wish to fight England the French will force his hand."

I smiled, "And as a loyal Scot that should suit you, yet I can see that it does not. Before I become embroiled in some plot which may hurt my land and my king, I would know your motives."

He laughed and nodded, "You are wise. Aye, I should be glad but Comyn also supports the French but for different reasons. He seeks the throne so you see I am opposed to the French plans because they aid my enemy. I hold Atholl but, as the King said, Comyn claims the title too. No-one wants a civil war and so Comyn uses his knights to lead bands to raid the border. He chooses knights who have nothing or have lost out to either English knights or King Alexander."

I nodded and looked to the river where I saw the dirty sails of small ships bringing goods to Edinburgh. It would be just as easy for them to bring French troops too. "It seems to me, Sir Alan, that you are asking me to inform King Henry so that he can bring an army hence and make war on your people."

He lowered his voice, "The Frenchman did not lie or if he did it was a lie to a king, and they have too much as stake for that. Your King did lose very heavily and he lost many knights."

My heart fell for my family were with the King.

"I do not think that your King Henry will be in any position to lead an army north. This will be down to the knights who defend the border, men like you, Sir William. So, what I am warning you of is danger coming to your very homes."

"Let us be honest, Sir Alan, for I am no Frenchman and I do not dance well. I like plain speaking. You are using fancy footwork and playing on my fears for my family. Tell what it is that you want and then I can leave Scotland for the cleaner air of England!"

He nodded, "I can see that you have a well-deserved reputation on the battlefield and you are right for it goes against my grain to be duplicitous. I would aid you but I cannot do so openly. When we dine this night, our squires will serve us. You will see my squire Robert and I will use him to bring messages to Elsdon." He turned to Geoffrey. "When you speak with Robert, as you serve, be as guarded as he is for the French and Comyn have knights here whose squires will watch every move that you make."

"And your squire can travel freely?"

His family lives not far from Ednam which lies close to Jedburgh. His father is unwell, in fact, I may have to knight my squire soon for he is the eldest and will inherit the manor. When he does then you will have a friend."

"And he will bring me news of..."

"Of all that I can discover. I will not betray my country, however, the French and Comyn do not work for the good of Scotland but for the good of themselves."

I sighed for this was that which I hated most, intrigue and deception yet I had little choice. Until I could speak with the King or my father directly then I had to defend this border. Perhaps that was why the King had elevated me. I said, "Very well, I will do all that I can to prevent this Comyn from gaining advantage and seek to thwart the French plans."

We walked back to our chambers in silence for neither of us knew who was to be trusted.

Geoffrey and I were preparing for the evening meal when a servant brought the chest of coins from the manor of Creca. If it was a bribe then it was a generous one. That evening, as we ate, I was largely silent. That was partly because I was seated amongst Scottish nobles who clearly did not wish to speak with me but it was mainly because I was deep in thought. Had we not gone on the pointless crusade then my father would still have been in the north and, who knows, we might have tightened our hold on Scotland. We had control over King Alexander who accepted that the King of England was his lord. King Henry's preoccupation with his Lusignan relatives might have cost England the north. I played with my food and used the bread and the meat to make a map of the north. It helped me to visualise it.

Berwick was in our hands and the Prince Bishop kept it well garrisoned. The castle of Jedburgh was, ostensibly English but had no garrison to speak of. Then there were the two fortified manors of Otterburn and Elsdon. Along the coast, we had Bamburgh Castle and then Warkworth and Alnwick. There was Morpeth and Prudhoe not to mention Newcastle but they just guarded the coast and the crossing of the Tyne. Between Elsdon and the west coast lay just Barnard Castle and Carlisle. If we were reduced then a Scottish army could sweep down, as the raiders had, into the heartland of England.

Geoffrey's voice brought me from my reverie, "Have you done, my lord? There is cheese as well as sweetmeats."

I nodded, "Aye, fetch me some cheese, Geoffrey."

I caught sight of Durward's squire, Robert. He was older than I expected and I could see that he would be ready for dubbing. He looked up and gave the slightest of nods. Sir Alan had trained him well.

We left, before dawn, without speaking to the King again. I did not try but I suspect that I would have been made to cool my heels outside the hall and it would have been pointless. Geoffrey and I slipped out like thieves in the night. We collected my men at arms and archers but I deliberately chose not to speak until we were well clear of the city and heading south.

Geoffrey spoke first, "There are many French knights in Edinburgh and most of them fought at Taillebourg. I did as you asked, my lord, and feigned ignorance of French. They are not here for peaceful purposes for all of them speak of defeating the English a second time."

"And that explains why I was seated amongst Scottish knights so that I would not hear the French knights speaking to one another."

"Alan Longsword, what did you learn?"

"That the Scots do not know how to brew decent ale and charge a small fortune for it." I laughed for my men measured the worthiness of a place by the quality of the beer. He went on, "The two factions, the Comyns and the Durwards are on the brink of civil war. The King has to tread a fine line between them and Master Geoffrey is correct, there are many French warriors in Edinburgh as well as mercenaries who come to sell their swords to the highest bidder. They are gearing up for war, lord."

Now I understood why the King was in Edinburgh. He could defend himself and his family there and did not risk being held hostage by one of the three parties who sought to use him. I needed to speak to my father but I could not risk leaving the borders. Sir Richard was in Stockton with Eleanor and that left me as the last sentry guarding the back door to England. I would have to send someone I trusted with a verbal message for him. It would have to be Edward of Yarum. He had been one of my father's men who had chosen to come to Elsdon with me. His family still lived by the Tees and it would make sense to send him. Then I would have to prepare the land for a war but it would not be a traditional war, I knew that now. There would be no armies to besiege us and to fight a battle. They would come as assassins and try to strangle the life from us. It would be the ordinary people who suffered and despite Alan Durward's promise, I knew that any message from the north would come a day too late. I would have to outsmart our enemies.

Chapter 7

I had to be honest with my wife when I reached home and told her everything that had happened. She took it all stoically. I suspect she knew better than any of the divisions which lay within the Scottish court. It was why she had had to flee and to marry me. She smiled, "I know that you paint a gloomy picture, husband, but I also know that you have plans in place already!"

I smiled. She was a warrior's wife. "I intend to use some of the gold from Creca to buy more horses. We need to be more mobile than the enemy but we have the next months to face first for it is harvest time and if I was an enemy who wished to wrest this land from us, I would make the people hungry. I intend to send groups of my men to camp close to the outlying farms. Until Richard returns, I cannot do that with the garrison at Otterburn and it may well be that the farms between Otterburn and the border may will suffer. I can do nought about that but Cedric's farm is the richest and most isolated of my farms. I can protect that one. If we have a signal fire then I can use my mounted men to reach them before they succumb to an attack."

She kissed me on the forehead as she went to Margaret who had just begun a milk demanding wail, "See, I knew that you would have thought this through. Fear not for us here in the castle. The Yalesham widows are tough women and we can ensure that while our warriors fight, we will keep them fed and their children warm and happy!"

I knew that I was lucky and for that, I thanked Queen Joan for it had been her decision which had changed my life.

I gathered my captains, Alan of Bellingham, Alan Longsword and Idraf of Towyn along with Edward of Yarum. My man at arms was surprised to be included in the meeting. I also invited Brother Paul. He was the rock of the manor. His church and his relationship with his flock would be vital if we were to survive what I anticipated to be a hard winter again.

I told them what I had told my wife. "Alan of Bellingham, choose ten men who have no family here in Elsdon. We need a mix of archers and men at arms. We will ride to Cedric's farm and I will tell him what we plan."

He nodded, "That will leave us weak here, lord."

I sighed, "I bear a heavy responsibility here, Alan, for if I am wrong then we can lose everything but I believe that our recent improvements to our defences have made Elsdon too strong for anything other than an army to attack us. I do not think that the French are yet ready to bring an army to invade. They wish to destabilise us. It will soon be winter and if they do attack then it will be in Spring by which time my father or the King may well be here." I nodded to Edward, "That is why you are here, Edward. I need you to ride to Stockton and to tell my father all that I am telling you now. I will commit nothing to writing. This will be in your head for I trust you and my father knows you. If any question you on the road then you tell them that you go to visit your father."

He nodded.

Alan Longsword shook his head, "But, lord, if we lost many knights in France then how can the King do anything about the French here?"

I leaned back, "Within these walls, it is not King Henry upon whom I rely but my father and I pray that he will hurry north, as he did two years since. It will be his name and standard which will make the Scots and the French think twice." I shrugged, "We will see. For the present, I make plans to protect this border and our people. I hope we will not have another wolf winter but I think that there will be beasts at the gate except that these wolves will be in human form and they will be Scottish brigands and French warriors."

Edward left that day and I guessed it would take him three days to reach Stockton. If Sir Richard returned that same day then within a week, we might have help. I looked at the skies; they were beginning to fill with clouds which suggested rain some time in the next few days. It was now almost September and the perfect time for an enemy to cause mischief. I rode with my chosen men to Cedric's farm. Alan of Bellingham had all but four of my men on patrol looking at the trails and hidden ways into the valley. Alan Longsword had ridden to Otterburn to warn those there of the dangers.

Cedric was in his fields harvesting his cereals. We had had a dry August and Cedric, like his father before him, was a good farmer. He and his men laid down their scythes. Most were family but he had two or three field labourers who were also handy with their weapons.

He smiled, "I see, my lord, that you have brought warriors. That normally presages trouble."

"It is ever so."

I dismounted and handed my reins to Geoffrey. Leading Cedric to one side I told him of my fears and my plans.

"It is good of you to offer me men but we can handle any raiders."

"Perhaps but I lost your father because he refused help and I will not see a stubborn son do the same and besides I need you to be the bait. You are the most isolated farm in the manor and the closest to the border; if any is going to be raided and animals taken it will be this one.

By leaving men here I guarantee that you will hold them up long enough for me to bring my horsemen and destroy them."

He rubbed his beard and then grinned, "Aye, my lord, I can see how that would work. If your men would build the signal beacon, we will finish harvesting this field. We have some animals on the upland pastures and we will bring them down and put them in the walled enclosure. The grass there has not been grazed this year. I was going to save it for winter fodder but we will have to use something else."

"Do not worry about winter fodder, Cedric. I plan to buy plenty for the manor. This has been a good summer and the lands of Durham will have a surplus. The Bishop wants us as sentinels and he can pay with winter feed!"

I spoke to Geoffrey as we headed back. "I will have much to occupy me over the next weeks, Geoffrey and I need you to be my eyes and ears. My people will try to hide their fears from me and I rely on you to let me know them. We are walking a knife-edge here and one false step can spell disaster."

"Aye, lord, but you should know the people have confidence in you and they trust you. You are a knight who has earned that trust. I have learned much since I came here. I am on a journey to become a knight and that journey is not a swift one."

I sensed an undertone in his voice and knew he spoke of his brother who, to save him, had betrayed his country and become a traitor. "Your brother did what he had to in order to save a brother."

"He betrayed his people and his land!"

"Until you have walked in his shoes, Geoffrey, then do not judge him. I have not had to choose and I know not what I would do. My father risked his soul when he slew a treacherous Bishop. That was his moment of truth. I have yet to face mine as have you."

We rode back in silence each wrapt in his own thoughts.

The patrols my men rode were punishing. These were not a cursory look to see if there was any sign of intruders, every path was examined for pieces of cloth in the hedgerows, hoofprints where there should be none. Anything that might indicate that someone, not from our manor, was in the vicinity. Dick sensed that something was different and he urged me to take him when I went on patrol.

"Richard, when you are old enough, I will have Geoffrey begin to train you at the pel. I will ask Idraf to find an archer to train you to use a bow and I will teach you to ride a bigger horse. Until then you stay close to home and you will be the one to guard your mother and your sister."

He looked shocked, "They cannot climb Elsdon's wall!"

"I am afraid that they can and if we give them half a chance then they will!" My young son began his journey that day. He was the son of a border knight and not the pampered heir of someone who lived a comfortable life further south.

Edward of Yarum had been gone exactly one week when we saw the smoke rising from the direction of Cedric's farm. We were all prepared for we knew that meant that there was an attack and we went to our horses almost silently. The four men we were leaving were already standing to on the walls and the bell was tolled to get the villagers into the castle. The same bell would warn Otterburn that we were under attack. They would close their gates and bring in their villagers. The only goodbyes we gave were waves. Those we left behind would prepare for the worst.

My plans relied on Cedric and my men holding the enemy up. If the enemy, whoever they were, knew anything about our plans, they would abandon their attack and flee, north. Our approach, therefore, was from the north; it added less than a quarter of an hour to the time it would take us but it meant we would be approaching from an unexpected direction as far as the Scots were concerned. We heard the sounds of fighting a few moments before we saw their sentries. They had left four men to guard the road from the north. My archers did not have time to string their bows but they were equally deadly with their swords and, being lighter than we were, they galloped towards the four lightly armoured men. The Scots shouted but they would not be heard and the four of them were slain where they stood without inflicting a wound on my archers. Idraf ordered the archers to dismount and, leaving one man to guard the horses, they each nocked an arrow and followed my men at arms and me.

There were less than twenty of us who approached the enemy and we had no idea of their numbers but we had surprise on our side and that was worth a great deal. Cedric's farm was just that but the dry-stone wall he had built and the ditch he had dug had come as a shock to the Scots. They had scaled the wall but the bodies we saw in the ditch showed that it had been at a price. Some of my men were better riders than the others and the better riders leapt the ditch and the low wall. Some of the stones had been pulled down by the Scots as they tried to breach Cedric's defences. As we landed in the pasture, we saw that Cedric's animals had all been driven by the Scots to the far wall but Cedric, his men and mine were defending his farmhouse. Here the wall was not dry stone, it was mortared and it was as high as a man for it was built upon a ditch which allowed the defenders to fight from height.

Even as I slowed Lion to view the battle I saw that the Scots had brought more than sixty men and would outnumber us, but Idraf and my archers held the balance of power for, while I raised my sword to order a charge, the archers began to rain arrows on the Scots. It was then I saw that these were not simple brigands for many wore mail and I saw a knight, identifiable by his spurs, exhorting his men to scale the walls. Idraf and his archers chose their arrowheads well and the knight was struck with a bodkin arrow as I shouted, "Charge!" I lowered my spear and rode for the wounded knight. He was the leader. If I could rid the field of him then the rest would succumb quicker.

The mailed men were closest to him and so Geoffrey and my men at arms closed up with me so that we had ten spears riding towards the fourteen of them. Once again, I was the tip of the arrow and I aimed my horse for the centre of the men who were now protecting the knight. The arrows from my men in Cedric's farm did not help them. There was no honour in what I was doing but, then again, the brigands had raided a farm and not sought battle. A lord did what he had to do to protect his people. Three of those in mail ran with swords and axes to hurt our horses. If they had been using pole weapons then they might have stood a chance. As it was, I leaned forward and, pulling back my arm, thrust my spear at the nearest Scot who flailed his weapon in an attempt to reach my horse's head. He slipped and my spear drove down between his shoulder and his neck. Alan Longsword and Alan of Bellingham were both good with a spear and they did not miss. I had to rein back with Lion for there was no way he could surmount the Scots before us. The Scot I had speared did not die immediately and managed to scramble to his feet. As I pulled back my arm, he also tried to wrench himself free from the spearhead. His blood showered and splattered over those around him and, as the head came free, I was able to thrust at the knight who, although he held his shield before him, had been hit by an arrow. My spear struck him squarely in the middle of his face. He may have been fatally wounded in any case but my spear ended his life. His dying act was to grab the spear with his hands and his falling body tore it from my grasp.

I drew my sword but the Scot who roared and used the bodies of his dead comrades as stepping stones came at my left side. I knew what was coming for Lion was no longer moving and I kicked my feet from my stirrups. His axe and then his flying body hit my shield but there was no resistance and I fell from my horse. He came with me, his axe held in two hands. I would have landed heavily but for the bodies which lay there and I just managed to turn my sword at the axeman who could not stop his fall. He impaled himself upon my blade. His bleeding body lay across me and I saw some of the Scots who survived rushing to get at me. The measure of the loyalty and courage of my men was shown at that moment. Men threw themselves before me in an attempt to stop the Scots. Then they struck so hard with their weapons that even if they had been wielding iron bars the men they struck would have died. When the would be killers were all dead then Geoffrey held a hand out and I pulled myself up.

The attack on me had been the last desperate act of a warband who had failed. Some ran off and I knew that Idraf and his archers would mount their horses and pursue them. None would return home to Scotland and that was part of the plan. It was cruel but necessary. Those at home, some sixty or more miles to the north would wait for a week for them to return. Even then, when they failed to return their anguish would not end, for they would hope beyond hope that the warriors who had gone south for glory and coin might have survived. With none left alive to tell the tale the grief would be unbearable. It was cruel but if we could make others fear to come south then that was an added part of the victory.

My first thoughts were for Cedric, his family and my men. Leaving Alan of Bellingham to organise the disposal of the dead and the clearing of the field I went through the gate to the farm. "Did you lose many men?"

Cedric shook his head, "No, we had your men watching from the roof of the farm and they spied the enemy. We had warning and brought all inside the walls."

He went on to tell me that it had been Ged Strongbow's suggestion and it had worked. It meant that the Scots had been spied when they were some way away. The signal fire must have been put down to stubble burning and by the time the Scots were at the dry-stone wall everyone was safe inside the inner wall and we were on the way.

I nodded, "Then the idea works?"

Cedric smiled, "I thought it unnecessary but I was wrong. Your men can stay here until the harvest is in and I intend to build a watchtower on my roof. Then you can have your men back. We have children who can watch! They know what a raider looks like!"

It was late afternoon when we headed back to the castle. Cedric had damaged mail from the dead he could make into farm tools as well as swords and four horses. We also had four horses and many weapons. I had a feeling that we would need them sooner rather than later. My wife was delighted and relieved to have us returned and I was pleased that my plan had worked. Now we awaited a message from Stockton.

It came in an unexpected form three days later. David of Wales led a column of my father's archers and two wagons through the village towards my gates. I had been in the new tower overseeing the completion of the plastering when I spied them. I hurried down to greet my father's oldest archer.

As he stepped down, I embraced him for David of Wales was like an old friend, no, he was more, he was like an uncle. "Well met, David of Wales."

"Aye, Sir William, but I wish it was under different circumstances." His tone suggested some dire news. I had dreaded having a conversation with one from Stockton for I had had no word of the losses from the battle in France and David's face and demeanour told a tale. He handed me a letter. I recognised my father's seal. "Your father has written all down and do not ask me to speak of it for it would unman me. I am a greybeard and I should be used to death but..."

I could see he was filling up and I waved him to the warrior hall. "You know where the chambers are. I will read this and then you and those who have come from Stockton shall dine with me."

"Read the letter first and then decide if we should dine with you or not. I also have a letter for Lady Mary from your mother."

David's words filled me with fear and I hurried to my hall with the letter, "Geoffrey, go and tell the cook to prepare extra food for the archers and ask Lady Mary is she is up to entertaining my father's archers."

"Aye, lord, what is it? You look as though the world is about to end."

"This will be news of the battle and I fear I have lost friends."

The Great Hall was empty and for that I was grateful. Beth had seen me enter and she brought me a beaker of ale. I shook my head, "Bring me wine, Beth!"

I opened the letter with my dagger. The blade cracked through the wax and the parchment crackled open. I would have known it was from my father even without the seal for he had a distinctive hand.

Stockton
August
My son,
This is a rarity, a missive from me to you and it is the hardest letter I have ever had to write. The King has suffered a loss, a disappointment for him but a disaster for the valley. He was defeated at the Battle of Taillebourg. There is no easy way to write what I must and so I must dip my quill into the ink and write that which I find hard to believe and can scarcely comprehend.

Sir William de la Lude and his son Robert, Sir Richard of East Harlsey, Sir Ralph, Sherriff of York, Sir Henry Fitz Percy all fell in the battle. That many of their men also fell is no consolation and if I was to enumerate them here then I fear I would need more parchment than I own. Sir Fótr was wounded as was Sir Peter. Although both will take some time to recover, they will and Ridley and Marguerite paid for a mass to thank God for that. I am just pleased that none were taken for ransom for that would have added to the worry. Henry Samuel survived and acquitted himself with great honour although he is terribly affected by the disaster. Sir Gilles and Sir Henry of Wulfestun also live., while your brother in law, Sir Robert of Redmarshal was also wounded.

You are no fool and I know you understand that this means I cannot leave the valley to come to your aid yet. That is why I have sent the best that I have, my archers. When time allows and all is settled, I will come with the new Lord of Otterburn and I will join with you in making the north safe.

Sir Richard and Eleanor were married and I thank God that they were married the week before the news of the disaster reached us for their day was happy as it was meant to be. Sir Richard will now be the Lord of Hartburn.

The King sent me a letter thanking me for the sacrifice our men made. It is cold comfort. Serving kings is something undertaken without any hope of joy! King Richard should have been a lesson I learned but I did not. I am sorry! I have written to him to tell him of the dangers in the north and I made sure that he knew the seriousness of the situation. I hope he will come north himself. Until then, my son, it is you who will bear the responsibility of guarding the north. Know that I have sent letters to the Bishop and the Sherriff asking them to support you but, with winter coming, I fear that the weight will fall upon your shoulders and for that, I am truly sorry. It is my fault that you are where you are. I promise that as soon as I can I will have other lords take on that responsibility and you and your wife can come home.

Your mother and I pray each night that God will watch over you,

Your father
Thomas of Stockton

I drank three goblets of wine and read the letter twice more. Even though the words of the French Count had prepared me for such news it still came as a shock. Poor Richard had gone home to give his father and brother good news and, instead, had received the worst. The fact that he was now Lord of Hartburn was no consolation. I was pleased that he had Eleanor at his side. My mother had said she was reckless and wild but I knew differently and now would be her time to shine. Sir

Ralph had been a great lord and I wondered how his family would fare. My father had said nothing about his sons. I folded the letter and put it to one side as though the news might disappear. I could not take it in.

"William." My wife had slipped into the room and silently closed the door. She was behind me and she put her arms around me and hugged me. She said, quietly, into my ear, "I know that this is the worst of news but you are strong. Your mother and your sisters told me how, after Alfred's death, it was you held the family together and you will do so again."

I stood, turned and held her to my chest. Her hair smelled of rosemary. "How did you know?"

"Your mother sent a letter to me. She said that your father has taken this hard for the men who died were all trained by him. They were a band of brothers. She also said that the wedding went ahead and that we were missed."

I held her at arm's length, "And you were not there. I am sorry."

I knew she was disappointed but she smiled, "It is God's will and besides I am not certain that a journey through this land at this time of year would have done Margaret much good. There may be more marriages. There are Alfred and Thomas who are almost of an age."

I led her to her seat and sat her down. "And it is good that my father kept them at home for had he not then I fear he would not have coped with any further losses."

We sat and spoke of the ones who had died. She did not know them as well as I had but she spoke well of them and it was good for me to think of them in that way. They were warriors and we all knew that death could be just a spearhead away but to die for the Lusignan family was a bitter pill to swallow.

She stood, "And I had better ensure that the table is properly laid."

"I am sorry, I have made work for you."

"David of Wales and these archers are like family and I have seen on their faces how they feel. This will be a time for reflection and the beginning of healing. I have invited Brother Paul and Father John. We will all need their wisdom and guidance."

My wife seated David of Wales next to me and he was able to fill in the gaps from my father's letter. "Both Sir Fótr and Sir Peter will live as will Sir Gilles but Sir Fótr broke his leg when he fell from the horse. The healers do not know if he will walk properly again for it was healers in France who mended his leg. Sir Gilles suffered a spear thrust to the leg. It missed everything vital and he will walk again. As for Sir

Peter?" He shrugged, "He had his arm broken by a mace. It was his left arm and if he had been an archer then I would have said that his days of war were over but he is as strong as his father, Ridley the Giant. Who knows?"

"And the men at arms and archers who were with them?"

"We were lucky in that they did not have many archers with them. Perhaps that was why they lost and the archers they took were quick thinking. They survived. Fewer than half of the men at arms returned to the valley. The knights' squires and the men at arms who guarded them all perished. The Lusignans fled and Sir William and the valley knights held up the French until the King was safe. The King is grateful!"

That left a sour taste in my mouth. Once again, the valley knights had paid the price for a King's ambitions. The last time had been at Arsuf and only my father had survived. Perhaps the one hope was that more than Henry Samuel had survived intact. "And my nephew?"

David smiled, "He is strong that one. I was not there but from what I have heard your nephew is the Warlord reborn. He rallied the knights and men at arms when Sir William fell. It took great courage to leave the bodies of his friends but he managed to save more than half of the men of the valley. I spoke to the archers he brought back and they told me of his skill. He used archers to shower the French and then withdrew to form a second battle line. He made the French charge his spears and then passed through the archers once more. In such a way he extracted his men without the loss of a single man."

That made me smile. It was what my father would have done and, I believe, what I would have done. Taking Henry Samuel to the Holy Land had been the making of him. He had changed from a youth to a man. I hoped that he would not suffer dreams as a result of the loss. I knew that my father had endured nightmares after Arsuf and, indeed, when we had been in the Holy Land, he had often woken sweating as he remembered that day long ago.

That night I prayed for a long time before I went to bed. I prayed for the souls of my dead friends and for their families. I asked God to allow the men at arms and archers to enter heaven. I knew that sometimes they might not always have been as righteous as one would have hoped for they were men. They were just ordinary men but they deserved eternal peace. And then I prayed for my manor and Otterburn. Through no fault of our own, we were now in great danger. The archers who had been sent to help us would be invaluable but there were few of them. As I crept into bed next to my sleeping wife, I knew that the next day I had to put the disaster of Taillebourg from my mind and plan how I would save the north!

Chapter 8

It had been almost a year since the winter had begun savagely early. The end of this year looked as though it might be a little more benign. It was still cold and we had heavy frosts but there was no sign of snow and whatever dampness there had been had come in the form of rain. The rivers were all high. That did not worry us for we had high ground and were at the headwaters of the river system. Others might suffer further downstream but not us. Selfishly, I gave no thought to them. I gathered my garrison in the inner bailey and spoke to them all. I had no doubt that the archers and Edward of Yarum who had returned with them would have told them of the disaster but they needed to hear the words from me and they needed the reassurance that I had a plan to cope with the impending danger.

"You will all have heard of the disaster which struck our brothers in arms from the valley. Brother Paul will say prayers for them but here, in the north, we have to go on. And I want you to be under no illusions, there will be no help until the spring. I tell you all that here and now! The men you see represent our only defence, you and the small garrison at Otterburn will have to do the work of many more men. We still have archer's at Cedric's farm and now that we have David of Wales and his men, I will rotate them. The Scots tried to attack once and this weather, kind though it is, actually helps the Scots more than we. Our patrols will continue. We have more horses now and while we will have little rest this means that the horses need only ride once every other day but for you, there will be no such relief. No matter what the weather we will be riding abroad every day. I know that there will be many days when we see nothing but if we relax our vigilance for a heartbeat then people will die. The ones who will die will not be warriors, like us, who expect to die, they will be children, women and farmers. My father will come but when…" I waved a hand. "What I see before me is all that we have but I know that all of you are the best of the best!"

They all cheered and I felt a lump in my throat. I looked along their faces and did not see a single dissenting one. They were all with me and I knew just how lucky I was to lead such men. I also knew, in that instant, that when my father came some of these men would be dead. I suspected that they knew it too but it would not stop them from doing their duty.

"I intend to divide the garrison into five. I will lead one section, David of Wales a second and Idraf of Towyn a third. Alan of

Bellingham and Alan Longsword will lead the fourth and the fifth. I will ensure that there are men at arms and archers in every section. One section will stay at the castle each day." I smiled, "That will be the easy duty. You will just have to walk the fighting platform and stamp your feet to keep them warm!" They all laughed. "When we are on patrol, we will cover the land for twenty miles around this manor and Otterburn. Each patrol will have a horn and if any finds signs of the Scots or the French then they blow three blasts on the horn and the rest of the patrols will converge. The bell will be tolled and the villagers kept safe in Elsdon. I will ride today and have the Otterburn garrison ride to the border and back as their patrol. I will speak to my leaders and the rest can prepare your war gear. Idraf of Towyn and his men will be the garrison this day!"

I had eight men with Geoffrey and myself; four men at arms and four archers. I rotated the two at the front for all of us needed to be experts in finding the signs of the enemy. Geoffrey had got over Eleanor and was, once more, the keen squire who wished to become a knight. He asked more questions than he had when Eleanor had preyed upon his mind. He was not put off by the deaths of the knights of the valley. That was partly because he did not know them but more that he had witnessed death at close hand in the Holy Land. Matthew had saved his life and lost his in the process. I think he wanted to be a knight because that meant he had more control over his own destiny.

It was almost December and we had established our routine. When we were in the garrison it was a time to recover from being in a saddle for five hours a day. Geoffrey said, as we headed through the woods to drop down to the road and head back to Elsdon, "Lord, we have seen no signs of the Scots! We could have stayed in the castle for all the good that we have done."

I laughed, "Not true. Robin Greenleg. Have there been no Scots?"

He shook his head but did not take his eyes from the trees. "We have not seen their signs but that does not mean that they are not here. They have been here, lord, but just one or two. They are the scouts and they watch us watching for them."

Geoffrey said, "Then why do we do this, my lord?"

"Because the scouts go back and say that we are vigilant and so they send more scouts. Each day it is a different patrol which travels the paths and that uncertainty means that the Scots cannot predict when and where we will ride. They need to be here, in numbers and then they can take our patrols but they have to get here and they wait for that one moment when we cease to be vigilant." I pointed to the north. "They wait beyond the border. They can get through the Otterburn patrol. That is not because they are not good men but they are not led by a lord and they have fewer men. One day they will find a way in and then we will have to fight them."

The ennui of the patrols was broken by the birthday party my wife threw for Margaret. She did so to bring light into the castle and showed that she was doing her part as much as I was. Our daily patrols meant that it was at night but I enjoyed it nonetheless. And then we had Christmas. That was a time when every man in the land would be in his home for it was the time of the shortest days of the year and, often, the coldest. December was cold but there was no snow and we still rode our patrols. We would keep watch on Christmas Day! That was the day we found the Scots, or rather, we discovered each other at the same moment for it was my patrol which was attacked. I now believe that they thought we would not patrol on Christmas Day and had travelled through the night of the Eve of Christmas to be in place so that they could ambush us on St Stephen's Day.

We were on the road and heading towards Bellingham when we came upon them unexpectedly for they were building some defences. They were clearing trees and we heard their axes. I knew that none of my people would be working on such a day. They had a sentry and he sent an arrow to hit Harold of Hart's horse. I shouted, "Roger Two Swords, the horn!"

Roger had spent each night adorning the cow's horn with carvings. The work had altered the tone slightly so that the other patrols would know that it was my patrol which was under attack. No patrol was more than five miles from Elsdon and the cold winter air meant that sound travelled. Even as the third note echoed, I was drawing my sword and riding towards the archer who had injured our horse.

He turned and ran. My archers dismounted and, grabbing their bows, they followed us into the woods. It might have been foolish for we did not know numbers but I always liked to take the fight to the enemy and to get them on the back foot. I heard a Scottish voice commanding the Scots and the fact that it was not in French but Scottish told me that it was unlikely to be a knight. An arrow slammed into my shoulder. It was a bodkin arrow but my surcoat, mail and the aketon I wore beneath meant that it just pricked my body. It was a warning and I shouted, "They are using bodkins!"

I urged Dragon, my horse, towards the archer who had sent his arrow at me. He tried to duck behind a tree but Geoffrey was on my left and his sword backhanded across the neck of the Scot, half severing it. Arrows flew from behind me as my four archers chose targets which endangered the six of us. I saw a Scottish archer draw back on a hunting

77

bow and I spurred Dragon towards him. To my right, Roger Two Swords was taking on a Scot with a wood axe. Even as I slashed across the middle of the Scot with the bow, I could see that we were greatly outnumbered. This was not the time for vainglorious heroics, it was the time to use discretion.

"Fall back to the road!"

My men were well-trained and they obeyed instantly. They slashed their weapons at the man before them and then, whipping their horse's head around, they turned and fled. Roger and I had already slain those before us and turned more quickly. We had surprised the Scots but now their leader saw that they outnumbered us and I heard voices commanding the Scots. I did not need to speak their language to know what they said. They would come after us. As we raced back, I felt arrows striking my back and clanking off my helmet. I was the knight and I was the target. The command had been to kill me! It meant that the rest were relatively safe.

Reaching the road, I shouted, "Archers mount and head back to Elsdon!"

They mounted quickly as the last of my men, Harold of Hart, emerged from the woods. His horse was hurt and I said, "Harold, get back to Elsdon! We will lead them there!"

I knew that Idraf of Towyn and his men were to the east and were the furthest away. David of Wales had the garrison and that left Alan of Bellingham to the north and Alan Longsword to the south. If we were lucky then they would flank the Scots.

The Scots were, largely, afoot but with frozen ground, they could move almost as fast as we could. They almost caught me and two of them ran from the woods ahead with axes they had been using to fell trees. Fortunately for me they both came at me from my left side and both swung at my leg. I lowered my shield and took the blows although it meant that my shield would be ruined. Using my knees to guide Dragon, I brought my sword over to split open the skull of one Scot and the blood, bones and brains splattered into the face of the other, temporarily blinding him. Spurring Dragon, I leapt away from the remaining tree feller.

The Scots were mainly on foot but they had four horses and mailed men upon them. They burst from the trees behind me and galloped after us. Their horses were fresher and they would catch us. Roger Two Swords looked over his shoulder and seeing the threat shouted, "Men at arms, protect Sir William!"

The other two men at arms and Geoffrey wheeled their horses. At the same time, my four archers stopped their horses and, even though they were on horseback, nocked an arrow and drew back. I was aware of the hoofbeats closing with me and saw my men riding towards me. The attack by the tree fellers had almost cost me, dear. An arrow struck my horse and his head dropped. Dragon was game but I would not have him ride himself to death for me. I wheeled him around to face the horsemen. That they did not expect me to do so was obvious for the first Scot had his sword behind him and I had a free swing at him. He barely blocked the sword blow and, as he had not managed to get his feet into his stirrups, he fell from the saddle.

I saw the leader who came for me. It was obvious that he was the leader for he had a coat of arms upon his shield. It was the livery of Atholl. Unless Alan Durward had betrayed me then this was a Comyn warrior. He was ready and as Roger Two Swords and Geoffrey clattered into the other horsemen and my archer's arrows whittled down the men on foot, I took the blow from his sword. It shattered my shield and numbed my arm. His shield was a smaller one than mine but it gave him an advantage. I drew my dagger from my belt, although my numbed arm did not inspire me with confidence. He pulled his arm back for another strike. With no shield, I think he expected to take my arm. I did the unexpected and lunged with the tip of my dagger. I aimed it at his face and he turned his swing from an offensive stroke to a defensive one. It bought me moments but, in a battle, moments are what decide life and death. My right arm was uninjured and my left arm was beginning to regain feeling and so I lunged again. This time he was expecting it and blocked my strike much more easily.

I had to think of a way to regain the advantage. Slipping my left foot from my stirrup I leapt at him with my sword and dagger held before me. I forgot that I still had the stump of an arrow in my shoulder and, as I hit him, I drove the head deeper into my body. It was too late to remedy my catastrophic error. The pain was excruciating. The combined weight of two men wearing mail meant that the Scot's horse was unable to stand and it fell. The Scottish warrior's leg was trapped beneath the horse and, as we fell, I heard it crack. His head was close to mine and he screamed. Momentum carried me over his body. Two Scots, hidden by the horses, saw their chance and ran at me. I barely had time to get to my feet but I did and my longer sword made the difference for they had short swords. However, as I connected with the sword of one of them, I felt a shooting pain in my shoulder. The arrowhead was biting! It was at that moment that Alan Longsword led his patrol and they fell upon the rear of the Scots who were trying to get at us.

One of the two men I was fighting glanced to the woods when he heard the clash of steel and my left arm, no longer numbed, darted like a snake's tongue to penetrate his eye. The other seized his chance and pulled back his arm. I was a dead man. Then an arrow flew over my shoulder to smack into his forehead. Even as he fell the warrior who had a broken leg managed to rise. He threw his shield at me and then leapt at me, holding his sword before him. He had great courage for I could see the two bones sticking out of his lower leg. My right arm appeared not to want to move and so I turned with my left hand to face him. His sword scraped and scratched across my mail but he drove himself into my dagger. It tore through his coif and into his neck. As we fell to the ground, I felt a shocking pain in my shoulder and then all went black.

I could not have been out very long for it was Roger Two Swords who pulled the dead Scot from me. "My lord! Where are you hurt?"

I gave a wry laugh, "At the moment, seemingly everywhere but I believe it is the arrow in my shoulder."

His fingers probed the arrow stump. "I dare not move it, lord. Master Geoffrey, fetch a horse for Sir William."

I could hear the sounds of battle as I lay there. "Forget me, get the Scots!"

"Alan of Bellingham has joined us and it is now a footrace to Scotland. We will get them but we need you to heed my words, my lord, for you are hurt."

I nodded for he was right and I did feel weak. "If you can, find out who led this band. They almost succeeded."

Geoffrey appeared with a horse taken from the Scots. "Here, my lord, let me help you to mount. Alan of Bellingham has taken charge and I will get you back to Elsdon!"

"Dragon?"

"He is hurt but he will recover. Forget him, it is you the men worry about!"

As I was helped on to the back of the horse, I saw the dead Scots. I noticed that I had lost men too. Two archers lay in untidy heaps. This Christmas would be one that we remembered but for all the wrong reasons. Geoffrey tied Dragon to his saddle and led the Scottish one by the reins. We were just three miles from Elsdon but he kept turning every few paces to make certain I was still in the saddle. I was about to tell him to watch the road ahead when Idraf of Towyn led my eastern patrol down the road towards us.

"You are hurt, my lord!"

"And I will live. The raiders are heading north and west. Ride across country and cut them off." He looked questioningly at me. "I am close to home and I have Geoffrey, now go lest more of them escape."

They went but I saw each one of his patrol stare at me as they passed. My surcoat was covered in blood and not all of it was my enemies'. Despite my words, I was uncertain if I would make it to the castle whilst still conscious and, to keep my mind active, I thought about the nature of this attack. There was no reason for us to keep watch on Christmas Day. It was a Holy Day which was celebrated by all in this land. If this had been close to Jerusalem then I might have understood for the Muslims did not celebrate the day. Our vigilance had paid off but, even so, we had come close to disaster. We needed larger patrols and that meant, until we received reinforcements, then we would have to weaken the garrison and use some of those who would normally guard the castle. And then it came to me. We could simply use the villagers to watch the walls. Until the end of February, they would have little to occupy them and I guessed that they would like to be seen to be doing something. My thoughts and plans kept my mind active until I reached the castle. Harold of Hart had warned them of the attack and when I rode through the gates Brother Paul and Father John were there already.

"His lordship is wounded and there are more wounded men to come!" I smiled for Geoffrey had come of age and his commanding voice was not that of the querulous boy we had rescued from the Turks!

My wife must have heard the shouts for she and Dick were in the Great Hall as Father John and Geoffrey half carried me in. I smiled, although it must have looked a pained one from my wife's expression, "It is just an arrow and I will live."

Brother Paul shook his head, "Let me be the judge of that, Sir William. Lay him on the table and fetch light and boiling water." The priest was a good healer and had some sharp instruments with which he could extract arrows but I anticipated pain. It was almost as though he was reading my mind for Brother Paul said, "Geoffrey, fetch wine."

Beth laid a cloth on the table to catch the inevitable blood spill and then my wife said, "Here, take Margaret and Dick. They do not need to see this."

"I want to stay!" My son wanted to be at my side,

I growled, "Heed your mother." The words sounded harsher than I meant for I had a sudden pain.

Beth said, "Come, Master Richard, this is not the place for you. I will take you to your chamber and tell you a tale of the Green Man!"

Such stories always intrigued my son and taking her hand he left.

"Pour Sir William a large beaker of wine, Geoffrey, and when he has drunk it, we will take off the mail."

I drank the unwatered wine in one for I knew that getting the mail from me would hurt. I lay back and Mary held my hand. "I fear the feast will spoil, husband."

I laughed and regretted it immediately for it sent shivers of pain through my body. "Lie back, my lord, and we shall begin." Brother Paul's voice was now the one which commanded.

Despite the effect of the wine, taking the mail from me hurt more than I cared to admit. The surcoat and the aketon were first cut from my body. We could always make new ones but mail was a different matter. I was given another large beaker and then Brother Paul began.

"My lady, if you would hold his right hand. Father John, Geoffrey, take his shoulders and prevent any movement. The arrow was driven in deep."

I was becoming a little drunk for I had lost blood and drunk two beakers in rapid succession. I giggled, "That was my fault, Brother Paul. I hurled myself at a Scot and it drove the arrow in… sorry!" For some reason, I seemed to find that highly amusing.

Looking up I saw the priest grinning, "I think the wine is working. Alice, pour some of the white wine over the wound. It will cleanse it and make it easier for me to see." He tugged a little on the arrow whilst keeping a wary eye on me. I felt a dull ache and I felt sleepy. I heard him say, "At least it was a bodkin. These are easier to remove." And then, as he began to work the arrow stump, I passed out.

When I came to, I was in my bed and Geoffrey was watching over me. He smiled, "The arrow is out and Brother Paul does not think that there is any hurt left in the wound. He has cleansed it with vinegar and rosemary and there is honey applied too. He has stitched it." I tried to rise and regretted it immediately. He smiled, "Brother Paul thinks that it will take a day or two for you to be ready to walk and a week before you can ride."

The priest did not know me. I would rise at my usual time; however, I was no fool and knew that I needed rest. "And Lady Mary?"

"She was determined that the Christmas feast would go ahead." He pointed to an empty platter. "I ate mine here."

"You could have left me to sleep."

He laughed, "Lady Mary knows you well, lord, and said that if you woke alone you would try to rise. Besides this is better. I did not have to serve at table."

"Then pour me some wine and tell me all that I need to hear."

He gave me a detailed account of the end of the skirmish. The Scots had been hunted but Alan of Bellingham was sure that some had escaped. We had six prisoners and they had told Alan that the leader had been Stephen of Atholl. I had slain Comyn's, right-hand man. That, I knew, would bring repercussions. I could do little about it. We had lost two archers and a man at arms and I was not the only one wounded. Had we not surprised them then it might have gone ill for us for they outnumbered us. Alan had discovered that they planned to build a defensive position in the woods where we had found them. Their plan had been to lure us there and then let us bleed while we tried to get over the barricade they intended to make. It was now obvious that they knew our exact numbers.

"Tomorrow, Geoffrey, I want you to have the prisoners sent to Morpeth. I will have a letter sent. I want these men tried and hanged but not here. The rest of the north must shoulder its responsibilities."

I had missed Christmas but I was still alive and, more importantly, my manor still survived intact. The men who escorted the prisoners to Morpeth arrived back three days later and brought with them snow from the east. The snow from the east and the north was always colder and tended to lie longer. The fact that it had come a month later than it had done the previous year was good news for it meant that as the days lengthened it was more likely that the snow would melt more quickly once the thaw began. Alan of Bellingham and my wife were both adamant that I would not stir forth for at least six days. The snow encouraged me to stay within doors for even if the Scots were abroad, a blizzard was blowing and we would never find them. As Idraf of Towyn pointed out, as soon as the blizzard stopped then if there were enemies then we would see their prints in the snow.

The first night of the two-day blizzard I lay in bed with my wife. Margaret had had some sleepless nights and we had the door to our chamber open so that Mary could listen for the child. She leaned her elbow upon my pillow and ran her finger down the scar on my face, "Where is the handsome young knight I married? He has two scars now which will mark him forever."

I smiled, "The one upon my face is fading, at least that is what my men tell me and the one in my shoulder will be hidden."

She sat upright, "But you are young and this will happen increasingly!"

"Then I will have better mail made. We have a good weaponsmith here in Elsdon and we have money to pay him. I will have a strong caparison made for my horse too."

She was silent for a while and then she said, "And one day Dick will wish to go to war and you will take him."

"I am a knight and a lord of the manor. It is my duty to have a son who will follow in my footsteps. I cannot give you any comfort, my love. Alfred died young and my mother never got over it. I fear that is the lot of all wives of knights."

She snuggled in to me, "Then I shall make the most of you while you are here!"

Chapter 9

When, after the storm had abated, my men and I rode my manor we saw no sign of Scots. I had been unable to ride, not because of my wound, but because with short days and incessant snow no-one could have ridden. In fact, the attack we had suffered on Christmas Day was the last one of the winter. We did not know that at the time and we continued with our daily patrols. I had Egbert, the weaponsmith, begin my new mail hauberk and I had him make mittens attached to it. I had seen some in the Holy Land and knew that they were effective. The caparison I had made was of heavy canvas with leather straps. It was painted in my livery and made my horses look magnificent. That was not the reason I had it done. The canvas would slow down a bodkin and might even stop a hunting arrow. When the snow had finally disappeared my father managed to send a message that King Henry planned a visit to York in the Spring and he would seek an audience with the Scottish King then. It seemed as though our isolation was coming to an end. All that we had to do was wait a month or two and we would have succour.

And then, at the very end of February, we had a visitor. It was the disputed Count of Atholl, Alan Durward. He came shrouded in a plain cloak and with just six men at arms as well as his squire, Robert. He was a brave man for I now knew that Walter Comyn wished him dead and travelling through the borders with so few men was dangerous and, as he made his way from his horse to my hall, I wondered what had brought him.

He clasped my arm and his greeting was genuine, "Good to see you, Baron. I heard about the attack and your wound. You are recovered?"

I smiled back at him, "Aye, but I have learned a most valuable lesson. Do not leap on a man when you have an arrow in your shoulder. He laughed. "We have a chamber for you and your squire but your men at arms will need to sleep in the warrior hall."

"And they will enjoy that, believe me, for your warriors have earned almighty reputation." He lowered his voice, "Some of those with Stephen of Atholl made it back to Comyn and they told tales of the battle they fought. You have frightened the wild men of the north, my friend."

My wife arrived, "This is my wife, Lady Mary."

He took her hand and kissed it. "I knew your father and a truer gentleman I have yet to meet. It is a tragedy that you cannot enjoy your own lands."

She smiled, "Sir Alan, these are now my lands and I am content to be at my husband's side. I fear the fare this night will not be what I would wish for the Count of Atholl but we will do our best to entertain you."

"Dear lady, I come here not for the food but to bring dire news."

She nodded, "Then I will make arrangements for the food and for your chamber. Alice will fetch your wine, husband."

I turned to Geoffrey, "Take Sir Alan's squire and show him the castle. I will speak alone with the Count."

This time of year, here in the borders, was still cold and we had a fine fire roaring in the fireplace. We sat on either side of the fire and I waited until Alice had served us wine and put a platter of ham, cheese and pork crackling from the pig we had eaten recently before I spoke. "Dire news, Sir Alan?"

"It is the French. The Count, as you rightly guessed, was here to suborn the King. With Walter Comyn so successfully fighting the Vikings in the north then the Scottish King was under pressure. He has agreed to bring an army south." He shrugged, "He does not wish to fight but, as I said, there is pressure and he hopes that the presence of a large army might encourage talks."

Even while I was listening to the words I was trying to work out when King Henry would be in York and, more importantly, when my father would arrive in Elsdon. I had enough men to stem an attack from a band of raiders but an army which was backed by the French was a different matter.

"And how long do we have?" I tried to keep my voice as calm as I could.

He sighed, "The French and some of Comyn's men are already gathering south of Edinburgh." My heart sank. The Scot leaned forward to speak confidentially to me although, as we were alone in my Great Hall, it seemed unnecessary but Alan Durward lived in a dangerous world and it was in his nature to be cautious. "King Alexander does not wish this but he is under pressure. I am not here as a traitor to Scotland but with the blessing of the King!"

"He wants me to stop it?" He nodded and I laughed, "Then a little more notice would have helped!"

"All of this was decided in the last ten days. You have a little time. I learned that the attack at Christmas was part of a greater plan. Comyn and the Count were planning this then. As you might imagine I am not privy to their plans, just the King's. The survivors who returned brought

86

the news that it was possible to bypass Elsdon and reach into the heart of England. Their plan is clever. The main army will approach down the coast from Dunbarre but a large column will head down the centre of the land to approach Northumberland from the west, north of the Roman Wall."

Suddenly the last two attacks made perfect sense. They had raided in numbers but their real reason had been to test my defences. We had thwarted them both but now they had learned of our weaknesses.

I nodded, "And if they are gathered now, south of Edinburgh and close to Dunbarre, then when will they begin their attack?"

"I will be with the King and the main army at Dunbarre. You should know that King Alexander will take as long as possible to bring the army south and I do not expect us to be close to Northumberland before the start of Spring. The Count and Comyn will also be with the King and I dare say that the evenings will be fractious for Comyn and I spar all the time. You slew the man who was, apparently, to lead this secret column and the Count has put in command his own man. Ferry de Lorraine. He fought at Taillebourg and it was he who broke your knights of the valley at the end. He had their heads displayed at his castle of Vendome!"

I quaffed the beaker of wine, "I thank you for your messages but I confess I think that we will struggle to hold them." I shouted, "Alice!" The housekeeper arrived, "Take Sir Alan to his quarters so that he can clean up."

Sir Alan downed his beaker and smiled, "And you will write letters!" I nodded, "Beware for there are scouts already abroad in the land to the east of here."

That made sense. De Umfraville was not as vigilant as I was. In fact, despite my pleas, he did not keep regular patrols between his manors and mine. I would have to send at least two men with each letter. I began scribbling and wrote my most important letter first. It was to my father. Then I wrote a second to the Bishop and a third to the Sherriff. I contemplated writing one to the constable at Berwick and then realised that the Scots would simply bypass that mighty castle which was a symbol of England in the north and could do little to stop an army.

Geoffrey arrived for Sir Alan's squire had joined his lord. "Fetch me Alan of Bellingham, David of Wales and Idraf of Towyn."

Left alone I thought about the Christmas attack. In the aftermath, my men had ridden the roads to the north, south and west of us for we knew that they had come that way. They had used the old Roman Road which lay to the west of the River Rede. The river could be forded easily but it crossed into England close to the tiny hamlet of Woodburn and then headed down to Corbridge in the heart of the Tyne Valley. My archers had found the houses there, in Woodburn, destroyed. That would be where a large force of men would cross the river and that was where we would have to meet them.

When Alan, David and Idraf entered I had them sit down and I gave them an outline of my plans. "You know that what I have just said is for your ears only. Alan Durward has risked all to bring us this news." They each nodded. "The letters I send are to ask for help but regardless of the response, I intend to take the men of Otterburn and Elsdon down to Woodford and to contest the crossing of the Rede. I can do nothing about the Scottish army which will pose the greater threat but I trust in my father. It will take him a week to muster his men and fetch them north. He will come directly to Elsdon and I am gambling that a small garrison at Elsdon and Otterburn can hold out if they are attacked."

Alan of Bellingham shook his head, "That is a mighty gamble, my lord."

Shaking my head, I said, "Not so, Alan. If they attack these castles then they have lost the element of surprise. This is a clever plan. With King Alexander threatening Newcastle from the north then a threat from the west would give them great bargaining power. Even if we fail to stop them, we will have alerted Prudhoe and the men of Northumberland. We have to buy time."

David of Wales nodded, "Fear not, lord, your father will not let you down. He came once before and I am just surprised that he is not here yet!"

I hoped that David was right but the knights of the valley had been hurt in France. "Idraf, tomorrow I want men to cross the border and to watch the Roman Road. They do not hinder any army but one reports to me and the others follow. We know where they will be going and it is just a matter of watching their progress."

"Aye, lord."

"I agree with David of Wales, my father will come but we all know that he cannot bring the numbers he might have in the past. This will be a severe test of our fighting ability but I doubt not the hearts and arms of the men of Elsdon," I smiled at David of Wales, "and of Stockton!"

While we ate, we kept the conversation light. My wife took advantage of Sir Alan for he was able to tell her about many of her friends. She had not seen any of them since before she had married me and the gossip was as necessary to her as bread for it linked her with her past. It also suited me for it allowed me to plan how to stop this French and Scottish column. The hamlet of Woodburn was now deserted. Close by were the foundations of an old Roman fort but they would not aid us as it had been made largely of wood and only the ditches remained. What would help us was the river. There was a bridge and the river formed a loop so that we could flank the column of men with archers whilst holding them up at the bridge. If we were trying to stop just a French army then that would be all we needed to do but there would be Scots there and they would happily cross the river further upstream for they were hardy and minded not a soaking in an icy stream. We would need to be prepared for a flank attack on ourselves. I could not stop them with the men of Otterburn and Elsdon. I would ride to de Umfraville and ask for his men. I was still unsure about his loyalties. Rothbury too and Sir Raymond would be another port of call. If they gave me men and knights then I could go directly to Woodford and wait. If they did not then I would need to wait for the Sherriff. I knew that the Sherriff and the lords of Bamburgh, Alnwick and Warkworth would not be able to send a large force to aid me. Their castles were vital for the areas they protected. We could not afford to lose one of our fortresses for it would cost northern blood to recover it.

I was suddenly aware that Alan Durward was speaking to me, "I am sorry, my lord, but I was distracted."

He chuckled, "Aye, and I would be too. When all this is over, I would be glad to hear how you managed to stop this attack. I will not ask you now for I am part of the enemy army although you know I am not against you." I nodded. "You fight for your king as I fight for mine. I suspect that King Henry is more secure than King Alexander! Although as both have sons who are but infants their succession is far from assured."

Our guests left before dawn and my riders and I left soon after. The castle would be almost empty for I had sent a rider to Otterburn to ask them to be prepared to join me. With our patrol on the Rede and my messengers seeking help, I took half of the remaining men with me.

Sir Gilbert, in Prudhoe, enjoyed his comfort. He had a rich manor and he also had four household knights but I was now a baron and could speak to him as an equal. I told him a version of the news I had. "How did you discover this, Sir William, for it is serious news?"

I lied about the source. "I was visited by a Scottish merchant who sought favour with King Henry. It was he who told me for he was in Edinburgh and saw the army gathering."

It seemed a plausible answer and he accepted it. "We must wait until the Sherriff can muster his men and then meet him with a large army."

I shook my head, "The attacks on my land and the nature of the enemy means that I fear a flank attack. I do not ask for all of your men, just a couple of knights, your archers and some men at arms." He did not look convinced, "King Henry will be in York soon and my father will come too!"

It was a veiled threat but it worked. Sir Gilbert might not take either advice nor orders from Baron Elsdon but the Lord of the North and the King of England were a different matter. "Very well. Whence do I send them?"

"I will ride to Rothbury. Send then directly to Elsdon for time is of the essence."

Sir Ranulf was a different kettle of fish. He had had Rothbury for a relatively short time and was eager to flex his muscles. He agreed to support me. He had no household knights but he left just ten men to guard his castle and promised to bring the rest to join me. As I headed back through the darkening gloom of twilight to Elsdon, I reflected that I now had enough men to slow down the column. Victory was unlikely but I counted on the Sherriff, the Bishop and my father acting promptly. They were three men that I trusted. Ultimately, however, victory rested with the arrival of the King!

Neither conroi reached me until the next day but as my watchers on the Rede had not sent a rider, I guessed that we were safe, for a while. It was just seven miles to Woodford. Upon reaching my castle I went to the tower to view the land. On a clear day, you could almost see the top of Otterburn Tower. Alan Longsword was there. He said, "Lord, why not call out the levy? They owe you forty days and this seems a time for that. The men of Bellingham, Elsdon and Otterburn would add two hundred men to the force you could muster."

"And they would be just that, Richard, numbers. I intend to tell the men of Bellingham of the danger and if we lose then they will be the ones to stop the enemy. Erik the Crusader is a good man and he will slow the enemy down but if we cannot hold them at the Rede then all is lost. We need professional soldiers and not farmers with pitchforks."

The men arrived the next day and we camped them in the fields we used for the winter grazing. The animals were now in their pastures. After telling the three knights and the captains what they would be doing I gave them a detailed outline of my plan. As I had expected Sir Ranulf was enthusiastic while the two knights from Sir Gilbert less so. It was while I was going through the plan that my messengers sent to Newcastle and Durham returned. They brought with them good news. Both leaders had ordered the muster and the Bishop was bringing his men to the Tyne. The Sherriff had promised me two knights and forty men. It was not enough but it would have to do. I knew that the messenger sent to my father would take another day, at the very least, to return.

That encouraged me. "Tomorrow we will head for Woodford. I intend to leave the garrison at Otterburn until we actually hear that the French and the Scots have come. I will send our archers first and then the men at arms. We will leave a day later for I am anxious to know the news from my father. As we have still to hear from my spies in Scotland the enemy is at least a day away from Woodford and we have time."

Sir John, who was one of Sir Gilbert's knights, a cousin, "Can you trust the archers and the men at arms to do that which you ask, Sir William?"

I laughed, "I know not the quality of the other men but mine will do precisely that which I ask. We will have defences in place and the bridge will be defensible."

Sir Ranulf nodded, "I know a little about the men of Elsdon and they are remarkable. They have thwarted two raids from north of the border in the last couple of years. The Scots marked their passage home with bodies. I, too, have confidence in the men of Elsdon."

The next day the castle gradually emptied as David of Wales led a hundred archers south. When my river patrol returned, we would have another eight. Later in the day, Alan of Bellingham led one hundred and twenty men at arms. The men of Elsdon came to my castle and took up sentry duties. I saw the three knights who were my guests taking note. The people and the castle were as one!

We were just finishing our food and preparing for an early night when I heard a shout from the gate. It was indistinct but I guessed it meant someone was approaching. Was it succour or news of the column?

"Geoffrey, go and see who it is!"

"Aye, lord."

I turned to the other three. "Well gentlemen, we may well get to ride off our dinner if this is my scouts."

While Sir Ranulf looked eager the other two did not!

Geoffrey burst through the door, "My lord! it is Sir Henry of Stockton and Sir Richard of Hartburn. They have come from your father and bring with them, fifty men!"

Before Geoffrey had spoken, I feared the worst but now it was like the shaft of light through a thick black rain cloud. There was hope.

"Mary, it is Sir Henry and Sir Richard! Food!"

The two of them looked exhausted as they entered my hall. They must have ridden their horses almost to death to reach us in time. I grasped my nephew and hugged him, "Thank God you have come!"

"But for Taillebourg I would have brought twice the men but the ones we have will have to do."

I held out my arm to Richard, "And it is good to see you too."

He nodded, "Have you a plan?"

That was Richard all over. He came to the point quickly and he knew this land as well as I did. "I intend to hold them at the bridge at Woodford. I have sent the archers and men at arms there already."

"Then I will borrow a horse from you and Garth and I will ride to Otterburn. It may not be my manor any longer but they are my men. I will follow you to Woodford tomorrow."

He turned and left. He was a true knight.

Sir Ranulf turned to the other two knights, "Come, we have an early morning ahead of us and I think that Sir William and Sir Henry wish to speak." I grew to like Sir Ranulf more and more.

My wife came in and embraced Sam. "I will fetch food."

He hugged her back. "It is good to see you, Mary, and I hope that I will see my new cuz before I leave."

Mary laughed, "Have no fear of that for she has a set of lungs on her and the ability to wake in the middle of the darkest night!"

Left alone I said, "Before you tell me of France, what news from my father?"

"He left for York before I left. He will speak with the King. Sir Geoffrey FitzUrse, Sir Gilles, Sir Peter and Sir Fótr are leading our men and archers to Durham."

"And are they recovered?"

He shrugged, "You know Fótr and Peter as well as I. They say that they are but we both know that the test of that will be when they test their arms in battle. You should know that both wished to come with Richard and I but my grandfather was adamant that you could manage." He looked directly at me to see my eyes, "Was he right?"

"We do not face the full force of King Alexander's army but we face a potent threat. If we can just stop them, we have won. We can lose the battle and still win but you know me, Sam, I will not lead men to certain death. You and your reinforcements might make all the difference. It is a good site I have chosen and I do not think that the French will have truly seen the effect of our archers."

He shook his head, "No, for at Taillebourg the fifty or so we took were the only ones and they were like pelting a fire with a handful of snowballs!"

"And Richard? It must have been a terrible shock for him."

"And his mother who almost lost her mind when she heard she had lost a husband and a son. The healers sent her to Mount Grace where the nuns care for her. It seems she knows no-one, not even Richard. Eleanor is with child and his mother will never know it. The King's decision cost us dearly."

I heard the bitterness in his voice. "Sam, guard your tongue. Here you can speak freely but there are many enemies."

"And that I know. We had Simon de Montfort with us and he is a treacherous snake. He feigns friendship and brotherliness but he seeks power. He was the first to flee the battlefield and yet now he belittles the King as a coward! If I were King Henry, it is de Montfort I would fear and not the French!"

The food arrived and instead of telling me about the battle, for Mary was there, Sam told us of the changes in the valley and the effect the battle had had on the men and families who served my father. "Sir Geoffrey is much changed. He is now the senior knight and the fact that Alfred and Geoffrey might have been in the disaster worried him. He is now grey."

My wife stroked the back of Sam's hand, "And you, Sam, what of you? You speak of others but I can see in your eyes a change."

He nodded and I heard a catch in his voice. "This was the first time that I fought without my uncle and my grandfather and I felt the weight of the valley upon my shoulders. That I was the youngest knight did not seem to matter. I did not want to be the one who slowed down the French but I knew that we had to and when the others fell, one by one, I was sure that I would be next." He looked at me, "Uncle, I wanted to run!"

I nodded, "I know and I have felt that too but you did not for you have the blood of the Warlord in your veins and that is a curse as well as a blessing for we stand and fight when, perhaps, we should run."

"But you do not and men know that. Riding north we heard the rumours of the Scots and yet the one hope from Durham and the north was that Sir William would stand firm."

I smiled, "And now you see the weight of responsibility I bear, here at Elsdon."

"And that may not be for much longer."

My wife and I exchanged a look. We knew nothing of this.

"Speak plainly, Sam."

"As soon as we reached home Grandfather petitioned the King to appoint a new lord of the manor here and at Otterburn. He was quite blunt and pointed out that you did not need to be a resident in Elsdon to enjoy the income and that as your wife has an income from the manor of Creca in Scotland, if you were not replaced, he would order you south."

I sucked in air, "That was foolish for you do not anger a king and besides, there was no need. I know my duty!"

"Grandfather is feeling his age. The losses turned him white overnight and he is bitter towards the royal family. You know how he felt betrayed by King Richard and King John. We see him as the kindly head of the family but remember this was the man who slew the Bishop of Durham. His waters run deep."

"And what has the King said?"

"By the time I left, he had said nothing but I think that things would have come to a head in York. If it is any consolation the King needs Sir Thomas for despite his tongue, he is the most loyal knight in the land and it is rumoured that having lost the chance to regain France, King Henry wishes to make Wales secure!" He yawned, "Uncle, I am weary beyond words and we rise early on the morrow."

"Of course." I stood and clasped his arm, "Know that I feel more confident with you by my side."

"And it will be ever thus."

When he had gone Mary said, "How do you feel about leaving Elsdon?"

Shaking my head, I said, "That is a bridge we will cross when we come to it. My father may make demands but I will not leave this manor to one who is unworthy. The people here are our people. We could not leave the Yalesham widows to a lord who would abandon them. Since we have returned here danger has never been more than a heartbeat away. I wish that my nephew had not broached the matter for it will hang in the air now like a sword of Damocles."

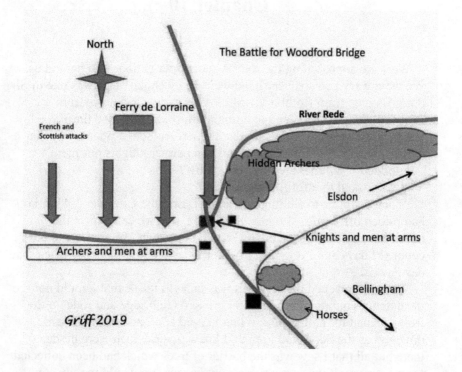

Chapter 10

We were approaching the river when a rider galloped up behind us. We were wary and so every hand went to a weapon but it was one of Sir Ranulf's men from Rothbury. "My lord, we have had news from Berwick. King Alexander and a mighty host have crossed the Tweed and they are heading south and the Sherriff has sent a rider to say that the host is so large that he can spare you neither knights nor men."

I nodded, "Whither are you bound now?"

"I was asked to inform Elsdon, lord."

"Then continue to Bellingham and tell Erik the Crusader." After he had ridden off, I said, "I think, gentlemen, that we can expect the imminent arrival of my scouts. We will be drawing swords in the next couple of days and I pray that my father has brought the King when that day dawns!"

When we reached the bridge, I was pleased to see that I could not see the defences but, to make certain I crossed the bridge and rode up the Roman Road for half a mile so that I could approach from the same direction as the Scots and French. I knew that my men were hidden there but all that I saw was the barrier of trees which had been collected from the river. It was not a permanent barrier and would merely slow attackers up but the archers who would be lining the riverbank would have more targets to thin.

My men at arms and archers said nothing as I inspected the work. In fact, most were busy speaking with the new men who had arrived with Henry Samuel. The three knights who did not know my men looked a little bemused. I dismounted Lion and handed the reins to Geoffrey. "David of Wales and Alan Longsword, divide the new men at arms and archers we have brought. I want a secure place for the horses and the spare arrows. I will go to inspect the riverbank."

I was not wearing my helmet but I pulled up my coif for I had to make my way through shrubs, bushes and tree branches. The side nearest the deserted hamlet was open and my archers had embedded stakes but it was the other side where the river turned north to run next to the road that I was interested in. My archers had used old honeysuckle, growing ivy and willow to weave a sort of net which hid them from view. David of Wales was busy and it was Will Son of Robin who nervously followed me waiting for my comments.

I pointed to the river bank. "There we need some stakes. If the Scots cross the river, I want it impossible for them to clamber up. Sharpen the stakes and cover them in mud and anything else which is slippery and wet. Keep them moist."

"Aye, lord. We should have thought of that."

"You have done better than I hoped and it was only riding down the road which made me see the danger." I had seen that some wild Scots would, in all likelihood, risk rushing into the river and it was narrow enough for them to attempt it. Our archers were the key to my plan to slow down and, perhaps, even halt the enemy.

When I reached the camp Alan of Bellingham had made, he asked, "Do we light fires, lord?"

I nodded, "The ambush is not the men on the bridge; it is the archers and, besides, our scouts have not yet returned. Have you organised the watches?"

"I have and put a good man in command of each one. It is good that we have fires for the men will appreciate the hot food. They have worked hard."

"I know and I will thank them. First, I need to speak with the knights."

My plans had changed slightly and I needed the knights to know them but before I could speak with them a sentry called, "Horsemen!"

Tools were dropped and weapons grabbed as we all looked north. It was getting on towards late afternoon and the sun was getting lower. I shaded my eyes. I recognised Sir Richard's horse, "It is the men from Otterburn! Clear the logs to allow them through and then rebuild the barrier."

I saw that there were just eight men on horses but another ten jogged behind. I heard Sir John sigh, "Just eighteen men! What use are they going to be?"

I whirled on him, "I would rather have just eighteen such men than one who carps and complains at everything. If you cannot show some spirit then take your squire and skulk back to Prudhoe!"

He recoiled physically and Henry Samuel restrained me, "Sir John has yet to see a battle, uncle, and he means nothing by his words, do you, Sir John?"

The young knight shook his head, "If I have caused offence, Baron, then I apologise. I just expected more."

I held his stare and said, "As did I but as Sir Gilbert just sent two knights and a handful of men at arms it seems we are both doomed to disappointment!"

I turned as Richard clattered over the bridge.

"Did you see any sign of the enemy, Richard?"

"No, but I only joined the Roman Road a mile or so north of here."
He looked around and nodded for he knew the country as well as I,
"This is a good site." Food had been put on to cook and he rubbed his
hands, "And there is food cooking! Better and better. Where do you
want us?"

"Alan of Bellingham will allocate the defensive positions to your
men. Have Garth put your horses to the rear where they will be guarded
and you can join us for a conference! We all need to know what we will
do when the enemy finally gets here."

Our camp was a good one hundred paces back from the bridge. We
used one of the large buildings from the hamlet. It was a farm which
had belonged to Gerald Osbertson. He and his son had been killed when
the Scots had raided and his wife and daughters had left for the south.
Geoffrey and Sam's squire, John son of Johann, had lit a fire and the
small room was cosy. We all fitted in, just.

Geoffrey had grown in confidence and he said, "We will fetch food
when it is ready, Sir William." He closed the door and I was left with
my handful of knights.

"My plan is simple but it will rely on the courage of the knights who
I see before me. We use our banners, and mine, in particular, to draw
the enemy to the bridge. We will stand behind the barrier of driftwood
and we will be backed by ten men at arms. We fight on foot and each of
us will have spears. David of Wales will command the archers in the
woods and Alan of Bellingham will command the rest of the archers
and the bulk of the men at arms to the west of the bridge. The squires
will watch the horses and they will be our only reserve."

Sir Robert, Sir Gilbert's other knight looked shocked, "Sixteen of us
will hold the bridge?"

Sam laughed, "Have you not read the history of early Rome, Sir
Robert? I have read of three Romans who held a bridge to save the
city."

I nodded, "Aye and one of our ancestors was at Stamford Bridge
when three Vikings held a bridge against King Harold and all of his
army. You crossed the bridge did you not?" He nodded, "And how
many men on horses can cross at one time?"

"Why it is only wide enough for three knights on horseback."

"And on foot?"

"Five!"

"Then we have three ranks and a man who is spare at the back. That
will be you, Sir Robert!" His mouth opened and closed like a fish. Sir
Richard and Sam grinned at his discomfort. I continued. "They cannot
get at us easily for there are logs and branches across the bridge. The

enemy will send men on foot to clear them and that is when the archers to the east of the river and the road will rain death upon them. They will, eventually, clear the bridge but by the time they do so, they will have littered the bridge with bodies. It is then that they can begin to cross but all the while archers from both flanks will shower them with missiles." I added, for the benefit of Sir Gilbert's men, "That is why we brought pack horses with so many arrows. It is the one arm in which we have superior numbers. Neither the Scots nor the French value the warbow. I hope, when this battle is over that they have learned a lesson!"

Sir Gilbert's men would say no more but Sir Ranulf frowned, "I do not mean to complain, Sir William, but all that we do is to hold them?"

I nodded, "For if we deny them the crossing then we have won but I expect it to get hotter eventually. Have you fought the Scots much before?" The three of them shook their heads. "They are a most resilient enemy. The French sometimes run when they are losing but the Scots seem to become more belligerent and stubborn when they face defeat. They will try to cross the river and if they close with the defenders on the west, it is then that we will see our mettle."

I saw the knight from Rothbury nod, "But if they bleed too much then even if they shift us from the road, they can do little against the Sherriff, the King and Sir Thomas."

"There you have it but as we do not know numbers until my scouts return then we will be in the dark." The door opened and Geoffrey and the other squires appeared, "Food is ready, my lord!"

"Then fetch it in and let us eat."

As we ate, I asked Richard about his defences at Otterburn. "I have left half of my men there. If I have done wrong, Will, then I am sorry but I could not leave my people undefended."

"You did right although I do not think that they will try to take Otterburn for even if they take it, they then have to reduce Elsdon and if they are attacked, they will sound the bell. We wait for our scouts." I nodded at Sir Gilbert's knights. "I hope this does not find them wanting. I am confident in the four of us but those two..."

Sam shook his head, "Give them a chance. You forget, Uncle, that we are all lucky and served under your father. You are cut from the same cloth. From what I can remember Sir Gilbert is a lord who likes his hunting!" That said it all.

When we had finished, I walked the camp speaking with the men at their posts. Those whom we had trained seemed confident and Alan of Bellingham and David of Wales had ensured that our men were spread out to give a steel backbone to our defences.

The scouts, when they arrived, did not come across the bridge but down the Elsdon road. They were all together and I saw that they had six spare horses with them. "Lord, the French and the Scots are camped six miles up the Roman Road. We rode to Otterburn and to Elsdon first. The folk are all within those two castles. There are forty knights, most of them French and two hundred men at arms, again, most of them French. They have forty crossbows. The other two hundred are the wild men of the Scottish north."

"Did you recognise banners?"

"The Scots are led by a Comyn and the French by a knight with three eagles upon his banner."

I nodded, "Ferry de Lorraine! And do they know we are here?"

"They will by now, lord. When we saw them approach, we remained hidden and then followed their six scouts. They died silently and we took their horses. When they do not return to the camp, they will know that something is up."

"Get some food, put your horses with the others and then David of Wales will place you where you can hurt them."

With sentries set, we went to get some sleep. There was a temptation to ride forth and to attack their camp but that would have meant using my men and I dared not risk losing a single one. Richard, Sam and I lay close to each other on the floor of the farm and it was Richard who broke the silence.

"I am sorry that I was not here when you were called upon to scour the land of the bandits."

"You had other worries and we managed. It must have been hard to leave your wife and come north."

He suddenly seemed to realise that I had missed much, "And neither of you was there for the wedding."

Sam laughed, "I think that a wedding is appreciated more by the womenfolk and besides, Richard, we were busy."

"And that is why I will make it up to you but we need a good lord of the manor for Otterburn. I hope that King Henry chooses wisely."

My voice was low, "I think that he will be guided by the Bishop and my father. It is not in the Palatinate but the Bishop has young knights who are like you two. My father needs every knight he can for the valley."

"Grandfather says he wishes you to come home, Uncle."

"And that will only be if I approve of the new lord. These are my people and I will not abandon them."

I slept for barely two hours and then I was up. The sentries had been changed and I walked amongst them, getting to know those whom I did not know. I watched dawn rise to the east and smelled the food that the night watch had begun to cook when they were relieved. I made water and then went to find Geoffrey who had my mail. The new mail hauberk I had had made was heavier than the old one for the weaponsmith had added two thin plates over the shoulders and there were more links than in the old one. My aketon was also new and I had better chausse. I donned my arming cap and slipped my coif over it. The effect was to square off my head! Geoffrey carried my helmet and spear. He would stay by my side until the enemy approached and then he would go to the horses and take charge. As we walked to the fire where the food was cooking, I said, "And you know what to do if the bridge falls?"

"Aye lord, I send one of the archers to Newcastle with the news and a second to Elsdon. Then we prepare to protect you while you and the others mount the horses."

I nodded, "And, hopefully, it will not come to that but we must be prepared."

"I would rather fight at your side, lord."

"I know and that does you great credit." We ate and then, as we heard to the north the sound of the horn ordering the enemy to move, I led my men to the barrier. The night watch had improved it by fixing sharp branches and brambles amongst it whilst also adding ropes and natural fastenings to hold it together. Determined men could destroy it but it would take time and time was on our side.

I took my helmet and spear and sent Geoffrey off. Sam stood on one side of me and Richard the other. Sir Ranulf flanked Sam and Sir Robert, Richard. Behind me was Alan Longsword next to Roger Two Swords, Wilfred of Sheffield, Edward of Yarum and Harold of Hart. They were all big men and solidly built. In the third rank, before Sir John, I had a line of men led by Erik the Dane!

It was Scottish scouts who appeared first and they came warily, expecting an ambush. They halted well beyond the range of the bows to the west of the bridge but had I so commanded then the hidden archers would have slaughtered them. That surprise would come as late as possible. Leaving two men to watch us the other lightly armed men rode back to the main column and a half an hour later the mailed snake appeared down the Roman Road. A slight dip meant that their standards rose first. The sun glinted off their helmets, spear points and mail. I recognised Ferry de Lorraine by his mail and his standard. Around him, he had knights who all had similar livery which showed they were close to him. The Comyn was a younger relative of the enemy of Alan Durward for he was carrying his helmet and had his coif down. He

101

would be looking to make his name and kill the Baron of Elsdon. I had insulted his family too much and slain too many warriors for it to be other. That information actually helped me for I knew that when they attacked, he would come for me and I could watch for him. The Frenchman was in command and I saw him studying our defences. The trees to the east of the bridge would prevent him from attacking in that direction. He had too many horsemen and he would not want to waste his Scotsmen until he had to. Turning to the Scottish lord he gave commands and when the Scot shouted, I knew what was coming. Fifty of his huge Scotsmen, most armed with a war hammer or a war axe suddenly ran down the road, shouting and screaming Gaelic curses and, no doubt, threatening to deprive us of our manhood.

David of Wales' voice echoed, "Draw!" The archers there each had an arrow nocked and they drew back.

A French voice gave the command for the crossbows to release. Our archers were sheltered by a wall of mailed men at arms sheltering behind shields. The Scots charging us drew closer and still no arrows descended while crossbow quarrels slammed into shields.

"Loose!" Fifty arrows plunged down and the result was terrible to behold. The Scots were just forty paces from the bridge when the arrows struck home and more than half found flesh. Even as men fell with a barbed arrow in their flesh a second flight was in the air and then a third. As I had told my men the Scots were recklessly brave and the fact that half their number lay on the ground did not deter the others. They ran at the barricade and began to hack and chop at the branches. Their ferocity was fuelled by anger that they had lost men and that they had yet to strike an Englishman. As the archers used a flatter trajectory more Scotsmen fell. The barrier began to crumble and I could see, just twenty paces from me, the angry Scots who cursed as they chopped and pulled at the wooden barricade. Their hands were torn by brambles and roughened wood. They were drenched in the blood of those who been struck and bled upon them but still they came at us.

I heard a Scottish horn and they launched an attack along the line. All but the French knights and four Scottish knights dismounted and closed with us. The crossbowmen had to come with the charging men for they could not release their missiles with men before them. David of Wales' archers shifted their targets and the men with axes and war hammers began to destroy the barricade. Seeing that the French knights began to move down the road towards the bridge, anticipating the destruction of the barricade.

Idraf and my hidden archers would judge the perfect moment to launch their arrows. There were just fifteen axe men left as it was and a couple of those were wounded. Even if they broke through then we could deal with them for they would be tired and their weapons blunted. More importantly, they wore no mail! One of the Scots brought his axe over in a mighty swing and it shattered an already damaged tree trunk; the timber had been pulled from the river and was soft. He pushed forwards and my right hand darted out and I rammed my spearhead into his triumphant and open mouth. He fell dead and his body blocked the gap he had made. It did, however, encourage the others and the French knights spurred their horses having decided that we were ripe to be taken.

"Fall back ten paces!" We all moved back for I did not want to become crushed by a falling barricade.

The knights were less than thirty paces from the barricade which was now on the verge of collapse when Idraf and his hidden archers let loose. They were so close to the French that every arrow hit something. Half hit horses and half hit men. Some of the arrows struck shields but enough French knights were injured to encourage me. A second and a third flight were loosed, by which time the French horses were behind the Scotsmen. The press of men and horses shattered the barricade. Four Scottish warriors were crushed by horses but some of my archers were just the width of the river away and at ten paces distance, the bodkin tipped arrows went through the helmets and the mail hauberks of the knights. Horses screamed as they found shards of the barricade embedded in their flesh. Dying Scotsmen also added to the chaos of the bridge.

I could hear splashes and knew that the bulk of the Scots had crossed the river and were engaged with Alan of Bellingham and my men at arms. The river was not deep enough to drown them but it slowed them and my archers poured arrow after arrow into them. Some of the Scottish horsemen were attempting to cross and to engage my men at arms but the press of men on foot impeded them. The crucial battle would be here on the bridge. Already we had thwarted Ferry de Lorraine's attempt to bring his men and flank King Henry. We had already hurt him so much that he would be ineffectual but that merely made things worse for us as they would want to slaughter us out of spite. Survival would be considered a victory!

Four knights were pushing their way through the barrier. They seemed not to care what damage it was doing to their horses. They were led by the young Comyn, a Scottish knight and two Frenchmen. The bridge was only wide enough for three horses abreast and the four knights were almost fighting each other to get at us.

"Lock shields and brace!"

I knew that my knights and men would understand the command but I had three knights whom I did not know. Our five shields interlocked and four spears were thrust over the top. Sir Robert failed to do so. I ignored two of the knights for I saw that the Comyn, in the centre, had pushed his way a horse's head clear of the other two. His spurs were the very long type that were now fashionable in France which meant he could not stand in his stirrups. That combined with the fact that there were other knights pressing behind him meant that when he pulled back his lance it caught on the man behind. I had no such problem and although his horse snapped at me, I ignored it and rammed my spear up, under his shield, through his mail and into his chest. I do not think I had ever had such a clean strike in a battle and I saw the Scot die before my eyes. He began to fall backwards and he pulled his horse's head up. Richard and Sam had both managed to draw blood and the enemy charge was halted.

As the knight slipped from my spear I shouted, "Push!"

The ten men at arms behind me needed no urging and with their shields squarely in my back, we pushed. The horse against which I pushed was already falling backwards and my shield in its middle accelerated the movement. The dead knight fell from the saddle and into the side of a French knight who could not help himself. He plunged into the river. The horse I had pushed crashed into the next knights and, at that moment, Idraf and his hidden archers unleashed such a shower of arrows that the horsemen must have thought the Devil himself had directed them. As Richard and Sam slew their opponents, I heard a French horn and knew that it sounded the retreat.

When the surviving knights on the bridge turned to flee, I shouted. "Fetch the horses! We have victory! Let us pursue them!" I rammed my spear into the face of one of the Scottish axemen who had, miraculously, managed to survive and he launched himself at me with his axe held in two hands. I punched with my spear at the same time as a green fletched arrow slammed into his back. He fell into the river clutching my spear which was embedded in his chest. Drawing my sword, I ran towards the fleeing Scots and French. It was neither a courageous act nor recklessness. I needed the bridge to be cleared for Geoffrey and our squires to fetch our mounts.

A man who runs away exposes his back to archers and mine were the best. I saw two knights fall to bodkin arrows sent at a range of less than fifty paces. These were the same knights who had defeated us at Taillebourg; now they learned of the efficacy of well-handled arrows. There were no enemies before me and so I sheathed my sword. Richard and Sam were there and Sir Ranulf and Sir John were too but Sir Robert had either been wounded or slain, I could not tell.

Geoffrey led Lion and I saw that he held a fresh spear for me as well as one for him. In contrast, Sir Ranulf and Sir John's squires just brought the horses and their knights would not have the advantage of a fresh spear. As I mounted, I shouted, "David of Wales, take command here. Alan of Bellingham, mount our men and follow!" The archers could take care of any prisoners and wounded and, more importantly, they could guard the bridge if I had miscalculated the attack and this was just a diversion. I did not think so but I had enough men and knights to pursue a defeated foe.

I mounted and Geoffrey handed me my spear, "Stay behind me for these are still dangerous men."

The ones on foot would disappear into the rough ground which flanked the road but the horsemen, and especially the French, would have to stay on the road for they did not know the land. I set Lion off at a steady pace and looked for targets to spear. If they surrendered then I would accept that but only a knight would surrender and that would be to save his life. I had the luxury, for there were none close to me, of looking over my shoulder. I saw four knights and their squires close behind me and Alan Longsword leading my men at arms. I would not be alone!

I had travelled half a mile when Henry Samuel and I came across three Scots who had tired of running. They turned and faced us with a broken spear and two swords between them. I spurred Lion and thrust my spear at the middle one. I hit his shield and bowled him over. Henry Samuel speared a second and the third was knocked to the ground.

We were now catching the stragglers who had stayed on the road. I would have to stop at the border; not because I wished to observe the niceties of such things but because I did not wish to be stranded in a potentially hostile land overnight! Sir Richard caught up with me so that the three of us were riding together. "You wish to catch Ferry de Lorraine?"

I nodded, "If I can."

"Why? Vengeance?"

"Aye," I said grimly.

"But you were not at Taillebourg."

"It does not matter for my brothers in arms were and if you hurt them then you make an enemy of me!"

Henry Samuel laughed, "It is good to know, uncle, that in an uncertain world you do not change!"

The conversation stopped because ahead of us some of the French knights who had not charged, the familia of Ferry de Lorraine, had halted and were facing us. It was now clear that they intended to buy their leaders the time to escape north, back to Scotland.

I slowed down Lion and that slowed the other two too. There were six knights and we would be outnumbered. These six had not fought and had sharp blades and fresh arms. The slowing down allowed Sir Ranulf and Sir John to join us. Sir John had the good grace to say, "You were right all along, Sir William, and I apologise. I should have known that you had a well-deserved reputation!"

"Aye, well, now you two must fight as though the five of us are one. Think not of ransom but of unhorsing or killing your opponent for he will try to kill you!"

My standard was back at the bridge, tied to the wooden handrail but they knew me by my surcoat and would want vengeance. We all wore short riding spurs and not the long ones favoured by continental knights. It meant we could stand in our stirrups and they could not. I spurred Lion for the last ten paces and then stood as two French knights thrust their lances at me. Being longer than my spear they struck me first. One glanced off my helmet and made it ring. The other splintered on my shield and hurt my arm. Had I not had a mask on my helmet I might have lost an eye as shards shattered and clattered into my helmet. I trusted in the design of my shield and my spear struck downward. It slid over the top of the cantle and tore through the mail hauberk and aketon into the right thigh of the knight. The combined speed of our horses broke my spear and I let go. I drew my sword and wheeled. The man I had speared was screaming and blood poured from the mortal wound.

Sir John had been unhorsed and lay at the mercy of the French knight who rather than use a weapon intended his horse to trample the helpless knight. I spurred Lion and swung my sword. It ripped through the mail links and the aketon. It tore through flesh and grated against the backbone. His dying act was to fall to the left, pulling his horse on top of him and saving Sir John's life. Two of the knights had surrendered and the other two lay dead.

"We have won and there is little point in thrashing our horses in a race. We have lost de Lorraine. We will make do with these prisoners and the booty from the dead knights. We have won. We will ride back to the bridge and tomorrow head for home."

Chapter 11

The two French knights we captured were young and, I suspected, not worth much ransom. I had them guarded in the warrior hall where they were more than intimidated by the men at arms and archers of my retinue. Sir Robert was hurt and he would need months rather than days to recover fully. Brother Paul healed the wound but the spear had scraped along his thigh bone and hip. He was unsure if the young knight would ever function well as a knight again. As soon as we had reached our camp, I had sent a rider to Newcastle to tell the Sherriff of the result of the battle. We had been back at Elsdon barely a day when a rider came back with the news that King Henry was at Newcastle along with my father.

Henry Samuel saw my face and knew what I was thinking. "Perhaps the King insisted upon grandfather and our men staying with him."

"That may be true but, if it is, then it tells me what the King thinks of me, that I am expendable. I am bait."

He shook his head. Now that Richard had returned, albeit briefly to Otterburn, we were the only two knights in the castle, "Are you telling me that if you thought your father would not reach us in time that you would have done things differently, uncle? If so then I do not believe you."

He was right, of course. It was the curse of the Warlord and so I said nothing.

"What else did the messenger say?"

"That King Alexander had a large army and they were camped north of Ponteland."

"So we wait."

Sam grinned, "And for me, that is a delight for I can play with my cousin, Dick, and make the googly eyes and silly noises which make Margaret giggle. I will enjoy the time that we can waste here."

His voice was riddled with humour at my expense and he was right. I wagged a finger at him, "I was too kind to you when you were a squire, that is my trouble! You should show me more respect but," I sighed, "you are right. I can now make the most of the time I can spend with my wife and children. The danger to Elsdon is gone and the danger to the kingdom," I shrugged, "is not my worry!" He laughed and I poured him some wine. It was my turn to have fun at his expense, "Of course one worry for you is finding a bride before my mother finds one for you."

He almost choked on his wine, "Grandmother would not do that!"

"You forget that you are the eldest grandchild and her favourite. Of course, she would do it!"

He looked as though someone had winded him. "But I do not know how to woo a lady."

"Neither did Richard but he managed. I know my parents and the loss of so many knights will make them worry about you and there is something about a knight who is married which appears to make him safer."

"And that is not true. You were married and an assassin tried to kill you."

I did not need reminding of that. "And has my father suggested a manor for you yet?"

"I did wonder if he would send me here in your place."

I shook my head, "That he will not do. I was sent here, as was Richard, to do a job and we did it but neither manor is suitable for a son or a grandson of the Lord of the Tees. The valley is richer than the Tyne and is the jewel of the north. No, King Henry will need to find another lord."

Two days later a rider came to summon me to Newcastle. I was going to refuse for I did not wish to leave my wife and family alone. Ferry de Lorraine had crossed into Scotland but I did not doubt for one moment that he harboured a grudge against me. The messenger handed me a letter from my father. It said that Henry Samuel could watch my manor and I would not be away long. It was in my father's hand but it did not feel like his words. I trusted Henry Samuel and I left all of my men with him, taking just Geoffrey.

This was the first opportunity that I had had to speak with Geoffrey since the battle and he had been silent more often than I was used to, "How was your first command, Geoffrey?"

"Command, Sir William?"

"You led the squires and guarded the horses; how did you enjoy making the decisions?"

I could see that he had not thought of it that way and he nodded, "I suppose you are right, lord, I did command." He shrugged, "I just said the words and they obeyed. To be honest, my lord, I was too concerned with how the battle was going for I thought when the barrier broke that the horsemen would sweep you from the bridge."

"It was the wrong place to waste such fine horses and the detritus on the bridge made it harder for them to move." He nodded. "And as for just giving the commands think about this. Did any hesitate? Did any question?" He shook his head, "Then you know how to lead and that is a big step to becoming a knight."

The journey to Newcastle was less than thirty miles and we had good horses so that we made good time. We were actually behind the Scottish army for while we had a narrow road to travel, they used the great Roman Road which suited their numbers better. However, as we neared Ponteland we saw, to the east of the road, the army of King Alexander camped to the north of Ponteland. Many men would have taken a detour or, perhaps, turned back, but as the messenger had actually reached us without harm and the army appeared to be just camped, we carried on. I kept a wary eye upon them. "That is a large army, lord."

"It is indeed and you can see how clever was their plan. The force led by Ferry de Lorraine was not a large one but with every eye on this army to the north then even such a small force would have disheartened the men who faced them."

He nodded, "So we saved the King and the North?"

I laughed, but it was sardonic in nature, "I doubt that King Henry will see it that way. To the kings of England, the north is not land which is of any worth to them save to be a buffer for those in the south. There they have the rich farmland and the fiefs which yield coins. Elsdon will never support more men than we have for if it was not for the money my wife earns from her manor in Creca I would not be able to pay for as many men at arms and archers."

Geoffrey nodded for he had already commented that Sir Richard, who had a similar-sized manor, had had far fewer men at his beck and call.

"That is not to say that the people are not worth defending. In my view, they deserve more protection than the pampered and privileged people who squat in London but I confess that I would like to be closer to my family. My mother and father have both seen more years than are allocated by God to man and I know that their time on this earth is short. I would like to spend more time with them while I may. I wish Dick and Margaret to get to know them both, especially my grandfather. None has done more in their life than he and none, I believe, has done more for England since the Warlord."

On the moor to the north of Newcastle was a huge armed camp but the King was not with the army and we were directed to the castle. The knight who directed me said, "And you have arrived just in time, Sir William, for we have been told to break camp and head north. You came down that road. What can we expect?"

I had to hold my tongue for scouts should have been out already and they should have known the answer. Instead, I waved a vague arm north and said, "It is a mighty host and they are north of Ponteland. I am surprised that they have not tested your defences."

"As are we."

Overlooking the Tyne and surrounded by not only a curtain wall but the town wall too, the castle which had named the town was a mighty defence of the mouth of the Tyne. I left my horses and Geoffrey in the outer bailey and was taken to the Great Hall. A sentry wearing the King's livery stopped me. I began to become annoyed. I had been summoned and I would not wait, cooling my heels while this officious man held his pike before the door.

"I have been summoned by the King and I seek admittance." There was an edge to my voice but, before the man could speak, I heard a familiar voice behind me, "I see much of myself in you, my son and not all of it good. Let us pass, for the King is anxious to speak to my son, Baron Elsdon."

The sentry's eyes widened and I realised that I had not told him my name.

"Sorry, my lord, I did not know who you were."

I nodded and, as we entered, turned to my father, "What do you mean, not good?"

"We both have a temper and both guilty, sometimes, of hasty judgements. I can see that you seethe within. Be calm and be guided by me. When time allows, I will speak with you and explain what, to you, may seem like poor decisions made by me."

I nodded, "Aye. You understand my mood."

The King and his advisers looked up from the table as we approached. The King did not smile nor offer me a kind greeting, instead, he said, quite simply, "Well, Baron, is the threat from the French in the west gone? We heard you stopped them at the River Rede."

"They are fled north, King Henry, but you should know that King Alexander has a mighty army north of Ponteland. They are untouched and they also have French standards."

He waved a hand at a pair of chairs. Obviously, my father had occupied one of them and the other must have been left for me. As I sat a servant came to pour me some wine and I saw the King cast an irritable look at me as though I was delaying him. I smiled at the servant and said, "Thank you, for your kindness. It is a hard ride from Elsdon!"

I saw my father roll his eyes and then the King continued, "The Baron has brought us good and bad news in equal measure. That the minor threat to our lines of communication is gone is good but the news that there is a large army north of here is more worrying. What, gentlemen, do we do?"

I recognised some of the lords who were present for they had fought alongside us before. What I did not see were either of the de Montfort brothers and that was concerning for they had large retinues. The King's brother, Richard of Cornwall, was there and I knew him from the crusade. It was he who spoke, "Brother, we have more than enough men here to march north and drive this army back to Scotland! I wonder at this delay. Had I delayed in the Holy Land then we would not have retaken the holy city. You have already given orders, brother, to move the army closer to the Scots now that we are mustered. Let us do more and engage them!"

That was unfair for he had done little to take it and the work had all been my father's. Worse, it criticised the King and was not helpful. Before anyone could speak I did so, "King Henry, alone out of the men at this table I am the only one to have met with King Alexander and, most recently, I have fought the Scots and the French. I have no doubt that his lordship is right. We could go north and battle them and we might even win but it would not be as easy nor as painless as he makes out." I saw the Earl of Cornwall frown at this challenge to his authority but he said nothing. "When we held the bridge at Woodford the Scots were as brave and ferocious as any Saracen or Turk I faced in the Holy Land." It would do no harm to point out that while Richard of Cornwall had been to the Holy Land he had not actually fought. I had and all men knew it. I saw my father smile.

King Henry said, "Then what would you do, Baron? It is well known that there are few knights in the realm as skilled in war as you and your father but we speak here not of a border raid but an attempt to take over this land!"

I sighed and, after sipping the wine, continued, "King Henry, let us march north as the Earl suggests but I believe we should try to speak with King Alexander for I do not think that he wishes war."

The Earl snorted a laugh, "Well he has a damned strange way of showing it!"

The King did not take his eyes from me but he waved a hand at his brother, "Peace, Richard, for the Baron appears to have a strategy in mind we had not seen. Why do you think this?"

"As I said, Your Majesty, I spoke with the King and I do not believe that this invasion is his idea." I realised that I was in great danger of speaking Alan Durward's name in public and that would be disastrous. I leaned back in my chair.

The King's eyes narrowed and then he, too, leaned back, "My lords, it is late and we have debated all day. The Baron has given me a new strategy and I would both eat and sleep upon it. Until we dine this evening, I beg you all to leave us." My father and I stood but the King said, "Sir Thomas, Baron, brother, I beg you to stay for I would have words with you about Woodford and the battle there."

As we sat down the others left us and my father said, quietly, "So, the cub is now the wolf, eh? I will back you, son, in whatever you say."

"Close the doors and stay without Sir James, we would speak in private." King Henry folded his hands before him. Henry might not be a warrior king like his uncle, Richard the Lionheart, but he was a cunning and clever king. "You know more than you were saying, Baron. Speak now where you know that you can trust all who are in this hall."

"The King is under pressure from the Comyn family and their allies, the French. He is under threat."

The King nodded to his brother, "Much as we are by the de Montforts. Did you know, Baron, that Simon de Montfort said, after Taillebourg, that I should have been locked up like Charles the Mad of France?"

He waved a hand at his own interruption and I continued, "I had warning of the attack from a Scottish lord who is loyal to King Alexander but sympathetic to England. I sent word of the threat."

"And his name?" I hesitated, "Baron, I command you to give me his name!"

"Sir Alan Durward, Count of Atholl, lord, but if word should get out of his involvement then we could lose a valuable ally."

"None shall hear it from my lips. I just need to know that the information is correct and that we are not being led into a trap. It is expensive to keep the army in the field and if we can avoid a battle... what does King Alexander want?"

"Peace, so that he can go north and defeat the Vikings who are the Lords of the Isles. That will secure his position. He has as little liking for this war as we do. Comyn and Ferry de Lorraine are the enemies we face."

"You are convinced of this? For if I went seeking peace and was shunned then that would be worse than a defeat on the battlefield."

I would be putting all of my faith in King Alexander and Alan Durward but sometimes a warrior had to trust his own judgement. "Aye, King Henry."

He stroked his beard. The Earl of Cornwall looked as though he had been brooding about my implied criticism but he said, "There is an easy answer, brother. We intend to move the army on the morrow. Why not send Sir William to the King as a herald to arrange peace talks. If the Scots are in a belligerent and intransigent mood then we will know before any talks can take place."

My father said, "And if they are belligerent and wish to make my son suffer for the battle at Woodford bridge then he might be used as a bargaining counter."

The Earl shrugged. "He goes as a peace envoy and if King Alexander does so then that gives us the moral high ground."

I sensed that my father was going to say more and I said, "I am content, father, and I trust my own judgement. I know how to see in men's hearts." I looked at the Earl of Cornwall as I spoke for he was being less than honest.

The King said, "And I will send the Bishop of Ripon with you for I would not risk losing such a valuable knight so carelessly." He nodded towards the door, "And now if you would excuse us, I will speak with my brother."

My father waited until we were beyond the door before he spoke with me. "Come, let us walk to the river wall and we can talk." He smiled for there was a brisk wind blowing from the east and the sentries were shrouded in cloaks, "We can speak without being overheard."

It was a raw wind. I had taken off my cloak when I had entered the Great Hall and now, I donned and pulled it tighter about my ears. I had a rabbit skin hat in Elsdon. This would have been the day to wear it. The sentries recognised my father and moved further along the fighting platform to allow us to speak. He turned, "You were angry when I did not come to your aid?"

"I was disappointed but I knew that there would be a good reason."

"The King and his brother were the reason. Since the defeat, there have been many lords from Poitou who have come to England having lost their lands in France. They are relatives of the Kings, the Lusignans. At the moment it is a trickle but it will soon become a flood. Already, in the south, there is talk of an invasion by foreigners. The situation is aggravated by the fact that the King has given away the manors of some knights who fell at Taillebourg to Poitevins!"

I shook my head, "All very interesting but how did this stop you from coming to my aid? I had but three knights in addition to Sam and Richard. It could have become a disaster."

"But it did not for you are a better general than you know. The King's brother wished to come north and to fight King Alexander and the French. We cannot afford another defeat. I have brought Sir Geoffrey, Sir Gilles, Sir Robert, Sir Fótr and Sir Peter with me. Three of those knights are yet to fully recover. I have no confidence in the

English army to defeat anyone at this moment in time. Had I not counselled caution then Richard of Cornwall would have charged into battle and we both know his weaknesses. I had to be at the King's side or we could have lost all that you had saved. Simon de Montfort and his brother are just waiting for another failure and then he can push forward his claim to the throne."

That made sense and I could understand why my father had done what he had done. "And will the King give away East Harlsey and Whorlton?"

"That is another reason why I stayed close to the King. I have yet to secure a manor for Henry Samuel but I will."

"And what of me and what of Elsdon?"

"You shall have Stockton! I need it not and your mother is constantly asking me to do less. If you were the Lord of the Valley then I could as she wished. As for Elsdon, we are yet to speak of it."

I nodded and looked at the cold grey waters of the Tyne. The bodies which had fallen into the Rede would have joined the Tyne and would now be far out to sea. The lives of the dead ended in a heartbeat.

"And how did my grandson fare?"

I smiled, "He is a warrior through and through. His father would have been proud. You need not fear for him but he needs a manor."

"I thought of Yarum. Since old Sir Geoffrey died it has just his widow there and I am certain that I could have a house built for her. There is no castle there but it needs not one. Do not say aught yet. We have time enough when we return south."

"If you find a lord for Elsdon."

"These talks will not be speedy. We have time."

The rest of the knights my father had brought with him were at the camp on the moor. Now that I was the herald of the King and his army, I was given my own, cramped quarters in the castle. We were not seated close to the King and that suited me for I wished to talk to my father. We had much to discuss. Most of it was about the battle as my father was keen to know how the French and Scots fought. Then we touched upon the valley and the changes there.

"Henry Samuel seems to think that you are tired of war."

He nodded, "I am not certain that I was ever enamoured of it. I know how to fight and I seem to be good at war but there are few men who enjoy war. Even though Sam is a young warrior it is just the adventure of war he seeks. He will enjoy discovering the courage of the men with whom he fights but the cause needs to be a good one."

"Like your crusade in the Baltic?"

He laughed, "That had even less to do with good than the Baron's Crusade! The Teutonic Knights lost their home in Outremer and sought a new one. The only ones they were allowed to fight were pagans. Defending your country is something worthwhile. That is what you did at Woodford and I find it sad that there were only three other knights who followed you. The rest of the northern knights sought the glory of fighting where their King could see them."

"I will happily sheath my sword but only when Elsdon has a lord of the manor in whom I have faith."

He nodded, "Amen to that but even when you are away from this border the King will call upon you. He is less likely to call upon me due to my age but with so many knights lost in France, he will have to turn to knights like you and Henry Samuel. Remember that so long as he is your liege lord, you cannot gainsay him and he knows your value."

The King rose and that was the sign for us to retire. I had been given instructions by his pursuivant who would accompany Geoffrey and me the following morning as we rode north to meet King Alexander. I was to rise well before dawn and meet King Henry in the chapel. There we would pray and he would give me my final instructions. That was one thing I liked about this King. He was, at least, religious, while his father had been almost the opposite. God would be more likely to favour a King who followed his law. King Louis was said to be even more religiously minded. Perhaps that was why they had won the battle of Taillebourg; God had been on the side of their King.

Once again, I had to manage on but a couple of hours of sleep. That was mainly because the bed I had been given was the most uncomfortable I had ever slept in. I would have been better off sleeping outside on the river bank where it would have been slightly softer. Geoffrey and I rose and dressed, keenly aware that we had to be well dressed and groomed for we represented the King! The King was at his prayers already and we joined him in the small chapel. My prayers might have been different from the King's, I know not for a man's prayers, even if he is a king, are private. I prayed for my family first and then my manor. England and the King came well down the list.

I followed him outside. Giles, his pursuivant, and the Bishop of Ripon, Edward, awaited us there. The King nodded to the Bishop, "Remember, Sir William, I just need to know that Alexander will speak to me of peace and that it will be meaningful talks. I have endured enough humiliation already. I would that my sister was still alive for then we would not be in this situation."

He looked at me for an answer but I remained silent.

"You do not agree?"

"I think, King Henry, that the King of Scotland has not changed but the pressures have. You yourself know what it is like to have a lord who seeks to undermine you."

He nodded, "Aye, that I do. Promise nothing save your word that your King will talk!"

"Of course, Your Majesty."

The vanguard was already moving north but they were ponderous compared with us. I waved at the knights and men at arms that I knew from the crusade. Soon we passed them and headed towards Ponteland which was still held for us. As we passed through the small town, we were leaving England and entering the land occupied, temporarily, by the Scots and their French allies. Our helmets hung from our cantles and our coifs were around our neck. The pursuivant wore the brightly coloured livery of the king and carried a mace rather than a sword. Geoffrey carried my banner. The Scots had erected a crude barrier on the road to stop men travelling along it. Seeing the pursuivant we were passed through and I saw a rider galloping ahead to speak with the King. I was not afraid but I felt nervous for I had never been asked to be a diplomat before and I was uncertain if I could pull it off.

I saw that men recognised my banner and surcoat as we rode through the camp. Some of the wild Highlanders spat as we passed. I heard some Scottish lords admonish them for the disrespect. I did not mind for if I was hated by the enemy then I had done as I had been commanded. As we neared the King's tent, I spied the banners of the French lords. Ferry de Lorraine's was closest to the King's and on the other side of King Alexander's was Walter Comyn's. I felt for the King. His guards took our horses and his steward, whom I had met before, greeted us.

"King Alexander will meet with you in his tent, Sir William."

It was a large tent and could have slept twenty or more men. There was a large table and the King was seated. I allowed the Bishop to enter first and then I followed. I saw, once my eyes adjusted to the poor light, that the Count and Walter Comyn flanked him along with the Abbot of Jedburgh. I was happier then for it meant I had two friends, at least, the King and the Abbot. The King's face was set in stone but his eyes danced. Those on the table with him could not see his eyes but I could. They confirmed that he wished peace and, even though I was a novice at this, I felt more confident.

The Abbot smiled, "Your Grace, Baron, please be seated. Let us hope that God will smile upon this visit."

I nodded, "As do I." I glanced at Ferry de Lorraine who was seated close to the Count, "There has been enough bloodshed on this border."

I saw the Count squirm. King Alexander said, "And what does our brother, Henry, wish to say to us?"

The King was making it simple for me and I dived in directly, "The King feels that enough blood has been shed already. We have kept the peace and the attack on Woodford was unprovoked as is the arrival of this army. King Henry wishes to speak directly with King Alexander so that the two men may bring peace, once more to the two countries."

Even as King Alexander nodded Walter Comyn burst out, "King Alexander, this shows we have them where we want them! Let me lead my men and tomorrow you will wake up the Lord of the lands north of the Tees and the Eden."

I hid my smile for the outburst was a mistake. The other lords and churchmen, de Lorraine excepted, all shook their heads at the Mormaer.

The King said, "I am the King, Comyn, and before I shed another drop of Scottish blood, I will speak with King Henry." He turned to me, "Sir William, we will meet at a place which is equidistant from Ponteland and our camp. King Henry shall bring you and a churchman, the Bishop here will suffice and I will bring my own two. I would also appreciate a scribe so that our words may be noted down for posterity." He glowered up and down the table, "My words have been twisted more than enough. I wish all to know what King Alexander says from his own lips!"

"At what o'clock, King Alexander?"

"The fourth hour of the day!"

And with that, we left the tent, mounted our horses and headed back. Giles was surprised at the speed of it all, "You have a gift for this my lord!"

I laughed, "No, Giles, for King Alexander wanted a private meeting with King Henry before he even came south. If I have a gift it is for knowing when a man speaks the truth!"

Chapter 12

The King was delighted, not so much with my news but the confirmation from the Bishop of Ripon. Perhaps he was too used to being surrounding by self-serving sycophants who could not tell the truth. My father appeared to be the only one who was not surprised. "Of course, William, it means that you will now be marked forever in the eyes of our enemies. The French and this Count whom you seem to have annoyed and Comyn will look to do you harm either in deed or in name. Be careful."

I nodded, "At least I have kept Durward's name from people's ears."

"At the moment but that may not last. He sounds like a good friend and I know, from speaking with him today, that the King is keen to meet him."

Shaking my head, I said, "Now is not the time. Alan Durward has little power but, if we can agree on peace, then he can begin to grow in importance."

As we rode towards the meeting place, the next day, the King said, "I am grateful to you, Sir William, and know that I will reward you. Where others have failed me, you have done all that you promised and more."

I nodded, "I would like you to appoint a good lord to Elsdon, King henry; one who will help the people."

He turned and gave me a shocked look, "I offer you a reward and you ask for something for ordinary folk? You are a strange creature but I respect you. I promise that I will do so." We were nearing the meeting place. A tent without walls had been erected to give us some shade from the thin sun. I knew why it was done. If the sun shone in the eyes of one king or the other then it would be seen to give them an advantage. This way they could look into each other's eyes.

As my eyes adjusted, I saw that the lord he had brought with him was neither Comyn nor Durward but the French Count I had chased from Woodford, the Count of Lisieux, Raymond de Courcy as well as Ferry de Lorraine! I saw hatred in both of their eyes and so I kept my face impassive.

"Well brother, it is sad that it has come to this sorry pass. What made you wish to come south to fight with me? Did your French allies persuade you that our setback in France made us weak?"

It was obvious that it was French pressure which had resulted in the attack for the Count averted his eyes, albeit briefly.

"Henry, we need to decide, once and for all, where will lie the border twixt our countries for there are too many men who will seek to take parcels of land one from the other. I am more than happy if we can decide on a clean border to give any disputed manors to England if England will do the same."

All apart from the French Count knew that most of the disputed lands were empty. There had been too many raids from both sides and they had stripped the people from the area in dispute. Men fought because no one had defined the border. The King glanced at me and then said, "Agreed, but where shall be this border?"

It was the Scottish Bishop who made the best suggestion, "Your majesties, why not let God decide?"

The French Count's eyes lit up, "Let God decide? Trial by combat?"

King Alexander rolled his eyes in despair and the Bishop shook his head, "No, Count. There are rivers which are natural boundaries. Berwick in the north and Norham have long been English and that is because they lie on the Tweed. Jedburgh, King Alexander's royal home, lies north of that river. Let us use the waterways to determine the border. Sir William here has ridden this border often," he gave a wry smile as he glanced at Ferry de Lorraine, "he must know the border well. Let him suggest waterways."

I was on familiar ground. My father had always set great store by maps. I too had an interest and on my various travels in the north hunting down brigands and fighting for the King, I had kept a record of what I had seen. Those maps were in Elsdon but, by closing my eyes, I could picture them.

King Henry said, "Are you able to do so, Sir William?"

"I can give a rough line but it would need to be clarified."

King Alexander said, "And that is the work of clerics and clerks. Speak, Sir William, for you have the trust of us all."

I knew that the Count would not agree. The scribe had a spare wax tablet which I had seen. I said, "May I?" He handed it to me and I made a mark at one side. "Here is the east coast and this is Berwick." I then scribed a line south and west. "Here is Bell's Burn and then Kershope Burn." There were gaps between them. "Then here is the Liddle Burn and finally the River Esk which feeds into the Eden." I made another mark. "And here is Carlisle. There is a border north of which there are few places with more than a dozen houses. There are no castles along it except at Berwick, Norham and Carlisle. The gaps between the rivers are high ground, natural ridges between the waters and none live there. If you wish my suggestion then here it is."

119

I placed the wax tablet between the two men. England had more of Northumberland and Scotland more of the land north of Carlisle but that reflected the population. I watched the faces of both kings. They knew not the geography of the land but they knew the manors and the incomes which were generated. I had thought of that as I had drawn the line. Neither would lose much money and it brought peace. When they looked at each other and smiled I knew that the border was safe, at least for a while.

The border after the treaty of Newcastle 1244

Griff 2019

They stood and clasped arms and then, moving to the side, embraced. It was a symbolic move. The two churchmen also clasped arms but I knew that despite my outstretched arm Raymond de Courcy would not move. King Alexander saw the refusal and shook his head, "Ungracious de Courcy. Come, Sir William, both countries owe you a debt." He grasped my arm as warrior to warrior.

King Henry said, "And to seal it, along with our signatures, what say we betroth my daughter, Margaret, to your son, Alexander. That they are both less than three years old does not matter." King Alexander frowned a little. King Henry said, softly, "When you were married to my sister, then we had peace. It worked once what say we try it a second time?"

King Alexander nodded, "Let it be so written." He looked at the clerks and scribes, "Have the treaty written as we spoke and then we shall sign it before the leading nobles of both armies so that all may see that there is peace and no discord." He looked at Raymond de Courcy, "At least not on this side of the German Sea!"

That this was a momentous occasion was clear to all. For the first time since the time of the Romans, there was a clear border between the two peoples. We returned to our camp where my father and the other nobles waited. King Henry himself told them the news. None in the camp had lost out and so there was great celebration.

My father came to me and said, "Of course, you have lost Creca, for that lies north of the border."

I shook my head, "It always did and I was keenly aware of that when I suggested the line but King Alexander, I think, will hold on to Creca and, while he lives, my wife will receive the income."

"While he lives?"

"This will not suit the Comyns. In one fell swoop, King Alexander has disarmed them. The French have no need to stay in this land and with peace along this border Comyn loses that threat to the King. This will enhance Alan Durward's chances of becoming confirmed as Count of Atholl."

"Have you been used by him so that he can get what he wants?"

"Perhaps but as it suits us who used whom?"

The next day we all met again on the field north of Ponteland and the treaty which became known as the Treaty of Newcastle was signed by the two kings and witnessed by the great and the good. There were two exceptions to that: Walter Comyn and Raymond de Courcy decamped with all of their men and headed north. That worried me but it was driven from my mind when, as the feasting began, King Alexander brought over Alan Durward to meet with King Henry. The two got on immediately. Alan Durward was very personable. His enemies called him sly and treacherous but in all of my dealings with him, I did not find him so. I think he took his chances when he could and he reaped the rewards. Within a few years, he had been given one of King John's favourite castles, Bolsover. That was still in the future and that day of peace just saw celebrations.

We returned, in the late afternoon, to Newcastle. I was anxious to return home but King Henry wished to speak with me. I rode with the King and my father while my father's knights and men at arms packed up their gear ready for the ride south. We rode behind an ebullient King Henry who had achieved more than he had expected. His daughter was now betrothed to the future King of Scotland and that was all to the good. He had a secure border and the French threat from the north had gone.

As I rode with my father I said, "I will speak with King Henry and then head for Elsdon."

He shook his head, "You must wait on his pleasure. You cannot leave tonight in any case. It will be dark when we reach Newcastle and I would spend as much time with you as I could."

"Are you ill?"

He laughed, "No, I am old and you are the only son I have left. I would spend as much of my time with you as I could. I was denied time with my father and with Alfred. There is much I wish to say to you."

That thought sobered me for I had thought, despite his wounds incurred in the Holy Land, that my father was hale and hearty but his words suggested that he saw his own mortality.

The feast north of Ponteland had been little more than the devouring of the food both armies had fetched for a long campaign. The King ordered a feast for the following day. "Until then, your time is your own."

The other nobles all left but I waited, "Yes Sir William?"

"King Henry, I am mindful of the fact that you wish to speak with me but I have been away from my family longer than I expected. I beg leave not to attend your feast on the morrow for I wish to return home."

He frowned, "This does not please me, Sir William. Most men would be happy to stay and hear the rewards a grateful king bestows upon them."

My father had not left and he said, "Your Majesty, you should know, by now, that my family never does things the way other men do. I apologise for my son for I, too, wish him to stay, but I understand his concern."

"But his lands are safe now!"

"Perhaps." He looked at me with questions in his eyes. "It is one thing to put a treaty to paper and I have no doubt that most men will adhere to the letter of the law but there are always those who seek to subvert and alter the words of their betters."

"And that is why you wish me to replace you with a lord who can keep the land safe?"

"Either that or leave me there."

He shook his head, "No, Sir William. I need you and your father's knights in Wales." He saw my expression of disappointment and smiled, "Not yet but I wish to make that border as secure as this one. The Bishop of Durham has two knights who have shown themselves to be worthy warriors. One, Sir James Buchanan, was a knight of St. John and served as a crusader. He has brought a wife from the east and wishes a small manor where he can raise a family. I believe your grandfather did much the same, Sir Thomas?" My father nodded. "I would give to Sir James, Elsdon. There is another, Sir Robert of Seggesfield. He is the second son and he served with you in the Holy Land."

I nodded, "He was a good man."

"He, too, has married and I would give him Otterburn. Now can you stay?"

It was what I had wanted and so I nodded, "Aye, King Henry."

He beamed, "Good! And you shall have the manor of Hartlepool that was once called Hartness for your own. It is a gift from the Bishop." He put his arms around my father and me, "And it is close enough to Stockton too, eh?"

That night my father and I ate in an inn in the town. The food was good and honest and the ale to our taste. He toasted me, "The Lord of Hartlepool."

I nodded, "Did I not hear a tale that the Warlord had enemies there?"

"Aye, and he rescued his bride, Adele, from the clutches of the then lord of the manor. It is strange how these threads tie us to the past. There is no castle there but the manor house is a good one and the town wall is the equal of Stockton's. Your family will be safe."

"And what of the men who have families at Elsdon? Will they follow me?"

"They may but if they do not it will not be out of disrespect. They have all served you well."

"I know but they are like brothers in arms."

"I know how you feel. When I sent David of Wales to aid you, I felt as though I had had a limb hewn from my body!"

It was as we were leaving that Sir Gilles' squire, Henry, came to tell us that my father's men were camped on the moor once more.

"Good, for once we have enjoyed the King's hospitality we can head south and get our lives back in some sort of order."

We were woken, in the middle of the night, by a sentry who banged so hard on my door that, leaping from my bed I drew my sword and dagger, fearing treachery. Geoffrey opened the door and I faced the sentry, "What is it that makes you disturb my slumber?"

"I am sorry, my lord, but Sir Geoffrey Fitzurse is at the gate and he demanded that you be roused. Your castle is under attack!"

"Go and tell my father! We leave now."

Even as we were dressing, I knew who it was. The Count and Comyn could not accept that they had lost and it was my fault. The men who attacked my castle might not fight under their banners but they would be their men and they would be intent upon mischief! As we hurried towards the gate, my father, still in his night attire, came to me. "The French?" I nodded. "Take my men and I will speak with the King."

"Then tell him this, also, that I will not leave Elsdon until his crusader knight arrives and I care not if he is offended!"

"Hush, my son! He will understand and it is right. I will wait here until it is over."

I shook my head, "If my castle has fallen then I will not return here for I hunt down and kill those who attacked my home."

My squire ran for our horses and I went to speak to my sister's husband. He began to speak immediately and his words poured out as though he could not say them quickly enough, "It was Ged Strongbow brought the news. The men who came were seen before they closed with the walls and the villagers in both Elsdon and Otterburn were ordered into their castles. They are safe but they have not enough food for a protracted siege."

I shook my head, "They will not wait for a siege to starve them. The enemy will attack. Sir Geoffrey, ride back to the camp and rouse our men."

He smiled, "It is done already and by now they should be on the road to Elsdon."

I reached up and clasped his arm, "Thank God! I am in your debt!"

Geoffrey and the grooms had saddled our horses and I threw myself into the saddle and followed Sir Geoffrey. As we rode Sir Geoffrey said, "Do you know who this enemy will be?"

"My guess would be that Comyn and de Courcy are behind this but they will make it look like brigands. They left the talks early. I am guessing that King Alexander will still be on his way north and will know nothing of this."

I rode Lion hard for we had thirty miles to travel and each moment would be precious. I had strong walls and good defences but determined men could hurt my people and I did not want one person to suffer for the death would be at my door!

It was still early in the day when we caught up with Sir Gilles, Sir Fótr, Sir Robert, Sir Peter and the rest of my father's men. In all we had one hundred men and, thus far, they had not drawn a sword or nocked an arrow. Comyn, de Courcy and de Lorraine would not be expecting such a rapid response. I made my way through the column, acknowledging the waves and comments from all and sundry. I wanted to speak to Ged Warbow. As I had expected he was at the vanguard with the other scouts.

"My lord, I came as fast as I could!"

I could see that he worried he had been tardy. That was the way with my men. "You brought us the news and that is all that counts. Now tell me all!" I hid the fact that I was worried about my wife and family.

"Alan of Bellingham had kept a good watch since you had been gone and it was Alf Broad Shoulders who saw them. At first, when he spied the knights and the horsemen, he thought it was you, returned with other nobles and visitors and then he saw that there were no banners. He has good eyes. He sent for Alan of Bellingham who decided to send me to fetch you. He sounded the bell and I heard Otterburn's even before I had reached the stables. As I rode south, the villagers were flooding through the gates and it was none too soon for a column of hobelars galloped up the road from Newcastle. I barely escaped with my life. I took off through the fields and managed to lose them in the high ground above the Rede but that added to my journey. I rejoined the road south of them and rode to Newcastle as fast as I could."

I nodded, "Then you have not slept and you will have ridden more than seventy miles in one day!"

He nodded, "But this is a fresh horse. Maria would not have made it."

"And how many men did you see?"

"Lord, I only saw the hobelars. I report that which was told to me by Alan of Bellingham. He said that there were knights and men at arms. The hobelars I would say were Scottish. They were well mounted and each of them wore leather armour and had a good helmet." He smiled, "I saw that when they chased me!"

The four knights had followed me through the column and Sir Gilles said, "We go into this blind then?"

"Not so. The houses which lie close to the castle walls will force them to attack from the eastern side which is more open. That defence was deliberate on our part and there are double ditches there. They have two points of attack: the gate and the eastern wall. My nephew has defended the castle before as has Alan of Bellingham. There is a good garrison and my villagers are all skilled with a bow. Last night would have been the hard time for if I was an enemy then that is when I would attack. Even if the outer wall and outer bailey fall, which I doubt, the inner wall and keep are much higher. We now have two extra towers."

We were riding hard and I was having to shout so that they could hear my words. I would not spare one moment more than I needed to.

"We have my father's men at arms. They did not ride to France and, along with the four of you are our best weapon. I will send the archers to the north of Elsdon so that they can flank the attackers on the eastern wall and we will charge those trying to assail the main gate."

Sir Gilles said, "Regardless of numbers?"

I nodded, grimly, "Regardless of numbers. There will be neither horns nor shouts." I looked at the sky. At this time of year, the days and nights were almost equidistant. "I am guessing that it will be when the sun is setting in the west when we arrive at Elsdon. We will be riding from the shadows even if it is not yet dark. They will not be mounted and I intend to sweep them from before the walls. We hit them hard. Do not worry about prisoners. Scottish lords will be absent. The knights will be French for then the treaty will not be broken. As much as Comyn might dispute the treaty and wished it had not been signed, he was there and attested to it. For a Scottish lord to break the treaty would be giving the King of Scotland grounds to take from them their manors and their monies. The Scots who fight will be the wild men, the mercenaries, French and the desperate men."

We had to stop about four miles from Elsdon. The horses needed a rest, no matter how short and I needed to give the archers, none of whom knew Elsdon, their instructions. There were fewer than I might have liked for my father's contingent were already in the castle. When we mounted, I saw that there was less than two hours of daylight left and so we rode for battle with helmets on our heads, shields upon our arms and spears in our hands. With Ged Strongbow to guide them, we bade farewell to our archers. Without armour, they would make much better time than we would. I led for this was my land and I knew the trails well. As we neared the village and the castle, we heard the sound of steel on steel as well as the shouts and cries from the fighting. I did not slow down. I had told the knights and their men at arms what we would do and it was time for action and not words.

We had my bridge to negotiate and if we had used horns then they would have been alerted. They had no sentries upon the bridge and it looked to me as though they were using the houses of my villagers for their camp. They had ladders and were attacking the gatehouse. They must have made some sort of bridge across the ditch for I saw the drawbridge was raised. To my right, I saw the east wall and there were ladders there too. I could rely on Ged Strongbow to choose his moment to attack. Sir Peter was next to Geoffrey and me as we clattered over the bridge. Inevitably the sound made the attackers at the rear turn. As soon as they saw us the Scots there shouted the alarm. Despite the fact that I saw Ferry de Lorraine and his household knights lounging outside the church I kept to the plan and rode directly at the men attacking the gatehouse.

I heard a huge cheer as we were recognised. The men who had shouted the alarm died first. My spear came back and, as I thrust, it found soft flesh close to the neck of the French man at arms I withdrew and spurred a tired Lion. As soon as I was able, I would dismount and fight on foot but first, we had an attack to thwart. Once we were over the bridge we could spread out. I saw Sir Gilles lead some of the men for the church. That made sense for there was not enough space for all of us. As I rode towards the ladders, I saw that the raised drawbridge was charred, they had tried to burn it. I pulled back my arm as two Frenchmen at arms, mailed and with shields, ran at me with swords raised. They led six Scotsmen who were armed with a variety of weapons. I was fighting, not for me but my family and I rode directly at the nearest Frenchman. I saw him swing his sword as the other held his shield to protect the two of them. I rammed my spear at them as Sir Peter did the same. Peter's father was Ridley the Giant and one of the strongest men I knew. Peter's wound had been to his left arm but his right was as strong as ever. My spear caught one Frenchman on the shoulder and a heartbeat later Sir Peter's spear hit the shield so hard that the two of them fell to the floor and as our horses clattered over them, I heard the crunch as a skull was crushed. Geoffrey knew how to use a spear and he struck the nearest Scotsman as Sir Peter's brother, Henry, took a second. The Scots who remained would not face our four horses and they ran. David of Wales and Idraf led my archers and the Scots who fled were slain.

The attack on the gate broke down as the men fled. A combination of our attack and a sally from the sally gate meant that it was ended and I wheeled a weary Lion to look for the French knights. They were trying to get to their horses which lay beyond the range of the archers from my walls and with Ged Strongbow leading the other archers to decimate the men attacking the eastern wall, Sir Gilles and the men he led were just containing them so that the enemy could not get to their mounts. These were not wild Scotsmen; these were French knights and men at arms who had axes and long swords and knew how to hurt horses and knights. It would be a foolish knight who would advance to a shield wall.

I dismounted and handed my horse to Geoffrey, "Form up on me! Wedge formation!"

I knew that I would confuse the enemy for they were French and I spoke in English. A wedge was rarely used these days and that was why I chose it. I stood at the head of the arrowhead and Sir Fótr and Sir Peter formed up behind me with Sir Robert behind them. I was mindful of Sir Peter's injured arm and Sir Fótr's injured leg as well as the head wound which Sir Robert had suffered in France. Next to Sir Robert were Sir Geoffrey, and Edward Long Leg. Four men were behind them, seven behind them and so on and so forth. Success depended upon the warrior at the point for he would have to face three men but once they were defeated then the wedge would drive through and split the formation asunder. That was the plan.

I shouted, "Stockton! Stockton! Stockton!" and banged my shield with my sword. Once the others took up the chant, I moved my right leg and, sure enough, the rest followed. That was the hardest part about a wedge, getting into the rhythm.

We were safe until we closed with them as their men with crossbows and bows had been close to the wall and now they were fleeing like startled deer. The knights and men at arms could not flee until they had their horses and for that to happen, they first had to defeat us. The French knights looked confident. They had avoided a fight at Woodford Bridge and the last time they had faced English knights had been at Taillebourg when they had not just defeated them, they had destroyed their foes. They had the look of warriors who thought they were going to win.

Ferry de Lorraine had six men at arms before him and his household knights. Two held spears while half of the others had axes. I knew that I would have to rely on Sir Fótr, Sir Robert and Sir Peter. This would be a severe test of Sir Fótr's wound. I heard Sir Gilles, who was still mounted, shout, "Half of you, get to the horses. The other half, follow me and we will join Sir William!"

It would only add ten or so men to the wedge but the weight of big men wearing mail might just give us victory. First, I had to penetrate the line of men at arms. Two spears were rammed at my head as one of the axemen stepped from the line to swing his sword at my right side. I took one of the spears on my shield while the second struck my shoulder. The plates I had fitted beneath the new mail worked and the spearhead rasped over the links. I lunged at one of the spearmen and braced myself for the strike of an axe in my side. It never came for Sir Peter's sword took the forearm of the man at arms. At the same time, Sir Fótr blocked the strike from another sword and his sword found the

128

unguarded neck of the second spearman. With three men dead we did not even have to pause for the wedge had broken their line. Now there were six of us engaged with the enemy and I was face to face with Ferry de Lorraine! I saw his eyes behind his facemask and they burned with hatred. I was the young knight who had thwarted all of his plans and he wanted vengeance.

His attempt to end my life in one blow might have succeeded if I did not have such quick reactions and if I was not confident that Sir Fótr's shield would protect my left side. The Frenchman's sword came from behind his head and that information was useful for it meant that the men behind the Count were not pressing into his back. My shield came up and I rammed my sword forward. I had no space to pull my arm back a long way and the blow would not hurt the Frenchman. My sword connected and raked through his surcoat to scrape and scratch along his mail. The wedge could not now be stopped. Sir Gilles and his men had added their weight and even if I had stopped moving my feet I would have been propelled forward. The French sword hit my shield and then Ferry de Lorraine was forced to take two long steps back as he was pushed by the mailed fist that was the wedge. As soon as he did then the French line was broken. It was like a branch which was bent and suddenly cracks apart. My wedge was able to turn out to face the French on both sides of us. We were all protected by each other and they were isolated groups.

As I approached Ferry de Lorraine, who had now regained his balance, I heard behind me, Alan of Bellingham's voice, "Surround the bastards and let none escape!"

I now had room to swing and, taking a wider stance than before, I held up my shield and then swung, not at his head as he expected, but in a scything motion aimed at his leg. He saw the movement too late and his shield did not come close to blocking the blow. My sword connected just above the knee, I heard the cry of pain from behind his mask as my sword struck and I drew back the sword sawing through the chausse. As I raised my sword for a second blow, I saw that I had drawn blood. He had not been idle and he tried for my head. My shield was before me and it was simplicity itself to, first raise my shield and then, deflect the blade down its face. The Frenchman's shield was now lowered and as I moved my sword back, I lifted it to strike down at his head and upper body, I used a diagonal stroke but it mattered not for he was slow to raise his shield and my blade hit his shoulder. He had no plates beneath his mail and the bones across his shoulder took the force of the blow. Something broke for I heard a snap. His left arm drooped and I pulled back my arm. This time I aimed at his neck and although he tried to bring his sword across to parry, he was too slow and my sword sliced into his coif. I put all of my anger into the blow and his head jerked to the side. Like me, he had a heavy helmet and I think that was what killed him as much as my blow. The weight of the helmet and the force of my strike snapped his neck and he crumpled at my feet.

I was aware that, around us, there was no longer the sound of swords and shields striking each other. Six of the French knights remained alive and they had no swords in their hands. They had surrendered. Five others lay dead along with almost all of the men at arms. Once our wedge had broken them and with Sam and Alan of Bellingham bringing the rest of our men from Elsdon then it was a foregone conclusion.

I took off my helmet and said to Sir Gilles, "Did any escape?"

He nodded, "David of Wales has mounted his men and they will scour the land for them." He pointed upwards with his sword and I saw that the sky was dark. Night had fallen. "Some, I fear, will escape but the danger is passed."

I walked to the knights. I could see that I had lost men at arms in the attack. They were not my men but they were warriors from the valley and that made them family. "On your knees, all of you!" There was such anger in my voice that they all obeyed. I put the tip of my sword perilously close to the right eye of the nearest knight, "Give me a good reason why I should not have you all killed now!"

He jabbered, panic in his voice, "We surrendered! There are rules!"

"The man you followed here signed and witnessed a treaty and that means that there are no rules for oath breakers! I am tired, Frenchman, and I wish to see my family! I await a good reason and if I do not get one then there will be six heads on spears atop my gatehouse when dawn comes!"

One of the others begged, "My lord, we have wealthy families and they will pay ransom! We did not sign the treaty and we were not party to it! We are knights who obeyed our liege lord!"

I nodded and sheathed my sword, "And your words have saved your lives. Take their mail from them and lock them away. They will be sent to Stockton!"

My men and the knights who had followed all cheered. Sam approached, bareheaded and he had a grin upon his face, "I knew that you would come, uncle. I just did not expect such a rapid end to the battle! We have not even put food on to cook!"

I laughed, "Then it will have to be cold fare but cold fare with warriors such as this is like ambrosia with kings and princes!"

Part Two
The Welsh War
Sir William

Chapter 13

It was June before Sir James, his wife and his men at arms arrived to begin to relieve us. Sir Henry Samuel and the rest of my father's knights, men at arms and archers had left three days after we relieved the siege. They took the knights for ransom with them. I had sent a rider to King Alexander with a letter which detailed the events. The reply told me that he would stand by the terms of the treaty and all those who returned to Scotland after the raid would be hanged. Of course, as they were all Comyn's men that suited the King but I felt reassured that Otterburn and Elsdon would be safer; they would never be totally safe but, as we had proved, they were defensible, even against great numbers. Sir Richard had left not long after my father's knights for Sir Robert arrived to take over Otterburn.

It was the day after Sir Robert arrived that I gathered the men and archers of Elsdon together in my Great Hall. They filled it.

"King Henry has given to me the manor of Hartlepool. I will be returning thence as soon as Sir James arrives. All of you here have a choice. You can return south with me or stay here. I know that many of you have families and land here on the border. None of you owes me any fealty! You have all discharged your duty many times over and now that I have a family of my own, I know that some of you will be torn. I cannot make any choice for you. What I will say is that when the ransom comes from the French knights my share will be split between all of you and those who follow me south know that there will be land there for you."

Alan of Bellingham said, "Lord, this is my land and while you were lord, I was more than happy to lead your men." He smiled, "Our men. This last battle was just that, for me, my last battle. I have my farm in Bellingham and I will retire there and hang up my sword. I will become a farmer. However, I know from talking to some of the others that they fear that Sir James will wish to reward his own men. What of those who wish to farm here?"

I had anticipated this. "I have had Brother Paul prepare the deeds and documents to give the land," I emphasised the word *'give'*, "to those

who wish to stay. They will still owe Sir James fealty but the land will
be theirs to sell or to give away. You can make your decisions knowing
that you have a legal entitlement to your land."

My men showed me great respect by each of them coming to me to
speak to me and explain their decisions. I was losing some good men.
Alf Broad Shoulders who had married Mariann and adopted Donal had
too many ties to the land to come with me. Those who had married the
Yalesham widows also stayed. In the end, I took with me just twenty-
one men and left twelve behind. It was a hard parting. Beth and Alice
came with us for they had married two of my men at arms. We left on
the longest day for the journey south.

Dick was old enough now to ride his pony for we would not be
travelling quickly. Margaret needed all the attention from Beth and
Alice, as well as my wife as she was learning to use her little legs and
riding in the wagon did not seem as appealing as either running next to
it or being like her brother and riding a pony. The men and their
families who travelled south with us had a variety of emotions. For the
women, they were going to an unknown country. Most had come from
the Rede Valley or Bellingham while one or two were rescued captives.
The men were sad to be leaving their brothers in arms and the land they
had defended but looking forward to what they considered home.

Hartlepool was less than thirteen miles from Stockton and my father
controlled the nearby manors of Norton, Wulfestun and Stockton. They
would each be given a farm for their families. With no castle, they
would not have garrison duty. Only Richard Longsword and Tom of
Rydal would live in the manor house with my family and Geoffrey.
Alan would be the captain of my guards.

The manor of Hartlepool was an important one to the Palatinate as it
was the Prince Bishop's major port. The taxes it generated accounted
for almost a fifth of the total income of the Palatinate. Thanks to my
father the lord of the manor of Hartlepool did not need to watch for
land-based raiders and the narrow entrance of the walled port kept it
safe from seaborne enemies. It was a generous gift and I knew that it
was for my father as much as me. My father had atoned for the killing
of a corrupt bishop and the present incumbent knew the value of the
Lord of the North. I rode next to my wagon and listened to my wife's
laughter as Margaret giggled at the faces Edward of Yarum pulled as he
drove the wagon.

"You are happy then, my love?"

She turned and nodded, "Aye, for as much as I liked the people of
Elsdon, danger was always just around the corner and it is such an
isolated manor. Sir James and his bride will be happy there for he

wishes a quiet life." She saw me shake my head, "I spoke with them. His wife is not noble-born and they do not wish a life with other lords and ladies visiting. They wish children and a good wall around them. Thanks to your efforts Elsdon is now much more defensible and, having lived in the Holy Land, Sir James knows that Elsdon will be safer than that land."

"And Hartlepool?"

"I shall not become comfortable there for I know that we shall move, eventually, to Stockton. Henry Samuel told me that your mother and father are becoming old. Your father has endured wounds which would have laid down a lesser man. He wishes to dangle his grandchildren from his knee." She smiled, "But it will be pleasant to look out on the sea."

Just after we had passed the hamlet of Elwick we stopped for the road turned and afforded a good view of the mouth of the river, the port and the manor. It was such a clear day that I could see all the way to the mouth of the estuary and the tiny village of Coatham on the southern bank of its mouth. Hartlepool was dominated not by a castle but by the huge church of St. Hilda. The church was larger than the one in Stockton and reflected the importance of the saint. The walls which ran around the town were also larger than Stockton's. I frowned as I looked at them. They would be hard to defend from a landward attack. The frown disappeared as I realised that any who managed to attack Hartlepool from the landward side would have to reduce Stockton first. All was well.

As we headed down to the town I said to Dick, "That was where your grandfather took ship when he went on his crusade to the north. He sailed in a ship captained by one whose grandsire had served the Warlord. Think about that."

"I should like to meet him."

I shook my head, "Henry is long dead but his son William, named after the first sailor of the family, William of Kingston, captains a vessel. Your grandfather uses him still. Always remember those with ties to our family for those bonds are strong."

He nodded, "And soon I will be old enough to be a page like cousin Henry Samuel was."

I looked at him. He had grown. "You have seen six summers. Aye, you could be ready but do you wish to be?" I saw his furrowed brow. He did not understand the question. "A page is more than a title it is the first few steps on a long journey. You will have to wait at table. Geoffrey will have to show you how to care for my horses, clean and sharpen my weapons. The time for playing will be gone. When

133

Margaret plays in the snow you will be standing by my side awaiting orders. You will have all of your lessons as well as new ones to help you prepare to become a squire and then a knight. You will have to learn to play the rote. Think on this and when we are settled into our new home then you can ask me again. If you do not then I will not think less of you." It was the first decision he would make that was of any importance and I saw the ramifications sinking in.

The Bishop had sent word a month since of our imminent arrival and the men who controlled the port for him, the priests and the clerks, had ensured that we had a warm welcome. There had been no lord of the manor for a little time. There were smiles and waves as we climbed the road towards the headland and the tower of the church. It was a busy port with fishing ships as well as cargo vessels. Women worked in long buildings gutting fish, for the herring and the mackerel they caught would be smoked and sent to Durham and Stockton to be sold in the markets there. Folk waved and smiled at us. My family's name was known and respected for Hartlepool relied on our family for protection.

The hall was a large rambling affair which sheltered below the mighty church built on the highest part of the headland. The hall had a courtyard and extensive stables. My warrior's eye took in the fact that it was indefensible. There was no ditch and no wall. The town wall was just a hundred paces from the entrance and was adjacent to the sea. Inside it was well furnished and comfortable as one would expect for the Bishop used it when he travelled to London by ship. The highway that was the sea was faster than the Roman Roads and more comfortable. My wife and I were well aware that if the Bishop came, he would have the best of the rooms.

Edgar was the steward and he had been a priest. He had fallen in love and left the priesthood. He and his wife, Matilda, were kindly people. He had four children but they were now grown and had families of their own. Matilda, in particular, was delighted that we had a young family. The welcome we had was as warm as I might have hoped. While my wife was shown around the hall and Geoffrey and my men saw to the horses and the weapons, I sat with Edgar and went through all of the tasks that I had to perform as well as reading the manor's books. It was much bigger than Elsdon and I would have more work. This was not a warrior's work and was merely dull rather than dangerous. Even while Edgar told me of my responsibilities, I was working out how to do them quickly.

That evening we ate our first meal in our new home. Mary was happy for it was not a castle and had been built for comfort and not defence. We had more rooms and they were both warmer and cosier than the cell-like chambers of Elsdon. "We will see the priest in the church tomorrow and I will send a rider to Stockton to tell my father of our arrival."

She smiled and put her hand on mine. "And then, perhaps later in the week, we can ride to Stockton for I would like to see Eleanor and her new home."

I nodded, "Aye, she must be almost at her time."

She laughed, "You goose! You men seem to think a woman has a seed planted and the baby comes within a short time. It takes nine months. Her child will be born in September!" I nodded. She gave me a mischievous smile, "Our baby, on the other hand, will be a Christmas baby."

It took a moment to sink in, "You are with child? When did you discover this?"

"Margaret of Yeavering examined me before we left Elsdon and I knew then. I did not tell you for I knew you would fret all the way south and I have managed the journey with no ill effects."

"Then that is cause for celebration." I then told her of the conversation between Dick and myself.

She smiled, "That is no bad thing for it will keep him out of mischief. Margaret is enough of a handful as it is. She is the wild child."

I could not help smiling for although my wife was right, I would not change one hair on my daughter's head for she made me smile. She was independent and took a reprimand badly. My wife said that Dick was a joy by comparison. What would my next child bring?

After I had seen the priest and prayed in the church I went with Geoffrey and Dick to walk the town walls and to meet the people. As we neared the fish market, I realised that we would have to get used to the smell of fish. It was an all-pervading stink! I also discovered that the people of the town had a clear sense of their own identity. They were fiercely independent. I became more confident that they would be able to defend their walls against any attacker. Each man practised every Sunday with the bow on the land to the east of the church. They were proud of their skills. It also became clear that they knew how to use swords. One or two of the men had swords which were Danish or Norse. They had been handed down from father to son since the time when this land was Viking. It showed the mettle of the men of my manor.

Three days after I had arrived, I began to feel comfortable. My men at arms and archers would need farms and land. I knew from the steward that there were some towards Greatham which were in my largesse and some around Bewley. The land had suffered a plague brought by a ship ten years earlier. For some reason, it affected those who lived outside the walls of Hartlepool more than those within. Some of the farmers and their families had died and the farms were almost derelict and would need much work. I was assured, by Edgar, that the Palatinate would fund the improvements for it was in the Bishop's interests to have prosperous farmers which generated a good revenue. Most of the farms were what one might call a smallholding rather than a viable farm. The men who had lived on them had eked out a living fowling on the marshes of the estuary. There were also seals and when I was told this I smiled, for it harked back to the days of the Vikings. My men were quite happy when I told them and for two days, I rode with them so that they could choose the type of farm that they would like. My archers all wished the lands which lay closer to the marshes. They would hunt the sea birds. My men at arms chose the farms which lay closer to the sandbanks on the river where they could hunt the seal. They would raise sheep for such animals raised on salt marshes had a taste which was unique. After seven days in Hartlepool, my men had their farms and they would begin to build and to farm. Of course, they would still be my men at arms and archers. Each Sunday they would come to church and then practise on the green which lay between the church and my hall. When I went to war, they would follow my banner.

Edward of Yarum was to be given a farm closer to Stockton. His family still lived in Sam's new manor and my father had given him the farm of a man at arms killed at Taillebourg. He and his family came with us as we went to Stockton. He drove the wagon which carried his belongings and gave a comfortable ride to my wife.

She saw my look of concern as she climbed aboard and shook her head, "You did not worry when we left Elsdon and I was in the same condition then! I am a hardy woman! Do not worry about me for a short ride in a wagon will do me no harm!"

My parents had been warned of our arrival and I found myself becoming quite excited. The last time I had been at home was when we had returned from the crusade. Much had happened in the intervening years.

After Elsdon and the manor house at Hartlepool, Stockton Castle seemed huge and yet it was so familiar. We had entered the town through the north gate and it took longer to reach the main gate of the castle than I had expected for we were greeted by so many people. Sir Mark's parents greeted us at the tannery which was at the far end of the town and then the weaponsmith gave us a long greeting. He seemed particularly taken with Dick my son. I realised then that his own son, John, had become my father's page when he was about the same age.

John was now a squire. The result was that by the time we reached the gate to the castle my mother and father were there to greet us. My mother burst into tears when she saw Margaret for this was her first view of her. Isabelle had been the youngest granddaughter and she was now nine. Margaret won her grandmother's heart as soon as they spied each other. Holding out her arms for my mother to cuddle her guaranteed the bond!

As I helped my wife from the wagon, she shook her head, "I swear that child has the mind of an adult. She will have your mother eating out of her hand!"

I laughed, "She has had no one to indulge since Dick lived here and you know what a fuss she made of him!"

Dick did not mind being ignored for my father had helped him down from his pony. Considering that my father was over seventy he still looked remarkably fit. His life had been hard and perhaps that had prepared him well. I saw my wife head towards my mother and Margaret. She would give my mother the news.

My father said the right thing for my son, "You have grown, young Richard! I would hazard that you will soon be training at the pel!"

My son squealed, "I have practised with Alan Longsword and he says I have a good arm!"

"Then we will let Ridley the Giant cast his eye over you for he is a good judge of warriors." I had dismounted and Geoffrey was leading my horse to the stable. "And you, my son, it is good to have you home! Our parting did not sit well with me. I liked not that you had to ride off to defend your family and this old relic had to watch!" He shook his head, "It is hard getting old and realising that all the hurts and wounds mean that I cannot do all that I once did."

"Now is the time for you to enjoy that which you did. You have deserved a time of peace."

He nodded, "I fear that it is you who will pay the price for peace. After you had left Newcastle I spoke with the King. He is keen to strengthen the Welsh border." I cocked an eye and he nodded, "He wishes to atone for the defeat in France. The battle of Elson and Woodford were not enough for him. With Llewellyn the Great dead he sees the chance of victory in the west which will restore his reputation. You, I am afraid, are his best choice to be the leader of the men who do this."

"Surely there are others?"

He gave me a knowing look, "De Montfort might have seemed a good choice but the King has given him the poisoned chalice that is Gascony. If de Montfort makes a success in Gascony then King Henry and the Lusignans will exploit it and he will reap the reward of de Montfort's efforts. If he fails," he shrugged, "then a potential rival is eliminated."

"So, I should make the most of my time here in my home?"

"Always do that, my son. I made the mistake of taking it for granted and I now regret it." He put his arm around me, "Let us go inside the castle. Your mother has been planning for your return for a long time. I know not how long you planned to stay but it will have to be at least a week or we will have so much food left over that it will be a crime."

It was obvious to me that my mother had been informed of the news. She was crying and hugging Margaret at the same time, "Another grandchild! God has blessed us, Thomas!"

My father smiled and looked at me. "We are to have a third child?" I nodded. "Then this is even more reason to celebrate. The rest of the family will come tomorrow. I know that Eleanor is looking forward to seeing you. She was upset that you could not be at the wedding."

For my son, this was all of his dreams come true in one fell swoop for Stockton Castle was a real castle. When my father had returned from the Baltic it had been a manor house only but he had improved it year on year and now it had, once again, a curtain wall, inner walls, towers and an imposing keep. The ditches and the river made it almost impossible to take without great loss of life and I knew that one day, it would be mine. I hoped that the day was a long time coming for it would mean that either my father was dead or incapable of caring for himself and neither was a prospect I relished!

The feast that first night was a quiet and conservative affair. That is not to say it was not joyful. On the way south Dick had asked me if he could be a page and that he was prepared for any hardship. The feast was his first time serving. My mother kept rolling her eyes for she did not think he ought to have to work when we had servants but, to be fair to him, he worked as hard as Geoffrey and I was proud of him. It was also the first time that Geoffrey sang to an audience with his rote. He had been nervous but I pointed out that it would be easier performing before just my wife and my parents and the audience was appreciative. I saw my son looking on with trepidation. It would be some years before he had to do the same but that day would come and I remembered my own experience. I think, in many ways, it helped me to become a better warrior. The fears you faced were different from those in combat but they were still fears which needed to be overcome.

The family reunion, the next day, was one filled with both laughter and tears. Not all the tears were sad ones. Eleanor was close to her time and my wife had told her that she, too, was with child. They were tears of joy. Remembering my dead brother Alfred, brought forth tears of sadness. Matilda had been with my brother for a relatively short time and she now had some grey hairs. My other nieces and nephews, with the exception of Isabelle and Geoffrey, were now young men and women and Dick and Margaret were the youngsters who filled the castle with squeals and laughter. Dick might be a page but he was still a child. Alfred and Thomas had now enjoyed more than a year of their lives as squires and I saw that they had broadened out. Working at the pel would do that to a man. Elizabeth was also looking for a husband for with her cousin Eleanor now married and with a child, she too began to seek a home away from the Valley.

When we left for my manor, after two weeks at Stockton, our new life began. This would not be the precarious existence clinging on to the border and riding forth each day clad in mail and helmet. Here I could ride from my new manor in surcoat only. I could ride with just Geoffrey and Dick, knowing that we would not be attacked and I travelled through a peaceful land. I could hunt with my men and not fear an attack by brigands or Scots. I had the whole summer to explore a land I knew a little already but would come to know well. There were the small hamlets and villages of Seaton, Stranton, Hart, Elwick and Dalton. There were the folk who worked on the fish quays. There were the sea captains who called upon me, often with gifts from exotic places. I was an important lord now and my favour was sought. The Bishop had given me one of his most precious jewels and it was my job to look after it.

As my wife grew and Margaret learned new ways to find mischief I began to worry. I suppose it was a needless worry but I had been given something which was valuable and I knew that there would be a price to pay. I did not enjoy that summer as much as I should have because I worried about what would come along to spoil it. That too was because of the change. At Elsdon, there had been no opportunity for me to either reflect or worry about shapeless threats. There the threat had been very real. When I had been in the Holy Land then danger and death had been ever-present. Now I was comfortable and wondered what would make my life less comfortable.

My niece, Eleanor, gave birth to a son in September. Both were healthy and the boy was named, as I had known he would be, after his dead grandfather, Sir William de la Lude. My wife was halfway through her term but in Hartlepool, we would not be isolated. Here there were doctors and midwives aplenty. That said, both of us would have preferred Margaret of Yeavering to be close at hand.

And then, in October, a missive came. I was to ride to Chester, there to meet with King Henry. My brief time of peace would be over and I would be going to war.

Chapter 14

I did not need a large escort but I needed good men and so I took
Alan Longsword, Stephen Bodkin Blade, Tom of Rydal, Idraf of Towyn
and Garth Red Arrow. We would be travelling across the high passes of
the Pennines and, with winter approaching, there might be some
desperate men who were willing to risk their lives to take a horse and its
rider. Dick would be coming with us. If his mother thought he was too
young she said nothing but that may have been because she was having
a more difficult time with the yet to be born baby. We also took two
servants to look after the spare horses. Harold and his son, Edward, both
worked at the manor and looked after my horses. They had shown me
that they knew what they were doing and, in truth, were keen to ride
across the land. Few of those in Hartlepool had ever travelled further
than either Durham or Stockton!

We wrapped for the cold in thick, oiled cloaks and we rode good
palfreys rather than coursers or destrier. I was on the service of the King
and I had a warrant from him which allowed me to stay at royal castles
and the religious houses which owed their existence to the King. King
Henry was a religious man, unlike his father, indeed, he had an
obsession with Edward the Confessor and had named his son after that
illustrious yet some said, unlucky, king. We snaked our way south and
west towards the bastion of the borders, Chester. That we had been
summoned there told me that King Henry was about to begin his attack
on that weakened Kingdom which was so troublesome to England.

As we rode, I explained to Geoffrey and to Dick the purpose of the
campaign. Geoffrey was French and did not know the history of the
western border of England and Dick was too young. His lessons had not
yet encompassed the wars with Wales. I knew that the three men at
arms who were with me were also listening closely for they had yet to
fight in this part of the world.

"The north of Wales is filled with mountains and passes where men
can be ambushed and attacked. It has little of value except that it guards
the breadbasket of Wales, Anglesey. If that was all there was to it then
we would not be going to war but, since before the time of an England,
the Welsh, like the Scots in the north, liked to cross the border and raid
England. They no longer take slaves but they do take from the rich land
which is Cheshire. They usually do this after the harvest has been taken
in. They are successful because they know their own land better than
the men of Cheshire and once they reach the valleys which surround

141

their mountains they disappear. I do not know what, exactly, the King plans but I am guessing that it will be a punitive raid to prevent them from attacking Cheshire."

Dick looked up. He was no longer riding a pony but the horse he rode was a smaller one than mine, "But we only have five men!"

I laughed, "This is not the time for war. The King summons us so that he can tell us his plans and give me the time when I bring my men. There is no Earl of Chester for John of Scotland died and that is why the King will be there. I have no doubt that he will have a constable appointed to keep watch on the border but his presence there will tell the Welsh that England has now turned its eye to them."

Alan Longsword asked, "Lord, what of the Welsh Marches and the Marcher lords further south? Will they not be involved?"

"In the days of the Earl Marshal then the Welsh Marcher Lords were a barrier to the Welsh and the strong castles there ruled that land. Since the Earl Marshal's son, William, rebelled then the Marcher Lords serve themselves. Their land is not Wales, nor, at the moment, is it England."

"How do you know all of this, lord?"

"That is simple, Geoffrey, my father told me before we left. He may no longer go to war himself but he keeps a keen eye on all that goes on in this realm. He has insight into the ways of lords. He has known treachery and deceit." I smiled, "I have much to learn!"

It was late in the afternoon as we rode through the gates of the City of Chester. My father had told me that Chester Castle had been a centre of power during the anarchy. Earl Ranulf and his wife, Matilda, had kept the castle as a bastion against the Welsh and against other enemies of England. As such it had almost been a palace. Now, as we rode through its gates, I saw that it was now much more functional and it had become a fortress.

Now that I had given such good service to the King I was treated well. He needed my help and he needed my skills. I was under no illusions. King Henry was a ruthless king and he would use me to his own ends but, for a while, I would be treated as an honoured guest. The fortress that was Chester had good accommodation and we were given fine rooms. The King was already dining and the three of us were ushered into the Feasting Hall as they were eating their first course. There was a place at the lower end of the table. I took no offence at my lowly station. My father had taught me that you could learn more from that end of the table than being seated next to the high and mighty. I was next to a young knight from the de Clare family, Robert. He was of a similar age to my nephew, Sam, and he was an affable knight.

"This is an honour, Sir William, the King has spoken of your heroic action on the northern border. Here in Wales, we get to fight bandits and poor Welsh knights. You fought and defeated the French!"

It would have been crass of me to point out that these bandits and poor knights had managed to keep the Marcher Lords from taking the rest of Wales. I just nodded, "To be honest, Sir Robert, the French we fought were little better than brigands. And where is your home?"

"Chepstow, my lord. I am the great-nephew of Gilbert de Clare who was Earl of Hertford. I never knew him but I heard he was a great warrior. I have little hope of land except through the good offices of the King and so I have come here as a sword for hire." He looked down at his platter and shook his head, "I am sorry if that offends you."

"My father was a landless knight and fought as a sword for hire. Do you have men who follow you?"

"Just my squire, Geraint. It is all that I can afford."

"Then take my advice, Sir Robert, and hire men to follow you. If you fight in Wales then they should be archers. It will be money well spent but I fear that if King Henry wishes us to fight the Welsh then coins will be in short supply for, as you said, there is not a great deal of money in Wales."

Talking to him I learned that none of the Marcher Lords showed the same fortitude as their forebears had. In Ireland, that branch of the de Clare family ruled the island with an iron fist. In South Wales, they lived comfortable lives in huge castles like Caerphilly where they were safe from any Welsh attack and they lived well.

"Are there many young knights such as yourself?"

He nodded, "Many take to the crusades. A few went with de Montfort on the Baron's crusade and now follow him to Gascony."

"I was in the Holy Land but it is not the place it used to be. I fear that whatever lands are held by Christians will soon be lost. It is a sad fact of life."

By the time the King retired and we followed I had a much better picture of Wales and the King's plan. It struck me he was encouraging knights like Sir Robert to come and serve him for that way he could avoid paying for them. He would feed and house them but that was cheap compared with what he would need to keep a large army in the field. I knew that when he spoke to me, I would have a much better idea of his plan.

I was sent for in the morning. I had not seen him when I broke my fast with the others. I was told that he was in the Cathedral, praying to God. He had with him just the castellan of Chester, Sir John de Vries, the Bishop of Chester and three scribes. Where were the earls and great lords who would lead his army?

"Sir William, how is your father?"

"He is well."

"And the other knights of the valley?"

"They prosper."

"Hartlepool is a manor to your liking?"

I grew tired of the inanities of the king's conversation, "Aye, I am grateful to the Bishop of Durham for his generosity."

That brought a frown from the King.

"The Bishop is a good man and heeds his king's advice. I assume your father gave you some indication of the reason for your presence?"

"You wish me to fight in Wales for you."

"More than that, I wish you to lead the knights of the valley when we begin to strengthen our hold on Wales."

That did surprise me and must have shown on my face for it made the King smile. "But Sir Fótr, Sir Geoffrey and Sir Peter are not only older than I, but they all also have more experience."

"True, they are older but you were instrumental in the capture of Jerusalem. I have spoken to my brother and know. You also managed to defend the northern border with a handful of knights and, more importantly, you are a baron!"

The reward of the title now became clear. King Henry had been planning this for a long time. I considered my next words before I spoke them, "If you wish the knights of the valley and their men," he nodded, "then that will only give you forty days' service, King Henry. As it takes seven days to reach here and return to the valley then you will only have just over three weeks of actual campaigning. Surely it would be better to use local lords."

He did not seem put out by my apparent impertinence, "Let me explain. I held Gruffyd ap Llewellyn as a hostage for the good behaviour of his brother Dafydd. However, the foolish Prince tried to escape from the Tower. He fell and he died. This Dafydd sees his chance to revoke any treaty signed by either his father or any of his heirs. He sees the French fiasco as a sign of weakness." This was the only time I heard the King even begin to admit an error. It showed me the effect Taillebourg had had on him. "Our English lords who are local have been beaten so many times by these Welsh wild men that they are defeated before they draw sword. We need new blood and you and the knights you lead have recent success so do not worry about the forty days. We will pay scutage for the rest of the time that you are needed." That meant that the knights and men at arms would be paid for by knights who did not wish to serve and also owed the King forty days. He looked me in the eye and I nodded my understanding. "I have simple objectives. Twthill Castle harbours the Welsh raiders who will come in the spring and steal from Cheshire. I wish it to be destroyed. I want the Valley of the Clwyd to be under my control. When Twthill is destroyed you will erect a stronger stone castle at the mouth of the river."

I stared at him, "And I do this with the knights and men of the valley?"

He laughed, "Of course not. Sir Robert Pounderling shall bring a large force of knights and he will be the one who will be responsible for guarding whatever you gain, but you will lead." He paused so that I could take in those words. "He is not here at present for he recently lost an eye in a tournament and is still recovering. I have promised him the castle that will be built at the mouth of the Clwyd. For this year that is all I wish you to do. I will have you return next spring to begin the work. This will be lucrative for you. I will pay you scutage and all that you can take from the Welsh is yours. However, you must be here by March for it is around that time when the Welsh warriors begin their raids. By stopping them you will give confidence to my lords of Cheshire and when you have taken Twthill their lands will be safer. I do not intend to bite off more than I can chew." He looked at me and said, carefully, "You will return each spring for three years until I have this part of Wales under my control. I am giving you command of this army. Sir Robert is a good man but you will be the one to win back my borders! You will do for me here what you did for me at Elsdon. That land is now safe and I would have you do the same for this border."

I leaned back, "You will be stripping the valley of both knights and men, Your Majesty."

"And you have successfully won a peace which will keep your lands safe. Besides, your father will be there and, I have no doubt that there are more squires who will soon be ready to be knights. The north, it seems, is a breeding ground for good knights!" He turned to his scribe, "It is decided and the warrant will be signed by myself and the Bishop. Richard here will deal with the scutage and other financial arrangements. I daresay that you will leave soon for you have much to do!"

I was dismissed. I went to our chambers and told Geoffrey and Dick to begin to pack and to tell my men of our imminent departure. I left them to it and went to the library in the castle. This was the repository of all manner of books and maps. I only knew of its existence because of my father. He had been told that the Warlord had been a close friend of the Countess of Chester and spent some time in the castle during the time of the civil war. The room was empty and, judging by the amount of dust I discovered, had been rarely cleaned. That suited me for it meant I could take whatever I wished and no one would miss that which I took. I found the maps I needed and carried them back to our chamber. The leather bags had been packed already, "Place these maps in one of the bags and be careful with them! We shall need them!"

By the time I reached the antechamber to the hall Richard, the clerk was waiting for me with the warrant. As I had expected King Henry had made it detailed and explicit. There was no doubt as to my duties and my commitment. I saw, in the inner bailey, the young Marcher knight, Sir Robert and some of the other young swords for hire practising. As Geoffrey and my men approached with my horses, he stopped what he was doing and came over to me, "Leaving so soon, Baron?"

"I have my commission and I shall return in March."

"Then you will be leading the army upon your return?" He seemed happy at the prospect.

Shaking my head, I said, "I am to lead men but not necessarily the army. And you?"

"We are taken on as knights of Chester and when Sir Robert Pounderling arrives, he will lead us into the Clwyd to become used to the land."

"Then beware the ambush and the Welsh archer. This is the country which suits them both well. Stay safe until spring for then we shall have archers ourselves. You fight fire with fire."

I was less than happy as I left Chester for King Henry was not being fair to the young knights. I knew not Sir Robert Pounderling but taking just knights in this land was tantamount to suicide. Riding north I waved Idraf forward, "Idraf, we return in March to rid the Clwyd of the Welsh threat."

He shook his head, "That you will never do. True the valley is not as rocky as the valleys closer to Wyddfa," he used the Welsh name for Snowdon, "but it is still far more dangerous than any valley in the North Tyne area."

"How would you control it?"

"Take the castles and then build stone ones. We, Welsh, are happier with wood than stone which is ironic really considering how much of our land is made of rock. Twthill castle is just a wooden motte and bailey and the Normans built it. Once it was good but now, I would put a stone one in its place."

It sounded like a good idea and told me that King Henry had thought this through well for that had been his suggestion too but building in

stone took time. I intended to spend as short a time as possible in
Wales. I did not know this Sir Robert Pounderling but if he was a
tournament knight then he was not necessarily a good general and I
could now see why King Henry was relying upon me. Then it came to
me, I would simply subdue the Valley and then let Sir Robert
Pounderling build the castle. The thought cheered me and I spent the
rest of the day, as we rode north and east, discussing the land with Idraf.
I would have the maps for my father and I to pore over but Idraf came
from Towyn which was at the mouth of the Clwyd. He told me of a hill
which sounded perfect for a castle added to which the Welsh did not
bother with such defences. The one at Twthill would not exist but for
William the Conqueror. By the time we reached our accommodation for
the night, a Benedictine Monastery, I knew the pitfalls and the problems
the campaign would bring.

Upon reaching Stockton, which was on the way to my new manor, I
spent the night with my father. Some of the maps were a little worse for
wear. They had not been cared for. Leofric son of Leofric, my father's
clerk, had a neat hand and my father and I took him through the maps
so that he could make a fair copy of each of them.

"My lord, this is the work of many weeks!"

I smiled, "And that you have. I need them in March!"

He seemed happy with that and went off to his chamber where he had
good light from a south-facing window. My father said, "March?"

"Aye," I told him what I had been asked and I saw my father
becoming angry. "Father, be at peace. I will be away for three months
and that is all; if I am successful it may even be less. It is too long but
not as long as we gave him in the Holy Land. I do not intend to waste
any time. Forty of the days will be free but with the scutage we receive
then we can hire more men at arms and archers. Do not forget that I left
many in Elsdon."

"But you do not need them. Soon I will give up my role and you shall
come here as Lord of the Manor!"

"And that is why I must obey the King for if I do not, he can take
Stockton away from me!"

"He would not dare!"

"His father did!" That silenced him. "It is almost like a penance.
Three months each year for three years. If you add the months up then it
is not even a full year. Then, if you still wish me to be Lord of Stockton
then I can do so knowing that I have fulfilled my promise to the King."

As I was staying the night, I went to his solar with him to enjoy some
wine. I told him all that I had learned but I saved the best piece of news
for the last. "And Alan Longsword discovered from the other men at

arms, that the Earl of Leicester, Simon de Montfort, had begun to upset the people of Aquitaine," I told him what I had learned. The King had sent Se Montfort there to stop him from persecuting the Jews, whom the King needed for their finance. De Montfort had made himself rich in the process and the King had made his brother-in-law the Lord Lieutenant of Aquitaine. De Montfort was using that title and his position to make more money and gain power. The local lords resented de Montfort using Gascony as his own fiefdom and they had complained to the King.

My father was a shrewd man, "The King may have miscalculated. When he, himself, failed in his French adventure, perhaps he thought de Montfort would too but the man is slippery and will not risk a battle! Believe me, the King needs to watch de Montfort. He has eyes on the crown."

My father had forgotten more about warfare than most men would learn in a lifetime and, while we waited for the food to be ready, he gave me advice about fighting in Wales.

"Of course, you realise the King is taking the knights from the valley?"

"Aye, Alfred will be ready for knighthood by then but I shall keep him here, this campaigning season. He will hate it but I am mindful of Taillebourg. I kept Sir Mark with me in Stockton and he will come with you for he is ready."

A servant came up the stairs, "Sir Thomas, her ladyship says to tell you that the food is getting cold!"

"Then we will join you directly." We emptied our beakers and my father said, "Talk not of this tonight. What your mother does not know will help her to sleep easier. She will worry enough when you are on campaign. Let her sleep until then."

I knew that Geoffrey would remain silent but I was less sure about Dick. As luck would have it, he had not been in the hall for Henry Youngblood had been schooling a new horse for him and Dick was still in the stable when I reached the table. I waved over Geoffrey, "Find Dick and impress upon him that he must not mention the campaign in spring."

"Aye, lord. I would not worry overmuch for he is full of his new horse!"

I need not have worried for my mother did not shut up about the new child in the family. She was a remarkable woman for she loved all of her grandchildren equally. Eleanor had been an aberration and now that was behind them. I found it hard enough to share my love equally with just Margaret and Dick. When she ceased going on about little William, she pestered me with questions about Mary and her condition.

"Why the King needed to see you is beyond me. Has he not other knights he can use." She suddenly stopped, "What did he want you for?"

I waved an airy arm, "Oh, he wanted advice. He seems to think that because I was a border lord in the north, I can offer him advice about how to deal with the Welsh."

She seemed relieved, "Well even I know that you do not fight the Welsh in winter! He is not a bad king like his father but I wonder if he was dropped on his head when he was a baby!" My mother did not suffer fools gladly and she thought King Henry a fool.

It was a cold, wet, almost icy morning as we set off on the last leg of our journey, the fourteen miles to Hartlepool. Dick insisted upon leading his new horse. He needed a saddle for it and that would need to wait until we had seen the saddler to have one made. Geoffrey was convinced that Dick would fall off as he tried to control two horses but I merely smiled, "Then he will learn a most valuable lesson for you offered to lead his new horse for him."

I did not fear for Dick as Henry Youngblood would not have let Dick have the new horse unless he was totally convinced that it was obedient. The experience taught him to concentrate for he did not utter a word all the long way home nor did he let loose of his horse.

Time passed and Alice and Beth became agitated as my wife's time drew near. This was one area where I could be of no help. What I did do was to spend more time with Margaret. I guessed that it would soon be her second birthday. I could not have remembered the actual date but my wife would. As a treat and as Mary was suffering with the unborn child, I took Margaret down to the harbour to watch the fishing boats landing their catches. I wrapped her up as well as I could but she seemed to be tougher than she looked. One thing I had noticed was that she always had a runny nose. Two green trails seem constantly to prey upon her top lip. She didn't seem to mind. Now that she could walk, she would not be carried, even though it was far quicker and she insisted upon holding my hand which made me move at her pace. The two of us were alone for Dick and Geoffrey were grooming our horses and walking them in the yard.

This was one of the first times that we had been alone. Normally either my wife or one of the women was with us.

Margaret was full of questions. Her speech was not always easy to understand but I had learned to keep saying things in different ways until I got a nod. When we reached the sea wall which lay just outside the town wall, I sat upon it and made a seat with my cloak. It was an icy east wind which blew and I thought it might be too cold for her but she seemed quite happy to sit there with me looking at the sea and the wildlife. She loved animals and birds. The seagulls which screamed and bickered over the guts which were thrown into the water amused her immensely. And then she saw the black gannets diving beneath the waves to take the treasure that the greedy gulls missed. It was a lovely time for me. She held my left hand while my right was protectively around her shoulders and she giggled and squealed with delight at the antics of the birds.

I know not how long we might have stayed there had not Geoffrey run to get me, "Lord, it is Lady Mary, your child is coming and I was sent to find you."

Sweeping Margaret into my arms I hurried back into the town and thence to my hall. I could do nothing to help except to be close in case I was needed. My new son, Matthew, took half a day to come and at one point we summoned a priest for it looked to be too hard for my wife to bear and that we would lose one or the other. Matthew proved a fighter and my wife showed me, again, that despite her diminutive size, she had the strength of a warrior. She fought through. The town had a doctor and while he did not deliver the baby, Beth did, he was present to examine her.

While the women cleaned up the mother and baby so that I could see them he took me to one side. "I fear that was a most difficult birth. I have spoken to the midwives who helped Beth deliver the babe and they agree with me. "Your wife will bear no more live children. She will take months to recover from this one and you may need a wet nurse for the child. Your wife will be weak for she lost a great deal of blood."

I merely nodded for I did not understand and could not take it in. I wanted to ask if he was certain but the man was a doctor and he had spoken to the midwives and I had to believe that they all knew what they were doing. I would have just one daughter. I would have no more children. I knew that I was lucky for some men had no children. That had been the lot of some knights I had known. They had died childless and their names had died with them. I would go to the church of St. Hilda and give thanks for the deliverance of my wife and son.

"Can I see her?"

"You can but do not mention to her what I have just said. There will be time enough for that in the future. For now, you need to be her rock."

When I entered the room, my new son, who seemed to be little larger than my hand, was sleeping. My wife gave me a wan smile as I took her hand and kissed her, "He fought, my husband. He may be small but he is a warrior."

I could barely speak for they both seemed so helpless and I was unable to offer anything other than a pathetic smile. "You are both warriors, now rest. Our son is resting and so should you."

She nodded, "I would name him, Matthew. It is a good name and Matthew died bravely. I would like to think that in naming him thus, we keep alive the memory of Matthew."

"You are too kind and it shall be so." I nodded to Beth, "Take the bairn, Beth and Alice, get my wife some honeyed wine. I will take Dick and Margaret and give thanks to God in the church!"

The preparations for Christmas were, of course, chaotic. My new son showed that he was tough and grew day by day. My wife was still weak and I had to do more of the household tasks such as speaking with the housekeeper and the cook. Geoffrey and Dick were rocks and were at my side helping me with tasks a squire and page did not normally encounter. If I had thought I would have complaints from Dick I was wrong and, looking back, I think it was my prayers in the church; they had been spoken aloud and it was then he realised how close he had come to losing his mother and new baby brother. He had taken his mother for granted, hitherto, as most men do and the realisation of her mortality made him grow up more than a boy who had seen but a couple of handfuls of summers should. I still do not know if I organised Christmas well but we celebrated and we ate. Geoffrey could not believe that, while we were just a few dozen miles south of Elsdon here in Hartlepool there was no snow. He thought it was like a different country.

He was seated at the table next to me when he asked me the question about the climate. As it was Christmas and my wife was still confined to her bed, I helped my son and squire to bring in all the food to my hall and after we had taken platters to my wife, daughter Margaret, Beth and Alice the three of us sat at my table, ate, drank and talked.

"Elsdon is further from the sea and the sea, I think, moderates the temperature. Do you remember when we were in Jaffa? There it was cooler than in Jerusalem. I do not think that the summers here will be as glorious as those in Elsdon."

The food was good for the manor had an excellent cook but I did not drink too much. With a wife who was still unwell, I wished to be available at all times.

Dick asked, "What if Mother is not well by the time we have to return to Wales, Father? The King will be angry if we do not arrive."

I had thought of this myself. "It may be that we have to take your mother, sister and brother to Stockton. That is a bridge we have to cross. What we do need is to ensure we have enough men with us. The warrant the King issued was quite specific in the number of men I was to bring. I am to supply ten knights, one hundred men at arms and one hundred archers." The fact that I only had ten if I counted myself seemed an insurmountable problem. I would deal with that if I had to. We would, of course, need far more men with us for we would need wagons for arrows, spare weapons, tents and cooking gear. There would have to be servants and men who, while they would not fight, would have to guard the baggage with the younger squires and pages. As we sat and celebrated the quietest Christmas I could ever remember I used my squire and page to work out where lay our shortfall. The battle of Taillebourg had stripped many of the knights of their most experienced men. Luckily it was not amongst the archers but I needed to make up the deficiency from my own lands. I had left some of my experienced men in Elsdon. I determined that once the days became longer, I would seek warriors from Hartlepool and the villages which surrounded it.

Once the celebrations for Christmas were over the port went back to its normal way of life and I went to find more men to follow my banner. I took with me, to select the men, Alan Longsword and Tom of Rydal. They were now the only unmarried men in my retinue and knew the sort of men we needed. Both spent time in the town for Hartlepool had some good alehouses and they knew the locals. Any port will have places which are frequented by sailors who are keen to have a good drink after the salty beer they had consumed at sea. Even as I was suggesting that we seek men I saw their minds at work.

"How many men would we need, lord?"

"King Henry is paying us scutage and we have all the booty which we can take from the Welsh. Let us say we look for fifteen men."

Tom of Rydal said, "We need more archers than men at arms, lord. We brought just eight from Elsdon."

"Then, Geoffrey, ride to the farm of Idraf and his wife outside Greatham. Ask him if he can join us."

I went with my two men at arms and page to the alehouses of the town. This was the time of year when there was little work for the men to do and so they sat in alehouses and nursed a beaker or two of ale. It took them from their own homes and they could dice and play nine men's morris. I could not understand it for I enjoyed being with my family but each to their own and it suited us. We found six straight away. Two were, indeed, archers and we were lucky. They had served in Durham and when their lord had died, unmarried and childless, they had returned to the place of their birth. The two, I suspect, were poachers. The steward had told me of a trade in the town; venison was sold secretly and the Bishop's men turned a blind eye. A good poacher was invaluable to a company of archers. The other four were sailors who had tired of the sea. While not as well trained as my men at arms they were tough, strong and, as their faces testified, they knew how to fight. I gave them a shilling each to bind them and two days to make their arrangements and then join me at my hall. Even as we left, I knew that the shilling would be gone in a day or so. Joining my retinue meant food, ale, clothing and lodgings.

When Idraf arrived, he had some good news. He had got to know the men of Greatham and he had found two young archers. They were brothers and both their parents had died not long before Christmas; there was nothing sinister in their deaths; they were just old. The two had already decided to seek their fortune and Idraf took advantage. When Geoffrey had told him what was needed he offered them employment immediately. Idraf knew archers. I had been looking for one day and had more than half of my number.

Seven days later and we had them all. We had found another four archers. Idraf took all of the archers back with him to his smallholding. He wanted to train them his way. I bought food for them and they seemed happy enough to live with Idraf while they trained. The rest of the men at arms were housed in my hall. The most interesting of them was a huge Norwegian, Erik Red Hair and his story was the most colourful of all of my men. He had come in on a Norse trader. When I met him, he was fighting with his captain and his crewmates. Not the best of beginnings but I never regretted hiring him.

It just so happened that we were looking for our last man and were seeking strong sailors who wished to leave the sea. We saw the altercation on the ship and I strode up, along with the Bishop's man, "Hold, I am Lord of this manor and I will have peace in my port!"

The Captain wiped the blood from his nose. I saw two other crewmen laid out and the man we came to know as The Viking stood facing them with bloodied knuckles. I saw the captain frown when I gave my title. He smiled and I saw deceit in his eyes, "Just a misunderstanding, my lord, it is all sorted now."

I looked at the huge man, "What is your name?"

He turned and spoke almost deferentially to me and that surprised me. I had expected belligerence, "Erik Red Hair, my lord, and this man and his brothers are trying to cheat me. I am owed a share of the profits and they are trying to send me hence without due payment."

I looked at the shifty-looking captain, "Is this true?"

"I have yet to sell all of my cargo. We will have a reckoning."

I knew that the reckoning would be a knife in the night and a body thrown into the sea. I turned to the clerk, "Brother John, what was the cargo which was landed?"

"Sheepskins, my lord."

I turned to look at the captain who was decidedly uncomfortable. "You are Norwegian?"

"Aye lord, from Tromso."

"I did not think that they raised sheep in Tromso."

"No lord, we picked them up from the Humber."

I was suspicious. The monks at the mouth of that river used their own ships to trade and the skins were normally sent to Flanders and France. It was a lucrative trade. I stepped back to look at the ship. She was a mixture between a knarr and an old-fashioned drekar. I recalled a conversation with King Alexander about the Vikings from the isles. They still raided as their ancestors had done. "Brother John, we will impound this ship until we can ascertain that the cargo was obtained legally." My two men at arms and Geoffrey had seen the furtive looks on the faces of the Captain and his crew. Like me, their hands went to their swords.

Seizing an axe, the captain shouted, "You cannot do that!" and he swung the axe at the rope holding the ship to the quay.

I had been in the manor long enough for men to come to know me and to respect me. As I ran aboard to stop them from leaving some of those who worked in the port grabbed weapons to help me and my men for the crew drew weapons. I saw one swing a boarding axe at Erik Red Hair, even as I blocked a sword swipe from another of the crew, I saw Erik grab the haft with his left hand while he swung his right hand into the side of the man's head. As I blocked the sword I shouted, "You will be punished for this!" I was aware that Dick had run on board too.

The Norwegian I was fighting suddenly pulled a seax from his belt. I grabbed his hand but the razor-sharp blade tore a long cut along my palm. Our swords were locked and so I drove my knee up between his legs. As he doubled over, I smashed the hilt of my sword against his head to render him unconscious. I confess that I was distracted by the wound and did not see the captain, wielding a two-handed axe, lurch at me. I was a dead man until Erik Red hair suddenly threw the boarding axe to split open the Captain's skull.

"Throw down your weapons!"

The death of their captain shocked the others and their weapons clattered to the deck. I turned and saw Geoffrey and Dick protectively watching my back with weapons drawn but they were unhurt. Tom and

Alan were also unhurt. As I surveyed the scene, I saw that the only death was the Captain.

I waved Brother John up the gangplank, "I am guessing that these are pirates." He nodded glumly, "And you did not see that. It means one of two things, either you are incompetent or corrupt. I will investigate and if I discover that you are corrupt then you will pay the price."

"I swear, my lord, that it was an honest mistake!"

"Such a mistake might be forgiven to another, lesser man, but the Bishop trusts you and you are paid a healthy stipend for your work. I want the ship and its cargo impounded. Send the crew to Durham for the Bishop's judgement. I will write out the warrant."

The priest looked relieved, "Yes, lord."

"Bind them all!"

I pointed at Erik Red Hair, "Not this man. He saved my life and if he had not begun this then these pirates would have escaped justice." The priest nodded. I said to Erik, "You are pirates are you not?"

"They are but I am not." The look on my face must have told him that I doubted his innocence. "It is true, lord. Let me tell you my tale. They do not come from Tromso. They are from the Isles and they fled to Tromso when King Alexander took over their island. They came to my home town which I had to leave for I killed a man. It was a fair fight but he was the brother of the jarl of Tromso. I took the opportunity to join the crew to escape the death sentence. It was only when we took the monks' ship that I knew they were pirates and I did not hurt any of the crew of that ship. It is why they were sending me from the ship without pay."

I nodded, for I believed his story. "Then you are free to go but, it seems to me that you are a man with talents and they should not go to waste. I seek men at arms to serve me. What say you? Will you join me?"

He looked and saw that Geoffrey and Dick still had weapons drawn and he smiled, "Anyone who can inspire a child and youth to risk their lives against Vikings is a warrior. I will join you…"

"Sir William of Hartlepool." I turned to Alan Longsword, "We have our last man. Take him to the hall and get him fitted with a surcoat."

Alan shook his head, "Best take the sail, my lord, for it will take a whole bolt of cloth to clothe this giant!"

I smiled for the words told me that Alan was happy. We now had our men and all that I needed to do was to weld them into one whole.

Chapter 15

My worries about leaving my wife alone proved to be groundless for Henry Youngblood and his wife arrived with four of my father's older retainers. Henry smiled, "Sir Thomas thought that my wife could help Lady Mary, lord and I can watch your home while you are away."

Although I was grateful, I was also a little worried, "Does my mother know yet what it is that we do?"

He laughed, "No, lord, Sir Thomas said it was to help your wife and nothing more. You and he have that maelstrom to navigate, yet!"

It proved to be the turning point. My wife now had a strong lady to help her and Alan and Tom had Henry Youngblood to help them. I had the problem of Brother John to deal with. I spoke to the other sea captains and they did not believe that he was corrupt. He just seemed lazy. A week after the pirates were sent to Durham I went with Geoffrey and Dick to speak with the Bishop. When I explained what had happened, he shook his head, "Brother John is a kindly man but he is not the man for Hartlepool. The revenues have been falling and the Palatinate cannot afford such losses. I have a new man but I am uncertain what to do with the priest. That is the trouble when you give a man a job paid for from the church's purse. They do not see the Church as a master and seem to regard the payment as something due just for being!"

I nodded, "Is he a healer?"

"He is a well-trained priest and he can heal, why?"

"I go to war against the Welsh and men fight better knowing that there is a priest who can absolve them before they fight. I could take him with us. It will be just for three months and would merely delay your decision, Your Grace, but, who knows, it may be the making of him."

"He may be a burden."

I laughed, "He can be as lazy as he wishes but he will have to march when we do, eat when we do, sleep when we do and endure all that the Welsh mountains can throw at us. It will either make him or break him. If he runs then you have one less problem, eh Bishop?"

He laughed, "You are a warrior, just like your father. And is all ready for this expedition on the King's behalf? The King told me, when he came last year, that which he intended."

"Almost. I have the men but I still need one knight. My nephew, Alfred, is young but we could take him if we had to."

"I have another solution if you will allow me." I waved an arm and he continued, "I have a nephew myself, Sir Gerard Tovington. My sister sent him north for he was a young man with young men's desires and he pressed his attentions too closely on a young lady who did not enjoy them. Here, he just cools his heels and gets up to mischief. There will be little opportunity for him to annoy ladies if he is fighting." I was reluctant to take such a liability with me. He saw that on my face and said, "As an inducement, I can let you have ten archers under my captain, Philip of Cheshire."

That decided me. Sir Peter and Sir Fótr could keep his breeches in check and even if he was just excess baggage then I would have fulfilled my commitment and the archers would be invaluable. "I will give him until July to see if he can mend his ways."

The Bishop looked relieved. "I will send them to you by the end of the week. My new port captain will be with you at the same time. Will Brother John be a problem for a week?"

"No, Bishop, since I spoke with him those who work in the port have commented that he is more diligent."

All was going well but I wondered what this new knight would bring with him. All the rest of the knights knew each other well. We were my father's knights and this would be something different. At best it would be like a new saddle which, while it might be better than a mere saddlecloth, took some getting used to. The phrase, 'a pain in the backside' was one my men often used to refer to warriors who irritated them until they were used to their ways. I was lucky in that the new men I had hired appeared to fit in well. Brother John seemed to accept the Bishop's decision and my recommendation with equanimity and stoicism. He saw it as a chance to redeem himself. I let Tom of Rydal help him to prepare for a life of campaigning. The sandals he wore in the port would not be of much use tramping the roads of Wales and he needed a good, oiled cloak. After a week I saw that he had changed and perhaps realised the size of the task he had taken on. He would be paying for his laziness.

When Sir Gerard arrived, I was not disappointed for he was all that I had anticipated. He was arrogant and he was pampered. The Bishop might not have approved of his behaviour and attitude but he had done little to change it. The atmosphere and the preparations for war came as a huge shock to him. His squire was also in for an unpleasant surprise. At the Bishop's palace, he had not served at table for they had young monks to do that. All changed when they arrived in my hall and Geoffrey ran him ragged. Sir Gerard also had to endure training with my men at arms and they took no prisoners nor did they make allowances for rich young lords who were ill-prepared for combat. They were just using wooden swords but by the end of the first day, Brother John's skills as a healer had been brought into play. Sir Gerard had a bloody nose, his scalp had been laid open to the bone and his knuckles had been so badly rapped that he could barely hold his knife as we ate.

"My lord, your men are a little rough! I protest at the treatment!" He wined and pouted neither of which endeared him to me.

I smiled, "Sir Gerard, they do this because they like you."

"Like me? They have an odd way of showing it!"

"Believe me when we go to war with the Welsh, the knocks you received today will seem like love taps and my men merely wish to toughen you up so that you may fight alongside them. I will tell you what, tomorrow you can try to fight Geoffrey, my young squire. He is no Alan Longsword nor is he the Viking. You should be able to beat him."

"Of course, that will be easy! Make it the day after, my lord, for my hand is sore."

I stared at him, "Tomorrow!"

They fought in helmets with shields and blunted swords without a point. An ill-timed blow could still break an arm. Geoffrey had become an accomplished swordsman. I could have knighted him but as I had no squire to replace him, he would have to remain a squire. Geoffrey was keen on the bout for he had not liked the knight's assertion that he could defeat my squire easily. My men at arms and archers, who had now left their farms to begin preparations for the campaign, were looking forward to it and money changed hands. They formed a rough square around them. It was quite obvious, within a few strokes, that Sir Gerard was not taking Geoffrey seriously and it was a mistake for it angered Geoffrey. The swashing blows which the knight used were both clumsy and predictable. Geoffrey blocked them easily on his shield. They both wore open-faced helmets and I saw the smile on Sir Gerard's face. He thought he was going to win. Geoffrey was merely working out the best combination of moves and when he suddenly launched his own attack then Sir Gerard was beaten. Geoffrey struck one blow which Sir Gerard blocked with his sword. He aimed another which Sir Gerard blocked with his shield and then, suddenly, Geoffrey feinted at Sir Gerard's shield again and when the knight brought his shield about Geoffrey spun around and brought his sword into the back of Sir Gerard's mail. He then used the flat of his sword to slam into the back of Sir Gerard's knee making him fall to the ground. He then dropped his own shield and grabbing the knight's head, held his sword at his throat.

"The bout is over, Sir Gerard; you are a dead man!"

My men cheered and the couple of men who had been foolish enough to bet against the squire handed over their coins.

I helped Sir Gerard to his feet. "He cheated!"

I laughed, "There are no rules in warfare, Sir Gerard. The Welsh will try to kill you any way that they can. Whoever trained you as a knight did a poor job of it. We have a short time to improve you. Heed Alan Longsword and Henry Youngblood's words or I fear I will be taking a corpse back to your uncle!"

It was the start of February before my wife was able to move around the hall as she had before the baby was born. As we sat before the fire with the children in bed and the servants departed I reached over to take her hand. I had been putting off this conversation for some time but I would be leaving in less than a month and the words needed to be spoken.

"You know, my love, that this last birth almost cost you your life?" She nodded. "We sent for the priest for we thought that neither of you would survive but you did and we thanked God for it."

"As I have thanked him each and every day since."

"When you were safe the doctor and the midwives spoke with me, they think it is unlikely that you will ever have children again." I shook my head, "I know not the reason and if any but the doctor had said it then I would have doubted it but they have collective wisdom and I believe their words."

I saw her looking into the fire and, as a tiny tear trickled down her cheek, I gave her fingers a squeeze. She turned to me and nodded, "In my heart, I knew so too. I would have been willing to give you another child, even though it might have cost me my life but…"

I left my chair and dropped to one knee so that I could hold her hand in my two, "I care not! I have a daughter and two sons. That is enough and even if it were not, I would not exchange your life for another child. Are you content?"

She wiped the tear away, "I shall have to be and besides Matthew is such a fighter that I believe he will be like two more sons for you." I nodded, "You will take care of Dick when you are in Wales, will you not, for he is desperate to emulate you?"

I remembered the fight on the boat, "Aye, and fear not, Geoffrey regards him as a younger brother. He remembers his own brother and the sacrifice made by him. Dick can have no better protector than Geoffrey of Lyons."

The time to leave came all too soon. It would take ten days for us to cross from Hartlepool, across the country, to get to Cheshire where we would muster. The rest of my men and knights were waiting for us in

Stockton. By now my mother would have discovered that the valley was going to war again and I expected a storm of biblical proportions when we arrived. It was a tearful parting for me and for those of my men who had families. The first fourteen miles were in silence. The icy wind which blew from the north was not in our faces but it was a lazy wind; it did not go around you, it went the shortest way; directly through you.

Stockton was like an armed camp. Although the castle was big it could not accommodate all of the men at arms and archers. They were camped by St. John's well. When we strode into the Great Hall the other knights were already there with their squires and I was given a warm greeting. Sir Gerard was viewed with some suspicion. Although Henry and Alan had knocked some of the edges from him, he still had a habit of looking down his nose at people. I could not worry about that. His presence meant I had fulfilled my quota and I had that most valuable of resources, more archers.

Sir Peter joined me, "I was watching from the battlements when you rode in. Who is that giant you have? He makes my father and I look normal-sized!"

I told them all his story. Sir Peter said, "Of course, as my father discovered, the tallest man on the battlefield attracts the most attention."

"You are right and finding a horse for him was not easy. He is not an accomplished rider but he has the heart of a lion."

My mother entered and she had a face as black as thunder. I had planned my strategy as I had ridden the Stockton road, "Mother, it is good to see you and now that Mary is recovered it would be a perfect time to visit with Margaret and Matthew. Margaret is changing and, each day, she looks more like you."

It was not true of course. As far as I was concerned Margaret looked like Margaret but grandmothers like to hear such things and her face softened. "As you are taking your father's knights away I might as well." She held her arms out, "Come and give your mother a hug!"

As I hugged her, she said, in my ear, "I like not secrets, William!"

"Sorry, I did not wish to upset you."

"Well, you have!" She turned to the rest, "We have a new guest this day. Welcome, Sir Gerard. You shall sit by my right-hand tonight so that I may get to know you!"

I think that Sir Gerard would happily have faced Alan Longsword and Henry Youngblood rather than endure my mother and her questions. For my part, it was a good night for I could talk with my father, sisters, nieces and nephews. One day I would be the head of the family and I had realised, whilst in Elsdon, that I barely knew my nieces

160

and nephews. I remedied it that evening. I made a point of talking at length to each of them. I found it both rewarding and illuminating. When I was not talking, I was observing. Eustace, Sir Gerard's squire, found himself working with other squires who knew each other really well. He could not cope with the banter and the humour. Things would get much worse when we were on campaign. Rebekah's daughter, Elizabeth, was now older than Eleanor had been when she had married and I saw her beginning to flirt with Sir Gerard. There was nothing in it, of course, but all the other eligible knights were either relatives or felt like relatives. Sir Gerard gave her the opportunity to try coquettish looks. As the alternative was talking to my mother Sir Gerard responded. I knew that Elizabeth would be reprimanded by my mother. Such was life in Stockton.

Most of the company retired early but I sat with my father before the log fire. Spring might be around the corner but in the northeast, it was still cold. "You have all the men you need? I can let you have more of my men."

"It is fine, father. Thanks to the Bishop I have more archers than are needed and I am loath to leave the valley undefended, but you, you need to take things easier. I have three years of campaigning and then I can lift some of the burden from your shoulders."

"It is no burden. You have the burden for it is you who now has to humour King Henry and not me! However, I beg you to be careful. King Henry looks to blame any for the disasters he endures. He got that from his father. At Taillebourg he would have blamed my knights except that their sacrifice was so obvious he could not. This Sir Robert Pounderling, I know not and I implore you to find out about him. If he is Henry's man then that is all to the good. Let him subdue the Welsh. Your place is here!"

We then spoke of the campaign and he and I devised a plan to take the castle. Perhaps it was the wine we had drunk or, more likely, that our minds were as one and the words flowed freely. It was late when we had finished but the bold plan we had concocted might just save many men's lives.

The weather was atrocious as we headed south. There were still patches of snow on the high ground and, with the wagons, it was slow going. I rode with Sir Richard and Sam. The main reason was that I knew the two of them the best and realised that I would need two lieutenants who knew my mind. Sir Peter, Sir Fótr, even Sir Geoffrey had fought in fewer campaigns than I. I also knew that those who had fought at Taillebourg had been damaged by the defeat. Only Sam seemed to have bounced back and I knew that his defence of Elsdon against Ferry de Lorraine and Raymond de Courcy had restored his confidence.

"You have a plan, uncle?"

I nodded, "I spoke at length with my father and I have studied the maps. We need to take the castle and the sooner the better!"

I made it sound easier than it was and Sir Richard shook his head, "Sam here told me how hard it was for the French to take Elsdon. We will lose many men."

"Twthill is made of wood and not stone and who said anything about taking the walls? I plan to use subterfuge. I do not know this Sir Robert Pounderling but the King has asked me to lead this campaign and I will. We will not be going directly to Chester. I intend to approach the Clwyd from the Valley of the Dee and do so in secret. I will send Sir Gerard, the wagons and a token force of men at arms and archers to Chester with the news that the rest of us are on our way to the muster. We are early in any case. I do not doubt that there are spies in the English court and in Chester who will know that we are coming and have informed the Welsh. I intend to secrete our men around the castle of Twthill and use a small number of men to enter the castle and then open the gates."

"They will be watching!"

"Idraf has told me that Twthill has houses in the outer bailey. More than is normal so that, during the day, there is ingress and egress. The gate to the inner bailey is watched more carefully. We have enough Welshmen to have them sneak inside the outer wall and then hide. Until our banners are seen then the Welsh will not be totally vigilant. I intend to take the largest obstacle before they know we are there."

They both nodded, "A bold plan."

"Aye, nephew and neither mine nor my father's. The Greeks did this at Troy."

Sir Richard shook his head, "And yet you ask much of archers. Have you spoken to them?"

I nodded, "I have and they like the plan. It will succeed."

"How can you be so sure, uncle!"

"For I will be with them!"

They both looked shocked and Sir Richard shook his head, "You cannot pass for a Welshman nor an archer; you will be captured."

"Richard, the plan is that the archers will play brigands. They will say that they recognised me as a lord and that I was separated from our army. They captured me but know that they could not ask for ransom. By the time I am captured then you and the rest will have surrounded the castle and any messenger who rides for help will be taken by our men."

"What if they suspect a trick? As far as I can see, Uncle, this only works if our men are free. What if they are imprisoned too?"

I nodded for my father and I had discussed this at length and it was the one risk we could not completely eliminate. "They will see what they wish to see, Twthill does not have a great lord nor a prince. Idraf believes that he is a member of the family who has ruled the Clwyd for the King of Gwynedd since before Wales saw it as one country. The present lord is Iago ap Gruffyd and he is not a young man. My father and I hope that the lure of a good ransom from a rich knight who is favoured by King Henry might well tip the balance. However, on the off chance that I am wrong, I would have the castle assaulted on the morning after my capture unless the gates are opened."

That seemed to mollify the two knights. Sir Richard was methodical, "So, let me get this clear in my mind. We surround the castle but stay hidden." I nodded. "You will be taken into the castle by our men."

"Aye, but it will be towards the end of the afternoon. We need darkness to aid us."

"Then we move closer to the walls and wait?" I nodded. "For what?"

"Idraf and his men will take the sentries at the gate and open it. They will signal three times with a light and you will lead the men inside the outer bailey."

They both nodded and then Henry Samuel saw the one flaw in the whole plan. My father and I knew the flaw but deemed it an acceptable risk. "But you will be in the keep! You will be in the inner bailey."

I smiled, "Aye, I will have an easy time, will I not? For I will not have to fight!" Sam looked shocked. "They will not try to harm me for I am valuable but know this, I will not be giving my word that I will not try to escape. We think they will assume that the words will have been given when I was captured for Idraf will have my sword. The keep will be hard to take but, if I can escape, then I will. That does not change the plan and you will reduce the castle as quickly as you can."

"And you will tell the other knights of this plan?"

Shaking my head, I said, "Not until we have Twthill surrounded and I am about to leave. The Welshmen I am taking I know I can trust. I would like to believe that I can trust all of the others too but there are new men recently hired and we cannot take the risk. The men Idraf leads have all been with us for years and I will not tell either Geoffrey or Dick for they cannot dissemble and I need all to think that we plan a traditional attack on the castle."

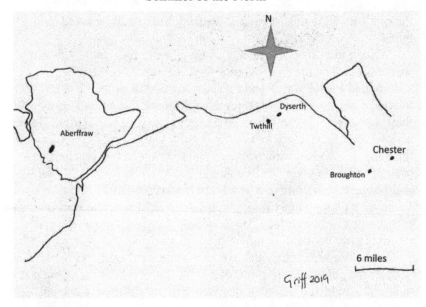

We parted just twenty miles from the head of the Clwyd and Chester. The men we sent to the muster at Chester appeared to be a considerable contingent but it was an illusion. With the exception of the Bishop's archers, Sir Gerard and some of the new men at arms, it was mainly made up of wagons and servants. I told Sir Gerard that we planned to scout out the land to the south and west and would rejoin him at Chester. He had not enjoyed the journey and seemed quite happy to hurry to a castle where he would be more comfortable. We headed south and east, seemingly away from the Clwyd but once we reached the small crossroads at Broughton, we then headed up the Clwyd Valley. This was now Wales. There were no castles nor fortified homes until Twthill and that lay twenty miles along the valley. We moved quickly knowing that we would be seen. We were all mounted and well mounted at that. A signal tower might have sent a message faster than we could travel or a pigeon but little else.

We stopped to water our horses and to enable me to change at the tiny huddle of huts called Rhualt. I gathered my knights around me and told them the plan. As I expected there were objections but I held up my hand. "Sir Richard and Sir Henry know the plan and the signals. When I leave you will all get into position and surround the castle. I have no doubt that men will try to get to the castle and tell them of our passing. You stop any from getting through. Idraf and the others will have the gates open before dawn. Now God be with you and I will see you when the sun rises."

Dick and Geoffrey rushed to my side as I mounted my horse. "My lord, this is foolish, take me!"

"Take me, father! I can be of assistance for I am small and can aid you!"

"It speaks well of you both that you offer to place yourself in such danger, but I am fine. Take care of my shield and helmet. I shall not be needing them."

Idraf and the other five Welshmen approached. They were wearing old and worn clothes. None wore mail and their swords were short swords. Their horses were not the palfreys they normally rode but sumpters and ponies. I handed my sword and baldric to Idraf. "Let us go, Idraf, they will not allow us in after dark."

He nodded and turned to the others, "Remember, this is the last time we speak English until after we have opened the gates!"

I was riding Dragon and that seemed appropriate for the Welsh standard was a dragon. He was a warhorse and they would take good care of him for he was a valuable animal. I did not look back as we headed down the narrow road which, eventually, led to Twthill. Dafydd Green Fletch had my horse on a tether. Rhys and Gareth rode behind me for we were all playing a part. While men might not have followed us and reached the castle ahead of us this close to the wooden walls of Twthill, there might be men in the woods who would spy us. Idraf and the men looked furtive and I adopted a grimace which I would keep until the attack began. We had prepared both my buskins, chausse and Dragon's saddle. I had weapons to hand. If I was searched then they would find them. Idraf would tell them that I had been searched... if they asked!

As we neared the castle, I was able to see that it had not been improved since it had been built more than a century ago. It had been maintained and the ditch kept clear of rubbish but that was all. There were sentries on the walls and at the gate but fewer of them than I had had at Elsdon. When we halted, Idraf began to speak and I understood not a word of what was said. I saw them pointing at me and then the gates were opened and, as the sun began to set over the sea, some three miles to the west, we were taken in. Once in the inner bailey, I saw that they had used every piece of space that they could. The castle's inhabitants had outgrown the walls. I wondered if there were so many inside for they anticipated a spring offensive. King Henry and the men of Cheshire had not been silent about the plans.

Idraf and the others dismounted and Idraf and Rhys led my horse through the haphazardly constructed buildings up the slope towards the wall of the inner bailey. The castle had a mound and a wooden keep. It would not be a large one. I had to duck as Dragon was led through the gate. We were kept waiting while the lord, Iago ap Gruffyd, was summoned. Idraf and Rhys were playing a good part. They never looked at me and they chatted to the sentries. They seemed at ease as would men who hoped to make a small fortune from a chance encounter.

Lord Iago ap Gruffyd appeared and I saw that he was about thirty or so years old. He looked than I was and there were hints of grey about his beard. He had with him a young knight of about twenty. Idraf spoke at length and was questioned by the lord. I saw the young knight studying me and my mail. Eventually, the lord nodded and spoke to Idraf and Rhys, giving them a purse of coins. They handed the reins of my horse to a man at arms and, without another look, left me to head back to the outer bailey.

When the men had gone, Iago ap Gruffyd smiled and spoke in French, rather than English. "Well, Sir William, it seems King Henry's plan to take the Clwyd valley has failed before it has begun. I now have the son of the illustrious Sir Thomas of Stockton and we shall have ransom for you. I pray you dismount. Your fine horse will be cared for and I think will make a good present for my son who is twenty-one on the morrow!" He smiled, "Do not worry, you shall see him again for your chamber this night will be the stables. However, you are in time for food and you can tell me, in detail, of King Henry's plans!"

As I dismounted the gates were slammed shut, I was in and thus far the plan was working. When the sun rose would I still be alive? I followed the lord and his son, with two men at arms close behind me, up the twisting stairs to the wooden keep.

Chapter 16

It was hard to keep the smile from my face. The first part of the plan had been achieved and my men appeared to have been accepted for what they were. When we had crossed the outer bailey, I had counted the sentries and could only see four. There had been four men at the gate and I could not see them keeping that number on the walls all night. If we held the outer bailey then we held the castle. True, I would be a prisoner but I had plans to remedy that situation. This was a small wooden keep and the area where they ate could hardly be called a great hall. The table could barely accommodate ten people. The wife of Iago ap Gruffyd looked to be my age and she also looked fearful for she nervously twisted a napkin in her hands. I bowed and the Welsh knight gestured to a seat. I was seated between him and his son. When we were all in place a priest came and said prayers, they were in Latin and I understood them. We sat and the food was brought in.

As we began to eat the knight spoke in English, "We have known since before the winter solstice that your King planned his attack! We even knew who would be leading it although, I must confess, you have arrived earlier than we expected. Sir Robert Pounderling has yet to reach Chester. You must be keen to impress the King!"

I smiled and ignored his words which were a fishing expedition, "This is good soup."

"You have failed! Even now I have sent a messenger to Aberffraw where the Prince has a large garrison. We will have the walls manned and ready to repulse your men when they arrive. Tell me, Sir William, for I am interested, what made you walk alone in the forest? Surely you knew that there were bandits there? Those outlaws who found you are cutthroats and it is lucky for you they saw your spurs and knew you for a knight. On the morrow I shall send a rider for ransom from your father but why walk alone?"

"It is something I often did when I was at Elsdon. When I walk then my mind becomes clearer and I thought to plan a way to take this castle."

His son laughed, "Then your walk was wasted. I should like to see the faces of your knights when they realise that their leader is taken!"

They tried, for the duration of the meal, to find out what King Henry had planned. I did not answer them but my mind was working out who it could have been who supplied the intelligence they had used. They knew that it was Sir Robert and myself who would be leading but that was all. That confirmed, if confirmation was needed, that it was none of my men. Sir Robert had not been at the meeting and as the King had given me the responsibility of taking the valley then the spy must be in Sir Robert's retinue. It was also obvious that there were men watching Chester. The most useful information was that the enemy would be coming from Aberffraw. That was the royal palace on Anglesey and by the time a rider reached it and the army brought back then at least three days would have passed. I could tell that I had annoyed the lord and his son by their increasing aggression and belligerent tone. They had me but that was all and it became clear that they did not have enough men to garrison the castle against a concerted attack.

Lord Iago ap Gruffyd stood, "Hywel, take Sir William to the stable and guard him closely."

I bowed, "Thank you, Lady Angharad. The meal was delightful."

The mouse of a woman nodded and I was taken out of the hall and back down the steps. The stables were built into the mound and were under the hall, the sleeping chambers and the fighting platform. There were just four horses within and, like Dragon, all were warhorses. Hywel, the man at arms, took me down where another man waited. "His lordship wants him watching. If he tries to move then restrain him." I noticed that he spoke English and wondered why.

The man at arms, I never did discover his name, was short and very broad. He looked to me to have the arms of an archer but when he spoke, I knew that he was English and that meant he was the stable hand and not an archer. His face showed where he had suffered from the pox. He nodded, "This means an extra coin, Captain."

Hywel shrugged, "Take that up with his lordship. I have been given my orders."

"But it is not fair if I have to lose sleep watching this Norman! I should have a reward."

"I am done!"

Sometimes you get an idea and you know not where it is from. This was a powerful man and I needed an edge. After stroking Dragon, I went to make a bed of straw and then I knelt. I made certain that I was facing my unhappy guard. I took out the silver cross which my mother had given to me when I became a knight. I kissed it and began to pray aloud. I saw that he had spied the silver cross and calculated that he would try to take it. When I had done with my prayers I stood. "Goodnight, friend."

"Just keep still and you might live until morning." As if to emphasise his point he took a wicked-looking dagger from his belt. I will get nothing from your ransom. You only live if I am undisturbed." He pointed to a lantern hung from the ceiling, "I will keep the light burning and I will see if you move."

I nodded and knew that to be a lie. I lay down in a foetal ball with my back to him. The position made it look as though I was afraid. The reality was that I wanted to reach the bodkin dagger I had in my buskins. I slipped it into the sleeve of my hauberk. I began to breathe regularly so that he would think I was asleep. I heard the horses moving around. There was a strange one in the stable and none of them was settled. When my erstwhile guard said nothing, I knew that he was planning some mischief. He would take the cross from my neck and if I fought then he would use the knife to end my life and claim I tried to escape. The cross was worth a year's wages to a stable hand.

The man was quiet but he could not disguise his smell. He had not bathed this year and when the smell grew stronger, I slipped my dagger into my right hand. My left arm was free and I had laid it out on the straw. When he came, he pounced like a cat with a mouse. He had his dagger in his right hand and I felt it rasp across my mail. I reached up and grabbed his wrist before pulling him all the way over. Had he not been so violent I could not have done this but I used his own weight and momentum to throw him. I was astride him in an instant and my bodkin dagger held close to his eye.

"Well, my pungent friend, your attempt to steal the cross has gone ill with you! Drop the seax or you lose an eye and then your life." He snarled and I said, reasonably, "This is a bodkin dagger. It will not catch on the bone but slide into your orb and then slip gently into what passes for your brain. Drop the dagger!"

I heard it drop. Keeping my dagger close to him I stood and used my left hand to pull him to his feet. I could see the perspiration on his worried brow.

"That is right, you have need to be worried. Now on your knees."

"I beg you, do not kill me. I am just a stable hand!"

"On your knees."

I heard him begin to mumble a prayer and I stepped behind him, moving my dagger in a threatening arc. I had spied a piece of timber on the ground and I reached for it with my left hand. While he still prayed, I smacked him hard, rendering him unconscious. He fell in a heap. I felt his neck and he was still alive and so I sheathed my dagger and found some harness with which to bind him. I used a piece of cloth to gag him and then looked for another weapon for I had his dagger in my belt. There was a spear propped against the wall and I took it. I stroked Dragon and then, after donning my dark cloak, made my way to the door. This would be the hard part for when the door opened there would be a shaft of light. I found the guard's cloak and hung it between the door and the light. It would not hide the light completely but it would make it a barely discernible glow. Opening the door just wide enough for me to slip through, I left the stable. Moving around the mound and keeping to the shadows I moved slowly so that I could see the main gate to the outer bailey.

All was quiet and I allowed my eyes the time to become accustomed to the dark. I was rewarded by a movement over the gate. I studied the movement and saw that it was two sentries. After a short while, they moved off in opposite directions. I took my chance when they passed the keep and ran to the gate. I now knew that there were just two sentries and that meant the hall contained the lord, his son, his family and his servants. If there were guards, they would be on top of the keep. I looked, belatedly, at the top of the keep. There were no movements. In Stockton, my father, even in times of peace would always keep men in the highest of our towers. I looked at the bar across the gate. It was heavy and I wondered if I dared risk moving it. I stared towards the far side of the inner bailey and I did not see the movement of the two sentries. They would probably stop and talk. I laid down my spear and took the two sides of the bar. Although heavy I was able to shift it a little. I bent my legs and then stood, using the strength of my legs as well as my arms to raise the bar. I managed to lift it clear but then I had to carry it to lay it down. My muscles were burning with the exertion and I had to lower it slowly despite the fact that I wished to drop it! I placed it on the ground and then I heard a cry. It came not from the inner bailey but from the outer bailey. Either my men had been discovered or our attack had begun.

Picking up my spear I moved myself into the shadows under the fighting platform. I heard the shouts from the sentries and then from within the keep followed by their feet as the two of them ran along the fighting platform to the gate. Suddenly there was a piercing scream and then a shout. I heard the roar of men and knew that my knights, men at arms and archers had begun their attack. A light flared from the keep as the door was opened and I heard Lord Iago ap Gruffyd shout something. I recognised Hywel as he raced down to the stable. Then there were footsteps rushing down the two ladders as the sentries came to open the gates for the garrison who were racing to get into the inner bailey to defend its walls.

One was faster than the other and as he ran towards me, I lunged with the spear. He was taken by surprise and fell to the ground clutching the spear. The other sentry saw me and shouted. He had a spear ready and ran at me. I tugged my spear from the dying man's fingers and whirled

170

it to clash into the Welshman's spear. I heard a roar and knew that Hywel had discovered that I had escaped. The flaw in my plan now became obvious. I had to guard the gate and stop the garrison from getting into the keep. I would have to fight the sentry, then Hywel and finally Iago ap Gruffyd and his son. As my father had taught me, you fight one enemy at a time.

I whipped the spearhead back across the sentry's face. He had been trained how to use a spear but not how to fight and win with one. I heard Hywel's boots as he ran across the inner bailey to get at me. I stamped on the ground as I lunged forward and the parry from the Welsh sentry was poorly executed; my spear tore across his hand and he dropped his spear I swung the spear so that the shaft smacked him in the side of the head and he fell as I whirled with the spear point aimed at the chest of the Captain of Iago ap Gruffyd's guards.

"I should have tied you up!"

The man had a sword but no shield. Behind me, I could hear the sounds of battle as my men fought their way through the buildings and warriors. Some of the Welsh would be trying to stem the tide of attackers whilst others would be racing to the safety of the inner bailey. I rammed the spear at his face and he slashed at me with his sword in an attempt to render my weapon useless. The fact that he missed gave me the measure of his skill. I was holding the spear in two hands which meant I could achieve greater power than a one-handed grip. I feinted at his face and he swashed once more. As he did so I turned the spear to jab at his leg. He brought his sword down and it hacked into the wood. When I pulled the bloodied spearhead from the wound, I knew that my spear could only take one more blow.

Suddenly the door behind me burst open as the Welsh who had fled my men raced in. I took my chance and rammed my spear at his other leg. I struck the thigh and my spearhead grated off a bone but in doing so I broke my only weapon. Wounded and bleeding badly he lunged at me. All around me was a sea of Welsh and English warriors fighting. Mine would have the upper hand for they were more numerous and were armoured but the Welsh were fighting hard. Fate intervened and I tripped over the leg of one of the sentries I had disabled. Captain Hywel brought his sword over his head as he attempted to end my life. Henry Samuel's sword hacked across the arm of the Captain, severing it below the elbow. Blood spurted and I knew, as he began to sink to the ground, that he was a dead man.

My nephew held out his arm and I pulled myself up, "Your job was just to get captured! We did not expect to find you fighting for your life!"

I nodded and picked up the dying Captain's sword, "Follow me, we can take the keep!"

Henry Samuel shouted, "Yarum, on me!"

He had led his own men and now they cleared a space to rush after us across the inner bailey. I had to lead for I knew the layout of the keep. I saw a dead Welshman with an axe in his hand. An arrow protruded from his back. One of my archers had hit him, "Grab the axe!"

I did not look to see if I was obeyed but, dropping my cloak I ran. A bolt flew from the top of the keep but it was in the dark and we were moving quickly. If any of us were hit then it would be pure luck. Once we reached the staircase, we were safe and I hurried up to the door. As I had expected, it was locked and was, I had no doubt barred, but I had seen the door from the inside and knew that the bar was a piece of wood as wide as a hand, as long as an arm and as thick as two fingers. One of Sam's men had the axe and I said, "Break it down!"

We stepped away to allow him the space to swing and I looked at the inner bailey. The fighting was dying out, but crossbow bolts and arrows still descended and even as I watched one of Sir Geoffrey's men at arms fell with an arrow in his leg. Iago ap Gruffyd had sent for help and he would have to hope that he could hold out. If he had not had women inside the keep then I would have threatened him with fire. I could not do that! Soon we would have the castle and I would send for Sir Robert Pounderling.

The axe began to tear splinters from the wooden door. The castle had been maintained but this was a one-hundred-year-old door and it soon began to show its age. The door gave way and, as we burst inside, I pointed to the right. There are stairs there."

Sam put his hand out, "And I will lead!" He had his shield and he held it before him. The wooden stair was for access and not defence. I knew that the defenders and the occupants would all be on the top floor of the fighting platform. We passed the sleeping quarters and came to the ladder. My nephew made to climb but I restrained him, "Iago ap Gruffyd, Lord of Twthill. You have no escape. Save further loss of life and surrender!"

A voice, I think it was his son's, shouted, "Never! Treacherous knight!"

Henry Samuel shook his head, "Whoever that is they are foolish!"

Holding his shield above him and his sword in his right hand he ran up to hit the trapdoor. I was right behind him and as his feet landed on the fighting platform, I pulled myself up. The son of the lord was not a good knight and he had attacked prematurely. Sam blocked the blow easily. I ran at the man at arms who tried to go to the aid of the young lord. His attempt was half-hearted. I saw that Iago ap Gruffyd was defending his wife and the women. The Welshman who tried to hack at Sam had a shorter sword than mine and a poorer one. My sword hit it so hard that it buckled and bent. As it dropped to the ground, I hit him on the side of my head with my mailed fist. He went down like a bushel of apples.

Henry Samuel's sword cracked against the blade of the young Welshman. I saw the look of horror on the young man's face. He was fighting a real warrior. I shouted, "Iago ap Gruffyd, drop your weapon and tell your son to do so too!"

Iago's sword fell to the floor but he remained silent. The two men prevented us from getting to the far side where four crossbowmen and archers were sending missiles to the inner bailey. I saw Henry Samuel swing his sword a second time and this time he not only hit the young knight's blade he also hit his mail and a piece of the hauberk fell to the ground.

"You men with the bows and crossbows, drop them or I will have you blinded!" That was a threat worth heeding and they obeyed.

The young knight panicked and he tried to split open Sam's head. My nephew's training took over and blocking the blow he scythed his sword across the Welsh knight's middle. I do not think that Sam meant to kill him but he had been well trained and every part of his arm and body went into the blow. The sword's edge was sharp and tore through the mail. It ripped through his padded aketon and opened his flesh. The Lady Angharad screamed as guts, intestines, blood and entrails poured forth. He looked at it as though he could not believe and then, sinking to his knees, he bled his life away. His mother ran to his side and I walked over to Iago ap Gruffyd, "This is down to you! You could have stopped it!"

He knew I was right but he was angry and he snapped, "And you broke your word! You said you would not attempt an escape! You have no honour!"

I walked up to him and put my face close to his, "I never gave my word and you never asked for it. You assumed because I had no sword that I had surrendered. Did my men say I had given my word?" I saw him wracking his memory to dredge up the conversation. He realised that I was speaking the truth and he, too, sank to his knees and put his arm around his wife.

Sir Peter had joined us, "Sir Peter, secure the castle and have the wounded tended to. Brother John has some work this day."

"Aye, Will and your plan worked. I did not think it would but I was proved wrong. The right man was chosen to lead this expedition."

When he descended, I said to Henry Samuel, "I will leave you to clear up here. You did no wrong. The boy should not have fought you but he was a knight and ill-prepared."

I threw Hywel's sword to one side and went down to the hall. There I found my own sword and baldric. I strapped them on. Dawn was just breaking when I left the hall and my men saw me. They cheered and I raised my hand in acknowledgement. Idraf and my co-conspirators joined me, "Well done! The plan worked!"

"Aye, lord but these men fought so poorly that it made me ashamed to be a Welshman. We lost but a handful of men wounded."

"You can only defeat the enemies you face. I think the next battle will be more of a test."

I waved over Sir Gilles, "Take two men and ride to Chester. You can return with our men and leave a message for Sir Robert to join us here. We have a piece of Wales here but an army is coming from Anglesey."

"I will. Well, done Will, your father would be proud and he must have had great confidence in you for he risked his son's life."

Shaking my head, I said, "No, I was never at risk of losing my life, just money if a ransom had had to be paid. That was the risk and what is money compared to a man's life? We took the castle and we did not lose many men."

As he ran to get his men and his horses, Geoffrey and Dick rode in with the rest of the squires, "You survived, my lord!"

I laughed, "Geoffrey, that sounds like you expected me to perish!"

"No, my lord, but the task seemed to me to be impossible."

"It was not. Now fetch Dragon from the stable and release the man who is there. He was my gaoler but he was ill-suited for the job!"

Chapter 17

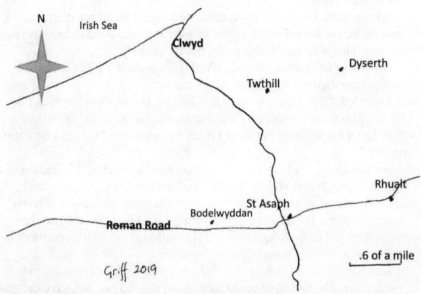

We buried the dead in the small cemetery attached to the castle. I sent Iago ap Gruffyd, his wife, servants and men under guard, back to Chester. I knew not if there would be ransom but I wanted them out of the way. I could have been mean-spirited and made them walk but I let them take all their belongings. The lady had lost enough as it was. Sir Iago looked like a shell of a man for he was broken; his world had ended when I had entered his castle. While we settled in to the castle I sent Sir Richard, Sir Fótr and Sir Mark to the coast to ride towards the straits which separated the mainland from Anglesey. If an army was coming, they would need boats to cross as there was no bridge. I told them not to dispute the passage with the Welsh but to let Sir Robert and I know when they were approaching us. If Sir Robert did not arrive then I would defend the castle against the Welsh. I did not want to for I had seen, already, its weaknesses.

While we waited, I found out how our men had behaved during the most unusual night attack. Even Sir Geoffrey was impressed that such a subtle strategy had worked. While our men began to clear the buildings in the lower bailey after we had sent all the people who lived there away, I rode with just the knights, squires and pages towards the coast. I had not had word yet from Chester but I assumed that Sir Robert was on his way or would be soon. Until we knew the exact numbers of the enemy, we could not begin to plan how to defeat them. I had already done half of the first task set to me by King Henry. I had taken Twthill but all of that would be for nothing if we were defeated in battle and the castle was retaken.

As we rode, I spoke to my remaining knights about the dilemma, "I am tempted to burn Twthill to the ground and throw the debris into the ditches. That way the Welsh could not reoccupy it."

Sir Henry of Wulfestun said, "And if Sir Robert wishes to build a castle there then we have done him a favour."

I nodded, "But I do not know this knight. He may not see it as I do. He might not see the need to build in stone. The King has promised him the Clwyd for his own but until I meet the man then I do not know my course."

Sir Geoffrey, my brother-in-law, was an older knight. He had fought alongside my father and me on the border and he was a methodical man. "It seems to me that, until we meet the man, we leave the walls where they are. If this army is too strong for us then we can use the walls until Sir Robert does arrive." He smiled at me. "But you think he will be here soon and seek a good battlefield!"

I laughed, "There you have it. I do not wish to fight from behind Twthill's walls. We have something the Welsh do not, we have knights and men at arms. We can also counter their most serious weapon, the war bow. I am looking for a place where we can use both to our advantage and not the Welsh."

We had forded the river and I looked up and downstream. I pointed to the tiny hamlet of Rhyl which lay at the mouth of the river. "Between here and the sea the river cannot be forded. It is why this was chosen as the site for a castle. It defends the river." I pointed upstream, "In that direction lies St Asaph. We know that St Kentigern is revered by the Welsh and that is seen as a holy place. There is also a bridge across the river."

Sir Peter, whose castle at Whorlton lay in a similar country, pointed to a tiny knoll to the southwest of us. "If we ride there then we can spy out the land. It all looks flat from here but I know that can be deceptive."

We headed towards the wood-covered knoll. When we reached it, I saw just six hundred paces from us, the old Roman Road which led from St Asaph towards Anglesey. There was a road which ran along the coast but the Welsh would not use it. It stopped at the mouth of the river. They would advance up the stone road built a thousand years ago. I dismounted and walked to the edge of the knoll. We had not seen the road because of the knoll and the trees. There were farms but they farmed livestock and trees had been left in the fields to provide shelter for animals in winter. Anglesey was the place to grow cereals.

I waved my knights to join me. "The Welsh do not know us. The men of the Tees Valley have not campaigned here in numbers. They will expect Norman knights. This knoll seems to me to be a perfect place to hide our archers. We can array our knights and men at arms to deny the Welsh the road to St Asaph. We either attack them, if we are superior in numbers or, if not, then we draw them on to our archers here on this knoll."

We rode down to the road and saw that the ground was perfect for horsemen. Although it undulated there were no serious holes to trip an unwary horse. We would be able to hold our formation. We headed back to Twthill. The smoke from the buildings we had destroyed told me that Alan Longsword and our men at arms had done what I had asked and burned the buildings from the outer bailey so that we had more room for our men. If we were forced to defend the castle then we would not be encumbered by buildings and we could now camp the whole of our army in what had been the outer bailey.

Sir Robert arrived that evening. He led thirty knights along with a hundred and fifty men at arms and forty archers. The archers were fewer in number than I might have hoped but they were Cheshire archers and they were good. We had to get to know one another quickly and so I led him into the hall of Twthill.

I confess that I liked Sir Robert straight away for he had humour. The orb he had recently lost was covered with a black eye patch and, as we climbed the stairs to the hall he said, "I see you have noticed my little wound! Damned Welshman who took it had the audacity to ask for a second bout! I told him that he had had one and I intended to keep the other. I have now done with tournaments!"

We entered the hall and I nodded to Geoffrey to fetch wine, ale and food. "There is food aplenty, Sir Robert, for they had laid in stores in anticipation of our attack."

He nodded, "Sir Gilles told me that you suspected a spy in my household." I nodded and he shrugged, "There may well be. I am not as lucky as you, Sir William, I have not campaigned with my men and come to know them. But forewarned is forearmed. I may look foolish but I am not. I have good men and I will find this spy. If any try to leave they will be followed."

Geoffrey served the wine and food, "Now see that we are not disturbed."

We toasted each other and Sir Robert said, "You have done that which was asked of you, Sir William, you could, with head held high, return home to your valley."

"I could but I promised the King three months and that I would make this valley ours. I have two more such campaigns to undertake and if I left early then all the good work we have done could be undone. You are to build a castle here and rule. I would not leave you in jeopardy."

He smiled, "I heard that you were an honourable man and I can see that it is so. What is your plan? Tell me yours and I shall tell you mine!"

I liked his openness, "My men watch for the Welsh. I have found a place where we can stop them just a few miles away. That is my priority. Lord Iago told me that he had sent to Aberffraw for reinforcements and so when this Welsh army is defeated then you can build your castle while I secure the land between here and the straits."

"You are confident then?"

"If we use our men to the best advantage then unless they have an army in the thousands then I think that we can prevail."

"Good, then I will place my men under your command. I have not been idle. I was late to the muster for I went in disguise to scout out the lands along the coast. The King wants a castle here and I thought to see what other sites were available. I found one on the coast at a place called Fflint but I realised it is too remote. I had not seen this one until today but I did see it at Dyserth, a good site which is both high and defensible. More importantly, it has rocks close by. At the moment I am torn between rebuilding this one in stone and building a new one at Dyserth. What do you think?"

I liked his thinking and I was impressed that he had taken the time to scout the land. It is what my father would have done. "If you were to build here then you would have to destroy what was already here. If this Dyserth is a place you can defend then I would burn this to the ground and then use Dyserth but it is further from the river, is it not?"

"But it is on the road from Twthill to Chester. Had you not ridden at night to make your attack then you would have seen it." He laughed and took a long drink of his wine, "By the way, that was a bold move. I thought that I was as mad as a fish, for that is what men say of me, but I can see that I have competition from you."

"Then if you are settled, we shall do that. We will begin to destroy the castle tomorrow for the Welsh cannot be far away and the pall of smoke rising from Twthill might hasten their arrival."

"Then let us enjoy a good feast here this night!"

We set the men to cook the food which had been left by the Welsh and we were almost done when a rider sent by Sir Richard and my scouts arrived. It was Roger Long Leg. He was brought into the hall and dropped to a knee. "My lord, Sir Richard sent me. The Welsh are camped on the other side of the River Conwy. By tomorrow they will be here. Sir Richard keeps his men a mile ahead of the Welsh and we have eliminated some of his scouts."

Sir Richard had not obeyed my orders but I understood why he had not done so. "They are following the Roman Road?"

"Aye, my lord."

"Go to the camp and get yourself some food. Send Idraf to me."

He hurried off and Sir Robert said, "So we fight tomorrow?"

"Perhaps. It is almost a day's ride to the Conwy. We may be able to attack them when they camp. However, I will send for Sir Richard and his men as we shall need every warrior we can muster. I wish to leave an hour before dawn. We will fire the castle before we go."

He stood for most of the knights in the hall were his, "Finish what is before you and then warn the men that we leave before dawn, tomorrow we test our mettle against that of the Welsh."

Idraf arrived, "I want you to ride to Sir Richard. Bring his men to the hill close to Bodelwyddan. You know where it is?"

"Aye lord."

"Discover from Roger Long Leg where they are camped. Take two men with you."

"Aye, lord!"

It was only as he left and Sir Robert and his knights departed that I realised I had not yet spoken with Sir Gerard. I spied him, alone, as the rest left and I waved him over. "Sir Gerard, it was remiss of me not to welcome you and thank you for bringing the rest of my men."

He shook his head, "Do not try to deceive me, lord, I know that you sent me there for you did not trust me."

"That is not true, Sir Gerard, although it is true that I know you the least of all of the knights that I lead. If anything, I was deceiving the spies who watched Chester for I wished to approach Twthill unseen. Now you are here and tomorrow you will have the chance to fight."

He nodded, "I have learned much on the road and while I was in Chester. I do not yet know what kind of knight I shall be. I now see that before I was sent to Hartlepool, I was a callow and untrained boy. I may still be and tomorrow will test me."

I shook my head, "You have still a long way to go. Tomorrow will be hard but I wish you to survive."

"I will try, my lord, but if I may be honest, I am fearful that I will be found to be wanting."

"And that is what all of us feel before we go to battle. Tonight, find Brother John and confess. It is always easier going into battle knowing that your soul is cleansed."

"Aye, Sir William, and I will try not to let you down."

I had much to do and I sought Geoffrey and Dick to tell them what was needed. Dick was now almost an old hand. Geoffrey had taught him well. He was a child but he knew his way around the camp and the castle. The two of them happily went to do my bidding. I would sleep in the lord's chamber for one last time. Before I retired for what I knew would be but a couple of hours of sleep, I went to the camp to speak to my men. It was as I approached the main gate when I heard an altercation. Drawing my sword, I ran towards the sound.

I found Sir Robert with four of his knights. On the floor lay a man at arms. Sir Robert had his sword at his throat. "Well, Sir William, I have discovered my traitor. This man, Edgar of Crewe, is the one who betrayed our plans to the Welsh."

The man protested, "My lord, you do me wrong. I am loyal."

"Then why were you leaving? What made you decide to depart? Was it that I had just told all of my men that we were going to fight the Welsh tomorrow?"

"No, lord, I just needed to make water."

Sir Robert laughed, "And for that, you needed a horse?" The man was silent. Sir Robert turned to his captain, "Captain Richard, you know Edgar better than any. Sir William here says that the Welsh knew I was coming. One of my men had to have told the Welsh so if it was not Edgar who do you think it was?"

"It is Edgar, my lord, for suddenly many things make sense. When we were told, before Christmas, that we would be coming here he begged leave to visit his mother in Crewe. When he returned, it was with a full purse. He told us that he had made the money gambling in his home town."

Sir Robert nodded, "No one else leaves this castle before we all leave. If you wish to make water or empty your bowels then do so inside the walls. Is that clear?"

The whole camp, it seemed, had been listening and they all shouted, "Aye, lord!" No one would have any sympathy for a traitor who had taken money to betray them.

"Captain Richard, have his shield brothers take him to the priest to confess and then hang him from the gate!"

"No, my lord!" The man's crimes had been discovered and he would die. Suddenly the coins he had been paid did not seem enough.

The six men with whom Edgar shared a camp dragged him, kicking and screaming to the priest Sir Robert had brought with him. "Thank you, Sir William, had you not warned me I might not have been as vigilant. Captain Richard here suspected Edgar once I told him your news. We had him watched and I had men at the gate. I think that we may well achieve surprise when the Welsh do finally arrive!"

I had just an hour of sleep. We moved all of the horses and wagons across the river having taken some of the timbers from the outer wall to make a crude bridge while we prepared the castle for firing. The body of the traitor swung in the gateway but once the castle was fired it would disappear. We lit the fire in the keep first and then the men put brands to the walls. The timbers were old and dry. They would burn well. As we gathered on the western side of the river, we watched the sky lit by flames. We were too far from the Conwy for it to be seen but as dawn broke, they might spy the tendril of smoke which would mark the end of Twthill Castle. We left the wagons at the river and they would be guarded by the servants and wagon drivers. I led the way as we headed the few miles to the knoll.

Sir Richard was there already and most of the men and knights he had taken were snatching sleep. He looked dirty and unshaven. They had been living rough. He gave me a wan smile, "I shall be glad to get back to Hartburn after this, Sir William." He turned in his saddle and pointed south, "I was not certain that any would be coming for we saw no signs of them. I am afraid we were forced to slay their first scouts for they did not come down the road as we expected and they surprised us. One spoke before he died and we learned that Prince Dafydd ap Llewellyn leads the army. Once we knew that they were scouts I sent archers to watch closer to the island. They are moving more slowly than we anticipated for they are largely on foot. We counted just eighty mounted men and most are knights. They have twenty or so scouts, and hobelars while the rest are men on foot. They have two hundred archers and five hundred men on foot."

I heard one of Sir Robert's men take a deep breath and I smiled, "Tell me Sir Richard, how many of the men on foot are mailed?"

"Less than a hundred."

"You have done well." I turned to my knights and Sir Robert. "We place the archers here on the hill and dismount the men at arms. We place their horses behind the hill so that they are not seen and then put our knights in two wings on either side of the dismounted men at arms. We will hold them a little back from the men at arms to tempt the Welsh forward. I will lead my knights and you, yours, Sir Robert. We place our banners with our squires on the knoll but above the men at arms. I want them to come for our standards."

"Then we fight a defensive battle?"

It was a simple question and I nodded, "If they do not attack us then we shall attack them but they are largely foot. They have to shift us, regardless of our strength. If they see us and turn to flee then we will slaughter them."

Satisfied, he said, "Sir Baldwin, go and give the orders."

I gathered the squires around me, "Today, you will pretend to be the knights which, one day, you will become. You will ride your master's spare warhorse and carry his banner. I want them to think that we have a reserve of knights mounted behind the men at arms. Pages, you will play at knights too. You will carry banners."

The way that they cheered me you would have thought I had honoured them in some way. They were the bait to try to draw the Welsh through our men at arms and up the hill.

It was late in the afternoon when the Welsh arrived and when they saw us on the knoll they halted. I recognised the royal banner and knew that Prince Dafydd was with them. Their levy, the men on foot immediately formed into a huge block in case we attacked them. They were a hedgehog of spears, pikes and homemade pole weapons. The nobles gathered around the standard and their leader, the Prince. I mounted my horse and headed down to my men. I had taken Tom of Rydal from my men at arms and he would sound the horn when it was needed. If we had to charge then he would charge as a knight. I joined my knights and I could tell that they were eager. They had fought together many times and Taillebourg was forgotten for here it was not a king who led them but a knight of the valley and a descendant of the Warlord. It was a great responsibility which rested upon my shoulders. The exception was Sir Gerard. He had no squire with him and was an outsider. I rode next to him. "Sir Gerard, come and ride on my right!"

"But that is the place of honour! You need a good knight to protect that side!"

I laughed to put him at his ease, "And all of these have already ridden to my right. Sir Richard will guard your right and we shall see how you do. You fight with the finest of knights and I am certain that you will rise to the occasion."

His voice dropped, "Lord, I have never fought in a battle!"

I nodded, "I know. Then this will be interesting for you, eh? Just remember all that my men taught you. Stay close and all will be well."

Then I put the novice knight from my thoughts for I wanted to view the Welsh. If they did not attack but made a camp then I would attack them. They would be tired and we had had time to scout out the land. I had set a problem for the Welsh Prince. Neither option was one he would have chosen when he left Anglesey but he had superior numbers and if he declined a fight then many men would desert and a man who deserted would be reluctant to fight a second time.

It soon became obvious that they would attack for horns sounded. Their priests arrayed themselves before the lines of men who formed for battle. I had my helmet on my cantle and I stood in my stirrups to afford a better view. The Prince was going to use the battering ram of his levy to try to break my men at arms. Their archers were forming up before the levy and they would rain arrows on my men at arms. Every horseman that they had was facing me and my handful of knights.

Turning in my saddle I waved over one of the mounted servants we had brought. "Ride to Sir Robert. When their archers form up, he is to attack them with his knights and then withdraw."

"Aye lord." I doubted that the messenger understood how I had known what the enemy would do but I had been fighting wars and battles for a long time. Some things were so clear to me that I often wondered how other men could miss them. I watched the rider head to Sir Robert knowing that we had time to prepare for their attack. This would be an attack on foot and they would take time to approach close enough to fight. Alan Longsword and our men at arms would know what was coming. They would hold up their shields and endure the arrow storm. They were all mailed and most of the Welsh arrows would be wasted. My archers would await the arrival of the Welsh levy. Our arrows would strike flesh for most of those approaching had no mail.

Once the priests had finished then the horns sounded and the archers moved forward. They scuttled and ran. To their front, there were no archers but that did not detract from the worry. Their very movement, however, created a weakness for they had no cohesion. They halted two hundred and fifty paces from my men at arms and that meant that they were just four hundred paces from Sir Robert and his knights. Every knight rode a warhorse and they could cover that four hundred paces in a very short time.

My messenger returned and nodded, "He will do as you command, my lord!" His reply told me that the outcome of that battle rested squarely on my shoulders. If things went awry then I would be to blame.

I saw the Welsh archers stop. Once again, they showed their lack of discipline. Had it been English archers then one would have commanded them. They began to release their arrows. They were strong men and good archers but that first shower, which should have been delivered as one black cloud of metal tipped death fell haphazardly. Some were short and some were long. My men at arms were able to track the flights of individual arrows and to block them with their shields. Of course, some arrows managed to get through and men at arms were hit but none were killing blows.

The archers had run towards our men but the levy marched. They were led by their own leaders, the headmen of the villages and towns from whence they had come. Their ranks were interspersed with men at arms. These were not professionals such as we employed. These were the richer men from the towns and villages; the ones who could afford a hauberk, helmet and good sword. These did stay together for they saw our two wings of horsemen. Once they were engaged then they would be happier and more confident.

Sir Robert was a tournament knight. One of his strengths was the judgement of pace and he chose his moment to charge perfectly. He gave no warning to the Welsh archers; he sounded no horn and he launched his warhorse and his men with a wave of his lance. He did not need to hit the line as one for the archers had, obligingly, spread themselves out to give them the space to pull back their bows. The thunder of the hooves of the knights alerted the Welsh and those on the left side of the Welsh line turned to send their arrows at the charging knights. Many of the leading horsemen had a caparison for their mounts. The thick material did not stop an arrow from penetrating but it slowed and sometimes diverted the arrowhead. They were some protection for the horses. The mailed knights shrugged off the arrows which hit metal, mail and strengthened leather. The Welsh had few bodkin arrows and the war arrows would struggle to penetrate mail and would do no harm to a helmet. By the time that the bulk of the Welsh knew they were in danger, the first archers had died. An archer wears no mail and his bow without an arrow is a stick! The lances and spears of the knights found flesh with each strike and Sir Robert and his men had almost reached us by the time that the survivors had fled. I saw him raise his visor and even caught his words as he shouted, "Reform!" He raised his lance in salute and wheeled his horse to ride back to his starting position.

When he had attacked the levy had halted, closed ranks and presented a hedgehog of spears and pole weapons. When the knights retired then they continued their march. The sun would set in an hour or so and if it did then this would be a most interesting battle for, in the darkness, it was hard to tell friend from foe. I knew that my archers would each have an arrow nocked but their bows would not be drawn. Their elevated position gave them extra range. More than half of them would be hidden by the mass of men at arms. Idraf commanded them and I heard his voice as he commanded, "Draw!"

I was close enough to them to hear the creak of yew as my powerful archers pulled the bows back prior to release.

"Loose!"

The arrows seemed to whistle like the wind and rose high in the late afternoon sky. This was not the haphazard attack of the Welsh; this was ordered and disciplined. I heard the second flight as I watched the first descend to strike the Welsh levy when they were just fifty paces from the men at arms. The Welsh knew the effect of arrows and they raised their shields. Even so, men fell for their shields were small round ones. Some were struck by arrows which were deflected by missiles which ricocheted from the shields and helmets of their comrades. However, the fact that some fell encouraged the rest to charge, somewhat prematurely. They knew that the archers would have to stop once they were engaged and they saw that they outnumbered our thin lines of men at arms. I saw, at the forefront of the men at arms, my men. The Viking stood head and shoulders above the rest and I saw that he was flanked by Alan Longsword and Kurt the Swabian. Any Welshman who manage to pass those three would be a worthy warrior!

It was at that moment that their prince committed himself to his attack and that meant he was trying to destroy me and my handful of knights. I heard the Welsh horn and, as he raised his own lance, I shouted, "Tom of Rydal, sound the charge!"

I heard Sir Robert's horn and knew that his men would charge the flanks of the levy and dismounted men at arms. All we had to do was to blunt the Welsh horsemen and Sir Robert would have the victory as he fell amongst the Welsh, like wolves in a sheepfold.

Sir Peter, next to me, laughed, "Here is a jest! Less than twelve men charge one hundred! There will be plenty for us all!"

My other knights cheered. I knew that Sir Gerard would be fearful but this was not a reckless gamble. The Welsh Prince had put his hobelars with his knights and that was a mistake. They could ride faster than the knights and they would be the ones we would strike first. Our smaller numbers meant that we could ride boot to boot and hit them like a war hammer. I spurred Lion and we began to canter. Looking down the line I saw that Sir Gerard was not yet in control of either himself or his horse and I said, "Steady!"

The hobelars rode smaller horses than ours and they were armed with a couple of throwing javelins. A well-thrown javelin could penetrate mail but to throw a javelin well from the back of a galloping horse was not an easy thing to do. We closed rapidly but while the Welsh were at full speed we were still accelerating. I was at the centre of our arrow and so the first horsemen came at me. To be fair that meant hitting the men who rode with me at the same time. The young Welsh warrior who charged at me had just a leather cap and jerkin for protection but he was brave. He pulled his arm back and hurled his first javelin at me and then tried to wheel away. He miscalculated. I watched a javelin come at me and flicked up my shield. There was no one behind me and the javelin which struck my shield and bounced landed on the ground. I pulled my arm back to spear the young warrior but his horse had slipped when he wheeled too quickly and he tumbled from its back. I managed to pull on the reins to make Lion jump while the other hobelars jerked their horses to the side to avoid crushing their comrade. Some managed to hurl their javelins but five others joined the Welsh warrior whose head was crushed by Lion's hoof as he landed. Thanks to the jump I was slightly ahead of the others and I reined in to allow Sir Peter and Sir Gerard to rejoin me.

The hobelars had been broken and now we faced the knights. These were more organised and ordered but some had urged their steeds forward. Here, our small line was an advantage for some of the Welsh were cutting in front of others to try to get at us. In doing so they baulked and blocked others. That, in turn, slowed down and congested their attack. Now that we were in one line again, I spurred Lion and he leapt forward. I had short spurs and I would be able to stand in my stirrups. If the Welsh followed the French fashion then they would have longer spurs, which were easier to use, but meant you could not stand in the stirrups. I had hoped to face the Prince but I saw that thanks to the disorder of the Welsh, I would not. He would face Sir Henry of Wulfestun. Sam was next to the young knight and would watch out for his friend. I faced a knight with a spear and a yellow shield with a blue diagonal line. The lack of a dragon told me that he was not related to the royal family.

I was twenty paces away when I stood in my stirrups and pulled back my right arm. I would be striking at his right side. Sir Peter would have to protect my shield side from the other Welshman who was riding at me. I would be striking down and the Welsh knight striking upwards. We both lunged at the same time. Our spears passed in the air and I drove mine down towards his middle. It struck the wood of the cantle and was driven into his stomach. His spear came towards my eyehole; it was a well-judged blow. I had good straps on my helmet but if my spear had not eviscerated him then it would have been torn from my head. As it was the spear fell from his dying arm and I allowed my spear to slip, covered in gore, from his body. I saw that Sir Gerard was still close by and that his spear was bloody.

I had no time for self-congratulation for the battle was at a crucial stage. I needed to break through the Welsh knights and halt their charge. I could not see Sir Robert Pounderling but I knew that he must have torn deep into the levy and that with our archers and men at arms on two sides of the Welshmen then victory would be ours just so long as I kept the Welsh Prince from attacking my men at arms.

I had managed to reach the third line of horsemen. These were the ones whose mail and weapons, not to mention their horses, were not as good as the ones we had just faced. As I pulled back my arm to lunge at the knight who faced me, I saw that he had an open-faced helmet and looked young. Once again it was spear to spear and this time, I did not stand for his horse was smaller than mine. As our spears crossed, I felt pain as his spear broke through the mail on my right arm and the spearhead scored a line along my flesh. My spear struck him squarely in the chest and he tumbled backwards from his horse. I had broken his mail and that saved me from worse injury than a flesh wound.

I heard a Welsh horn and knew that we had won. We needed to make it a complete victory. If Sir Robert was to build a castle and subdue this part of Wales then we needed all opposition to be ended. I reined back a little and looked along my line. I saw an empty saddle. I also saw that the sun was setting behind the knoll. The Welsh levy was streaming back towards the Roman Road and Sir Robert, as well as my men at arms, archers and squires, were pursuing them. It would not be a pleasant sight for Dick and the other pages. The Welsh who fled would be speared and hacked in the back. If they turned to face their pursuers then they would be overwhelmed. Their Prince had gambled and lost; he was mounted and would escape but his people would pay the price.

I raised my visor and shouted, "Try to get the Prince!"

If we could capture Prince Dafydd then he could be imprisoned in the Tower and I would not need to return in a year's time.

The Prince had his household knights with him and there were also knights who sought an honourable end. As the Prince and his closest knights hurtled towards the road ten or so of the others turned to try to halt our pursuit. We were both almost at a standstill when we met. The Welsh knights were being brave, if not realistic. Already some of Sir Robert's knights were racing to join us and the Welsh knights would lose. Sometimes it is more about honour than realism. The Welsh knight who rode at me still had his lance and he rammed it at me. A wooden lance only caused damage if delivered at speed and this one was not. It shattered and splintered on my shield without hurting me at all. My spear had a metal head and I rammed it at him. As he threw away the broken stump of the lance, he blocked my strike with his shield. As he was attempting to draw his sword, I feinted at his shield which he promptly raised but my thrust was aimed at his thigh and it tore through his chausse; blood spurted. He rammed his shield down and broke the shaft of the spear, which had more than done its duty.

We drew our swords together and I spurred Lion to close with him. The blades clashed and rang. Sparks flew. The Welshman had a good sword and this one would neither bend nor buckle. I stood in my stirrups and brought it down towards his head. Although he raised the shield and blocked the blow it was such a clean strike that it split the shield. He attempted a sideswipe at me but my shield blocked it easily and, delivered from a seated position, it lacked the power of my strike.

"Yield, Sir Knight, for you are wounded and your shield is split. Your Prince has escaped and you have done all that honour demands."

"Never!" He raised his sword again.

I saw that most of the other knights had surrendered but this one was going to fight to the death. He did not have the chance to deliver the blow for Tom of Rydal rode up and, reversing his spear, slammed it into the side of the knight's head so that he fell unconscious to the ground. Tom grinned, "Just helping him to make the right decision, my lord!"

I saw that the battle was over. Darkness had almost fallen and there was little point in further pursuit. We would not be able to catch the ones who had fled but we had won and Sir Robert could build his castle. We had, however, paid a price. I saw that some of Sir Robert's knights had fallen and of my knights, only myself, Sir Geoffrey and Sir Henry Samuel were unwounded. I did not count the minor flesh wound as a wound! That the wounded knights could still speak and were conscious told me that their wounds were not life-threatening but King Henry had, once more, cost the men of the valley their blood.

Epilogue

It was July by the time we reached, first, Stockton, and then
Hartlepool. We had little more fighting to do. Once we had secured the
prisoners in Chester, we began work on the castle at Dyserth which lay
just a mile or so from Twthill. It was, as Sir Robert had said, a better
site for a castle. He had his men begin the work with the captured men
at arms and the captured levy. There would be fields in Anglesey which
would lie untended. The wounded knights were left to recover while I
rode abroad with Sir Henry Samuel, Sir Geoffrey and our men. Dick
grew up rapidly during those long summer days as we travelled as far
west as the Conwy river and as far east as the estuary of the Dee. We
patrolled the length of the Clwyd scouring it of all who might threaten
Sir Robert and his new castle. We were harsh. We sought buried
weapons and that meant disrupting the houses and homes of the farms.
As we found hidden weapons in half of the homes then it was more than
justified.

The ransoms were paid by the middle of June and all of our men
benefitted. The King sent a messenger to congratulate us on our victory
and confirmed that Sir Robert Pounderling would be Lord of the Clwyd.
Sir Robert was grateful to me and I could use that at some point in the
future. It was summer and we lived outdoors while the castle took
shape. We enjoyed a remarkable dry period and were able to talk in the
open where we would not be overheard. He had been happy to take
orders from me and told me that he would do so when next we
campaigned.

"What do you think we should do next, Sir William? You will be in
Hartlepool and by winter we will barely have walls up but I need to
know what we do next."

"When my men rode to the Conwy, they pointed out that it would be
a good place to build a castle. I know that is not possible until Dyserth
is finished but we could cross that river and, perhaps, make this side of
the straits ours. There is no bridge and if we keep a watch there, we can
forestall any attempt to land men." I pointed to his castle, "And I think
you are wrong. By winter you should have the base of the keep finished
as well as the curtain wall. While you cannot dig foundations in winter
you can put a second floor on the keep and build a gatehouse. The
Welsh farmers you use will be keen to finish their part and to get back
to the farms that they have neglected."

I left him with the promise that he would send riders to keep me regularly informed of his progress. Our journey home was more pleasant than the one coming south. It was as we went home that we discovered what we had suspected, Sir Peter would never go to war again. He had hurt his leg and this time, more seriously. The Welsh knight he had fought had managed to strike his kneecap with a mace and shattered the bone. He would be a cripple who would only walk with sticks. King Henry's wars had cost him dearly.

Sir Gerard, too, was a changed man. His wound had not been serious. He had had his left arm broken. He kept training with his right arm while his left healed and he insisted upon coming on patrol with us. The battle had been the making of him. He had been terrified of death and he had emerged, if not unscathed, then alive and aware that he had defeated three knights while doing so. I could send him back to the Bishop knowing that I had done what I had promised. He asked to be considered for the next campaign and there, indeed, was a change.

My mother was just pleased to see that none had died and she fussed over Dick whilst glaring at me as he told her of his part in the battle with the Welsh. I did not mind that he exaggerated his part but it made my mother think I was a bad father. My father, in contrast, knew that I had done all that I could to keep Dick safe and he was pleased our plan had worked.

"All of this is good, my son, and you are another year closer to becoming Lord of Stockton!"

I just wanted to get home to see my wife, new son and my daughter. I had nine months to spend at home and I intended to enjoy every moment of those nine months. For a short time, I would no longer need to be a border knight and that pleased me!

The End

Glossary

Buskins-boots
Chevauchée- a raid by mounted men
Courts baron-a court which dealt with the tenants' rights and
duties, changes of occupancy, and disputes between tenants.
Crowd- crwth or rote. A Celtic musical instrument similar to a
lyre
Fusil - A lozenge shape on a shield
Garth- a garth was a church-owned farm. Not to be confused with
the name Garth
Groat- An English coin worth four silver pennies
Hautwesel- Haltwhistle
Hovel- a makeshift shelter used by warriors on a campaign-
similar to a '*bivvy*' tent
Marlyon- Merlin (hunting bird)
Mêlée- a medieval fight between knights
Pursuivant – the rank below a herald
Reeve- An official who ran a manor for a lord
Rote- An English version of a lyre (also called a crowd or crwth)
Vair- a heraldic term
Wessington- Washington (Durham)
Wulfestun- Wolviston (Durham)

Historical Background and References

Henry III did embark on a failed war with France to support his Lusignan family and lost to King Louis at the Battle of Taillebourg where King Louis' 4,000 knights defeated King Henry's 1,600 and effectively ended King Henry's French ambitions. He was lucky that the Welsh and the Scottish borders were relatively quiet but it did take many nobles to the continent to fight for their king and that allowed others to prosper at home. This was when Simon de Montfort began to increase his powers and those powers would eventually bring him into conflict with King Henry.

King Alexander did bring an army into Northumberland but he did not fight King Henry. The two forces faced off and then the Kings met at Ponteland where they signed the treaty of Newcastle. It restored the status quo where King Alexander acknowledged King Henry as his liege. The French involvement in the incident is of my own creation but after their success at Taillebourg, it seemed to me a logical extension. The dispute between Comyn and Durward is well recorded and Durward was given the manor of Bolsover by King Henry. As this had been a favourite castle of King John, King Henry's father, it suggests that Alan Durward did King Henry a great service.

Scutage was a sort of tax. Some knights and lords of the manor did not wish to obey the King's command for service. They paid scutage which was used to reward those knights who gave more service than they owed. The amount varied but there were increasing numbers of knights, especially in the south and the midlands, who had a comfortable life and did not bother to supply their own men. They were more like men of commerce than warriors. The King would take his cut and then give the rest to the men who fought for him. Eventually, this would lead to the Free Companies. (See the Struggle for a Crown series. Book 1, Blood on the Blade.)

- Norman Stone Castles- Gravett
- English Castles 1200-1300 -Gravett
- The Normans- David Nicolle
- Norman Knight AD 950-1204- Christopher Gravett
- The Norman Conquest of the North- William A Kappelle
- The Knight in History- Francis Gies

192

- The Norman Achievement- Richard F Cassady
- Knights- Constance Brittain Bouchard
- Knight Templar 1120-1312 -Helen Nicholson
- Feudal England: Historical Studies on the Eleventh and Twelfth Centuries- J. H. Round
- English Medieval Knight 1200-1300 Christopher Gravett
- The Scandinavian Baltic Crusades 1100-1500 Lindholm and Nicolle
- The Scottish and Welsh Wars 1250-1400- Rothero
- Chronicles of the age of chivalry ed Hallam
- Lewes and Evesham- 1264-65- Richard Brooks
- British Kings and Queens- Mike Ashley
- Ordnance Survey Kelso and Coldstream Landranger map #74
- The Tower of London-Lapper and Parnell
- Knight Hospitaller 1100-1306 Nicolle and Hook
- Old Series Ordnance Survey map 1864-1869 Alnwick and Morpeth
- Old Series Ordnance Survey map 1868-1869 Cheviot Hills and Kielder Water
- Old Series Ordnance Survey maps 1863-1869 Hexham and Haltwhistle

Griff Hosker
January 2020

Other books by Griff Hosker

If you enjoyed reading this book, then why not read another one by the author?

Ancient History

The Sword of Cartimandua Series
(Germania and Britannia 50 A.D. – 128 A.D.)
Ulpius Felix- Roman Warrior (prequel)
The Sword of Cartimandua
The Horse Warriors
Invasion Caledonia
Roman Retreat
Revolt of the Red Witch
Druid's Gold
Trajan's Hunters
The Last Frontier
Hero of Rome
Roman Hawk
Roman Treachery
Roman Wall
Roman Courage

The Wolf Warrior series
(Britain in the late 6th Century)
Saxon Dawn
Saxon Revenge
Saxon England
Saxon Blood
Saxon Slayer
Saxon Slaughter
Saxon Bane
Saxon Fall: Rise of the Warlord
Saxon Throne
Saxon Sword

Medieval History

Sentinel of the North

The Dragon Heart Series
Viking Slave
Viking Warrior
Viking Jarl
Viking Kingdom
Viking Wolf
Viking War
Viking Sword
Viking Wrath
Viking Raid
Viking Legend
Viking Vengeance
Viking Dragon
Viking Treasure
Viking Enemy
Viking Witch
Viking Blood
Viking Weregeld
Viking Storm
Viking Warband
Viking Shadow
Viking Legacy
Viking Clan
Viking Bravery

The Norman Genesis Series
Hrolf the Viking
Horseman
The Battle for a Home
Revenge of the Franks
The Land of the Northmen
Ragnvald Hrolfsson
Brothers in Blood
Lord of Rouen
Drekar in the Seine
Duke of Normandy
The Duke and the King

Danelaw
(England and Denmark in the 11ᵗʰ Century)
Dragon Sword
Oathsword

195

Sentinel of the North

Bloodsword

New World Series
Blood on the Blade
Across the Seas
The Savage Wilderness
The Bear and the Wolf
Erik The Navigator
Erik's Clan

The Vengeance Trail

The Reconquista Chronicles
Castilian Knight
El Campeador
The Lord of Valencia

The Aelfraed Series
(Britain and Byzantium 1050 A.D. - 1085 A.D.)
Housecarl
Outlaw
Varangian

**The Anarchy Series England
1120-1180**
English Knight
Knight of the Empress
Northern Knight
Baron of the North
Earl
King Henry's Champion
The King is Dead
Warlord of the North
Enemy at the Gate
The Fallen Crown
Warlord's War
Kingmaker
Henry II
Crusader
The Welsh Marches
Irish War
Poisonous Plots

Sentinel of the North

The Princes' Revolt
Earl Marshal
The Perfect Knight

Border Knight
1182-1300
Sword for Hire
Return of the Knight
Baron's War
Magna Carta
Welsh Wars
Henry III
The Bloody Border
Baron's Crusade
Sentinel of the North
War in the West
Debt of Honour
The Blood of the Warlord
The Fettered King

Sir John Hawkwood Series
France and Italy 1339- 1387
Crécy: The Age of the Archer
Man At Arms
The White Company
Leader of Men

Lord Edward's Archer
Lord Edward's Archer
King in Waiting
An Archer's Crusade
Targets of Treachery
The Great Cause
Wallace's War

Struggle for a Crown
1360- 1485
Blood on the Crown
To Murder a King
The Throne
King Henry IV
The Road to Agincourt

Sentinel of the North

St Crispin's Day
The Battle for France
The Last Knight
Queen's Knight

Tales from the Sword I
(Short stories from the Medieval period)

Tudor Warrior series
England and Scotland in the late 14th and early 15th century
Tudor Warrior
Tudor Spy

Conquistador
England and America in the 16th Century
Conquistador

Modern History

The Napoleonic Horseman Series
Chasseur à Cheval
Napoleon's Guard
British Light Dragoon
Soldier Spy
1808: The Road to Coruña
Talavera
The Lines of Torres Vedras
Bloody Badajoz
The Road to France
Waterloo

The Lucky Jack American Civil War series
Rebel Raiders
Confederate Rangers
The Road to Gettysburg

Soldier of the Queen series
Soldier of the Queen

The British Ace Series
1914

Sentinel of the North

1915 Fokker Scourge
1916 Angels over the Somme
1917 Eagles Fall
1918 We will remember them
From Arctic Snow to Desert Sand
Wings over Persia

Combined Operations series
1940-1945
Commando
Raider
Behind Enemy Lines
Dieppe
Toehold in Europe
Sword Beach
Breakout
The Battle for Antwerp
King Tiger
Beyond the Rhine
Korea
Korean Winter

Tales from the Sword II
(Short stories from the Modern period)

Other Books
Great Granny's Ghost (Aimed at 9-14-year-old young people)

For more information on all of the books then please visit the author's
website at www.griffhosker.com where there is a link to contact him or
visit his Facebook page: GriffHosker at Sword Books